LIES

NEW YORK TIMES BESTSELLING AUTHOR

KYLIE SCOTT

Cover Design: By Hang Le
Cover Photograph: Brian Kaminski
Interior Book Design: Champagne Book Design

ISBN: 9781072014669

PLAYLIST

"Fake Love" by BTS

"It's a Heartache" by Bonnie Tyler

"Tear Me to Pieces" by Meg Myers

"Secrets" by Mary Lambert

"Here You Come Again" by Dolly Parton

"Bad Guy" by Billie Eilish

"Barracuda" by Heart

"Cuz I Love You" by Lizzo

"Piece of My Heart" by Janis Joplin

"Little of Your Love" by Haim

LIES

ONE

"**Y**OU'RE GOING TO BREAK HIS HEART."

"No, I'm not," I say. "That's sort of the whole point. If I really thought leaving him would break his heart, then I probably wouldn't be leaving him in the first place."

My best friend, Jen, does not look convinced.

Boxes fill a good half of the room. What a mess. Who knew you could accumulate so much junk in only twelve months? At least we weren't together so long that I can't remember who owns what. One year is about the sweet spot for this issue in relationships, apparently.

"The fact of the matter is, we're not in love. We have no business being engaged, let alone getting married." I sigh. "Have you seen the packing tape?"

"No. He's just such a nice guy."

"I'm not debating that." I climb to my feet, then head up the stairs to the second bedroom. Thom's unofficial workout room/home office. Not a room I normally go into. But it only takes a bit of rummaging to find what I'm looking for. Whatever else might be said about them, insurance assessors are organized. The bottom drawer of Thom's desk has a neat stash of stationery. I grab a couple rolls of thick tape.

"And leaving him this way…" Jen continues as I head back down.

"How many times have I told him we need to talk? He's always putting it off, saying it's not a good time. And now he's away again. I've been messaging him for the last week and he barely replies."

"You know he has to drop everything once a job comes up. I realize he's not the most exciting guy, Betty, but—"

"I know." I smack down a line of tape with extra zest, sealing the lid of the last box. In this Operation Abandon Ship Posthaste, I know I'm definitely slightly the bad guy. But not totally. Say sixty/forty. Or maybe seventy/thirty. It's hard to tell to what degree. "I do know all of that. But he's always busy with work or away on some business trip. What am I supposed to do?"

A sigh from Jen.

"When you realize you've made such a monumental mistake, it's hard to sit and wait to fix things. Nor is it fair on either of us to keep up the pretense."

"Guess so."

"And the fact that he's yet again made no effort to prioritize our relationship and make a little time for me in his busy schedule is just further proof that I've made the right choice in ending this now before it gets any more complicated. End of rant."

Nothing from her.

"Anyway, you're supposed to be on my side. Stop questioning me."

"You wanted to get married and have children so badly."

"Yeah." I sit back on my heels. "I blame it all on playing with Ken and Barbie's dreamhouse when I was little. But it turns out that being in a relationship with the wrong person can be even lonelier than being alone."

Jen and I have been friends since sharing a room in college. We've witnessed the bulk of each other's dating ups and downs.

For some reason, I'm the type of girl who guys will go out with, but don't tend to stick with. Apparently, I'm fuckable—just not girlfriend material. Maybe it's my smart mouth. Maybe it's the whole not fitting current societal expectations of beauty i.e. I'm fat. Maybe I was born under an unlucky star. I don't know; it's their loss. Like anyone, I have my faults, but all in all, I'm awesome. And I have a lot to give. Too often in the past few months, I've had to keep reminding myself of this fact.

"There are just so many jerks out there," Jen says. "I was happy that you'd found a good one."

"I think I'd prefer a jerk who was genuinely into me than a nice guy phoning it in. Honestly, I'd rather go adopt a dozen cats and settle into old age and isolation than be with someone who treats me as if I'm an afterthought."

She looks at me for a long moment, then nods slowly. "I'm sorry it didn't work out."

"Me too."

"Time to start filling up the cars. Boy, do you owe me."

I smile. "That I do."

Jen stands and stretches before picking up one of the boxes labeled *kitchen*. "I just didn't want you to do something you'd regret, you know?"

"I know. Thank you."

Alone in the two-bedroom condo, everything is silent. My parting letter sits waiting on the coffee table with his name written on the front. A slight bulge in the envelope betrays the shape of my engagement ring. It's a sweet, simple ring. One small diamond perched on a band of yellow gold. My hand feels wrong without it. Naked. They say there are different love languages and you have to take the time to learn your partner's needs. It's like he and I never quite got there. Or maybe I'm just crappy at relationships.

The bridal magazines I'd collected are in the trash. Perhaps I should have taken them into the florist shop where I work so someone could get some use out of them. But this feels more symbolic, more definite. My family are a couple of states away, and I have only a few of what I'd classify as good friends. Being an introvert makes it hard to meet people. A boyfriend, a husband, would mean I'm no longer alone. Someone cares about me and puts me first. At least part of the time. Only Thom doesn't any of the time, so here we are.

I tighten my ponytail of long dark hair. Then, in a rare display of dexterity that my yoga instructor would be proud of, I stack three boxes in my arms and head outside into the hot afternoon sun. Jen's Honda Civic is parked at the curb, the trunk standing open as she moves things about inside. My old Subaru sits in the driveway waiting to be filled. Birds are singing and insects chirping. It's your typical mild autumn day in California.

That's when the condo blows up behind me.

I come to on the front lawn, sprawled across crushed boxes. Guess they cushioned my fall. A ringing fills my ears, smoke billows up into the sky. The condo is on fire. What's left of it, at least. This cannot be happening.

"Betty!"

I try to turn in the direction of Jen's voice, but one of my eyes won't open. When I touch the area, my fingers come away bright with blood. Also, my brain hurts. It feels as if someone picked me up and shook me around hard.

"Oh my God, Betty," she says, falling to her knees beside me. She's fuzzy for some reason, her familiar features indistinct. "Are you all right?"

"Sure," I say as blackness closes in.

The next time I wake, I'm lying down in a moving vehicle. An ambulance, by the looks of it. Only things don't seem quite right. A woman shines a small light in my eyes before tossing it over her shoulder. And instead of a uniform, she's wearing tight black pants and a tank top.

"Lucky girl. Just a mild concussion and a small cut on her forehead," the woman says with an English accent. Next she rips an antiseptic wipe out of its packet and starts cleaning up the blood on my face none too gently. "She's certainly not his usual type."

"What were you expecting?" asks the driver.

"I don't know. Something a little less plump and homely, perhaps."

A grunt.

"And she's awake," the woman says.

"That's inconvenient."

"I'm on it." She drops the wipe and reaches for a syringe.

"W-wait," I say, my mouth dry and muscles hurting. "What's going on?"

Without any preamble, the needle is plunged into my arm, the stopper depressed. It all happens so quickly. I try to move, to push her away, but I'm no match for her strength. Not in my current condition. As darkness closes in once more, I see a discarded paramedic uniform sitting off to the side.

"Who are you?" I mumble, my lips, face, and everything else going numb.

"Friends," she says. "Well, sort of."

The driver just laughs.

Consciousness comes slowly. It's like I'm underwater in an ocean of night. This time, however, I'm upright, seated on a chair in a large and dimly lit room. My feet rest on the cold bare floor since someone's stolen my shoes. Everything's woozy and horrible. My hands are tied behind my back, the restraints painfully tight. The shadows disappear as a blinding light is shone in my face. It's dazzling and awful, shooting pain through my already pounding head. Next comes a bucket of ice-cold water thrown in my face.

"Wakey wakey," yells the shadow of a man. "Time for us to talk, Miss Elizabeth Dawsey."

I cringe and shiver. "Wh-where am I?"

"I ask the questions and you give me answers. That's how this works."

"Is all this really necessary?" the woman with the British accent asks. Her voice comes from farther back in the room. "He's not going to be happy."

"Keep your mouth shut," growls the man.

With the light blinding my eyes, there's little I can see. My bare feet rest on concrete and the air is dusty and still. I could be anywhere. "I don't understand. Who are you people?"

Heavy footsteps come toward me; then *smack*! His hand connects with my cheek. Fothermucker. I've never been hit before. It's a hell of a shock. My face throbs and there's the taste of blood on my tongue. I must have bitten it. But then everything pretty much hurts to one degree or another.

"I wouldn't have done that if I were you," says the woman.

But the man just ignores her, stepping back beyond the light. "What does the word 'wolf' mean to you?"

"Wolf?" I ask.

"Answer the question."

"I don't...what do you mean?" I shake from more than fear, ice-cold water sliding down my skin beneath the drenched clothing. "As in the animal?"

"What else?"

"Fur? Teeth? House Stark? I don't know."

Laughter from the woman.

"Tell me about your fiancé," he demands. "Everything you know about the man."

This makes no sense to my already-addled brain. "But why? Thom hasn't done anything. He's an insurance assessor, for Christ's sake. Whenever there's a fire or a flood or something, he goes and helps people with their claims. That's where he is right now, assessing damage from that hurricane in Florida. It was on the news and everything."

"Are you sure about that?"

"What are you saying?" A sudden surge of fear grips me. "Thom's okay, isn't he? I mean, he couldn't have been in the explosion. He's on the other side of the country."

"He wasn't in the explosion, no. Tell me more about him."

"Ah, we met in a bar downtown, been together for just over a year. He's a hard worker. He likes watching football and going for morning runs. His favorite food is lasagna and he drinks Bud Light even though it's trash."

"MORE."

"I don't know what you want," I cry. Never in my life have I been so scared.

"Describe him to me."

"He's just an average guy. Average height. Fit, but not bulky. He has brown eyes and hair. Thirty-one years old."

"Tick-tock, tick-tock," says the woman. "You're running out of time."

"Whose fucking fault is that?" hisses the man.

"Guess I gave her more sleep juice than I meant to. Oops."

A grunt. "Keep talking, bitch."

My head pounds. "I, um…he sleeps on the right-hand side of the bed."

"What weapons does he keep in the house?"

"Like guns? None. I hate the things. We both do."

Again, the woman laughs. "Not the brightest, is she?"

"Keep talking," repeats the man.

"Thom's a decent person. He's nice...polite. Doesn't do social media. Has no close family." Nothing I'm telling them is damning or even particularly interesting. Still, I feel guilty for answering at all. But what the hell else am I supposed to do? "Is this what you want to know? I don't understand; what's he done? What's he involved in?"

"Who says he's involved in anything?"

"The fact that I'm here and you're questioning me says something's going on."

"Watch it. I don't think you appreciate how nice I'm being," says the creep. "Things could get much worse for you very quickly. You have no idea exactly how bad things could get."

"I don't know what you want. Are you the ones who blew up the condo?" My heart is pounding and I can't seem to get enough air. "Are you going to kill me?"

"Asking me questions again. Tsk tsk. You just never learn. Perhaps you'd like to try some waterboarding, hmm? Does that sound like fun?"

I choke on a sob.

"Got to say, it really messes you up. Feels just like you're drowning. You start suffocating and water gets in your lungs, which fucking stings, let me tell you. And your sinuses feel like they're going to explode. Eventually, Betty, you'll lose consciousness. Then I'll wake you back up not so gently and we'll start all over again." The sadistic prick laughs. "I hate to do it. But I just don't think you're being entirely truthful with me, you see? It's sad, really. All of this football-and-lasagna bullshit, it's just surface information. You must know more about the man you live with, the man you're going to marry. You'd have to know all his secrets by now, wouldn't you?"

I shake my head. "Thom doesn't have any secrets."

"Everyone has secrets."

"No, not Thom. I mean, he hates his boss and he takes his coffee black." I'm babbling now, the words tripping over themselves in their haste to get out. "He's a bit of a loner. Only has a couple of friends f-from college, work...I don't...oh, God."

"Do you talk to your friends about Thom?"

"Well, I talk to my friend Jen. Wait, where is Jen? Have you taken her too?"

"The friend checks out," says the woman. "She's clean."

"Is Jen okay?" I repeat. "Did you hurt her?"

"Your nosy little friend is fine. Took a lot of talking to keep her out of the ambulance," says the man. "Maybe we should have brought her along. I think you just need a bit more encouragement to help your memory."

"Are you sure about this?" asks the woman.

"Use your head," he snaps. "If they've found the condo, then they know about this one. If they know about her, they'll have tried to compromise her. Get her on the floor."

"Oh, no. I'm observing only," says the woman. "You're on your own with this."

The light clicks off and white spots dance before my eyes. I blink and blink, but it's a while before I can see anything. In the meantime, there are noises. Water running from a tap. More heavy footsteps. The near-silent hiss of the frigid air-conditioning turning on.

Slowly, gradually, things swim into focus. We're in an empty basement by the look of it. Small barred windows set high. Bare brick walls and a concrete floor. Over by a laundry tub, the man stands with his back to me. He's tall with a shaved head, dressed in all black. Meanwhile, the woman leans against a wall inspecting her nails. She's petite with short dark hair and golden-brown skin.

This isn't real. It can't be real. Everything hurts. And it's about to hurt a lot more.

Someone jogs down the stairs, coming into view a bit at a time. First are the black boots. Next is blue jeans. Then a gray T-shirt hanging loose. Finally, I see his face...

And it's Thom.

Relief rushes through me. He's here. He's okay. Oh, thank God. Though, now that I really pay attention, he seems different than normal. My addled brain can't figure it out exactly. As if it's Thom's doppelgänger. Because it looks like him, but the expression on his face...

Oh, shit. What if they're going to hurt him too?

"Thom," I gasp. "No."

He spares me only the briefest of glances. "What's going on?"

The creep turns, mouth set in a distinctly pissy line. Water keeps pouring out of the faucet into a bucket, presumably, and he's holding a piece of ripped towel. "Wolf."

"Spider," says Thom.

"Since we had to pick her up, they wanted a threat assessment." The woman continues to lean casually against the wall.

"It's sanctioned," snarls the man. Spider.

"And you decided that meant tying her up and torturing her?" asks Thom. "I don't think so."

The woman sighs. "For the record, I told him it wasn't a good idea."

"You were right."

"Hey, now." The man lifts his hands in a pacifying way. "I wasn't actually going to do it. I was just messing with her head. You know how it works, you've got to—"

It all happens so quickly. The work of a moment, no more. Thom's hand lunges for Spider's throat, crushing his windpipe. The man doubles over, choking.

Unhurried, Thom draws a gun from his belt. One smooth, graceful arc, and the gun's butt strikes the side of the man's head. He drops to the floor.

"I've been wanting to do that for years," the woman says. "He always liked hurting women a little too much for my tastes. Such a rubbish human."

It's the last straw for me. I'm not used to all the threats and fear and violence. In movies maybe, but not actual real-world stuff. Acid climbs my throat and I lean to the side to throw up. Vomit splashes the side of my leg. I'm too freaked out to feel the usual disgust. Instead, I feel frail and hollow. Like I might cave in on myself at any moment.

"Fox, get him out of here," orders Thom in a calm voice.

"Fuck's sake. I hate carrying dead weight." The woman, Fox, pulls out a cell, thumbs moving across the screen, sending someone a message instead of following orders. Perhaps she's checking her social media first. I don't know. Nothing about this makes sense.

Thom strides toward me, his face hard, eyes cold. I've never been afraid of him, but I am now. He produces a knife out of nowhere and squats down to cut the ties on my wrists. Then he grabs my chin, inspecting me.

I push him away, wipe my mouth clean with the back of a hand. My world has suddenly turned upside down. Thom the kickass fighter and me almost blown-up and waterboarded. What the hell?

"Thom…" I breathe.

His dark hair is this cool artful mess instead of following its usual dull, neat lines. And there's a focus to him, a determination.

No, a confidence. That's the difference between this man and my former fiancé. He stands tall and strong. Ready to conquer nations, to take on anything and win.

Holy shit. Who is this guy?

Because this isn't my Thom. It can't be.

"Your eyes are blue," I say.

"I wear contacts around you."

"No. You're his evil twin or something." This makes total sense. Sort of. "That's it."

"Don't be silly," he replies shortly. "It's me, Betty. Your fiancé."

"I know Thom. He's nothing like you. He would never…"

He pauses, then sighs. "You've seen my scars. You know them."

"I know Thom's scars, but…"

Without a word, he pulls his T-shirt up and over his head. Thom's always been fit, but in the shadowy light, with the gun tucked into the waistband of his jeans now exposed, the rippled body before me looks hard and dangerous. However, the scars are indeed there. Every one of them. One on the shoulder. A slash on his upper right arm. Four across his stomach, like a little constellation.

I shake my head. "Thom would never take his shirt off in public. He's too self-conscious. We didn't even have sex with the light on."

"Self-conscious about the damage from the car accident, right?"

"Yeah, and the scars from playing sports and a surgery when he was younger."

"I don't care about them." He sighs. "It was just too much of a risk that someone might recognize gunshot, knife, and shrapnel wounds if they saw them."

Huh. "Thom?"

"Hi, babe." He gives me a sad, sort of contrite smile. For the first time, he looks exactly like my Thom.

"What the hell is going on?"

He says nothing. But his gaze moves over me, taking in my battered face, my bruised body. It stops, however, at my hands. "Betty, where's your ring?"

"I—I took it off. I was leaving you."

For the first time, this scary alternate version of Thom seems almost surprised. A little shocked even. "You left me? Why would you..." Then he looks over his shoulder at Fox, who is carrying Spider away, holding him over one shoulder, fireman style. She's obviously stronger than she looks. Thom leans in close, his voice harsh and low. "Tell no one. Do you understand?"

"What? But why?"

"No one. Your life depends on it."

Returning without Spider, Fox wanders over. "All organized."

"Good," answers Thom.

"Of course, this is all your own bloody fault," says Fox. "You're the one who wanted a white picket fence and suburban family for a cover. Yawn."

Thom draws me to my feet and I sway like I'm caught in a storm. He slides a strong arm around my waist, drawing me against his body. I don't want to touch him, this stranger who uses violence so easily. But my options for staying upright and getting out of here are limited.

"The internal leak is being investigated," says Fox. "We should have something for you soon."

Thom just nods.

"What do I say to Spider when he regains consciousness?" asks Fox.

"Tell him if he ever touches my fiancée again, I won't be so diplomatic next time."

Fox snorts. "Whatever. Cheerio, Betty. No hard feelings, yeah?"

Thom hustles me out of there as fast as he can.

"I know you've got questions."

What an understatement. We're upstairs in one of the many bedrooms inside the sprawling old ranch house. It's somewhere in the wilds of one of the canyons, at a guess. No neighbors are in sight. Apart from Fox, the unconscious Spider, and a man working at a serious array of computers in the great room, the place seems empty. There's basic furniture only. No pictures or keepsakes. Nothing to indicate it's a home.

And it's all so surreal. I want to keep pinching myself, but I hurt enough already. Which reminds me: "Was anyone else harmed in the explosion?"

"No."

"It was meant to kill?"

"As best we can figure, the bomb malfunctioned. Went off early."

"Someone actually tried to blow us up. I wonder...I went into your office looking for tape. I don't usually go in there."

His nostrils flare. "That could have been it."

"So there's a leak in your organization and someone wants to kill you," I say, voice shaking. "Or you and me both?"

"You were paying attention back there."

"I'm not as stupid as you think I am." I almost laugh. Or cry. One or the other. "At least, I hope I'm not."

"Babe—"

"Do not *babe* me."

He takes a deep breath, pushing a hand through his hair. The past few months, he's been so busy it's longer than normal. Way overdue for a cut. "I never thought you were stupid, Betty."

"No. Just desperate."

He says nothing. Confirmation enough. Not that I needed it.

"Well?" I ask.

"Until we can identify who's passing off information, we won't know if the target is just me. It would, however, make the most sense."

"Unless they wanted to kill me to hurt you. Though it wouldn't hurt you, would it?"

His lips thin ever so slightly. "Given I cold-cocked the last person who harmed you, I think we can assume I care at least a little."

"A little. That's big of you." I sit on the side of the king-size bed, trying to ease the nerves, tiredness, and pain. What I wouldn't give for Tylenol or something stronger. A bottle of medicinal vodka, maybe. "What happens now?"

"Now we wait to see what the searches Badger's doing on the computers dig up. We're safe here for the moment."

"Badger." I snort. "Is there an Otter?"

"Not that I'm aware of."

"You and your friends are a regular fucking zoo."

The following silence is thick and heavy. Not comfortable at all. And to think I'd planned to spend my life with this man. This stranger.

"She referred to me and our life together as your cover. Does that make you a spy or a government agent or what?"

"Something like that."

"Oh my God, are you a traitor?"

"No, Betty. The ones I work for...they're an international

group dedicated to keeping things as unfucked as possible. That's really all I can say."

"And these people, you kill for them?"

There's the slightest of pauses before he answers. "When it's necessary. There are some dangerous people out there. But other times I just gather information. Each job is different."

"They usually involve you pretending to be someone you're not, though, right? Lying to people?"

"Yes."

"Hmm. You're very good at it." I watch him carefully. "So are you doing this for the good of humankind or for the money?"

"Can't it be both?" he asks all smooth-like. New Thom is slippery.

"What did you mean, my life depended on not saying anything about leaving you?"

"You know too much now. The only thing keeping you alive is that they, the people in charge, think you're loyal to me and that I'm committed to you. If those beliefs change, then they will review their risk-reward calculation about keeping you alive."

"All I know is that you name yourselves after animals and answer to some mysterious organization referred to as 'they.'"

"That's enough."

"It's ridiculous they'd want me dead just for knowing that." I want to beat him with my fists. Scream and howl in rage. Maybe later when I've got the energy. "Is Thom Lange even your real name?"

"Thom is my name."

"But Lange's not your surname."

"No." He pauses. "Why did you want to leave?"

"Does it matter why I attempted to dump you, since we're apparently now stuck with each other?"

"I thought you were happy." The weird thing is, he sounds almost hurt. Which is crazy. "I know I've been busy lately, but—"

"You do remember this is a fake relationship you're talking about," I say between clenched teeth. "A lie that you manipulated and tricked me into believing."

For a moment, we just stare at each other. Neither of us is happy.

"Given how badly I held up under pressure, I can almost forgive you for not telling me the whole truth. But I really don't think I can ever forgive you for starting this relationship in the first place."

"Everyone breaks under torture; it's just a matter of when." He doesn't address the second issue. Doesn't even go near it.

"Great."

"You're exhausted; you should sleep." He nods to a door on the other side of the large bedroom. "Bathroom is through there if you want to clean up. I'll check on you later."

"Okay."

"I'll be right outside. You're safe, Betty."

I don't know what to say. This new Thom doesn't feel safe at all.

And then he's gone.

I have no idea where we are or how far from civilization we might be. And I have neither money nor shoes. My chances of making a successful getaway are slim to none. For now, there's no other real option but to stay put and figure out this situation. My supposed fiancé seems to want to keep me alive and in one piece. It's something, I guess.

The woman in the bathroom mirror is pale and pasty, battered and bruised. I turn on the shower, testing the temperature with a hand. Red marks line my wrists, further reminder of the crazy and violent day. My clothes stink of smoke and vomit, but there's soap and shampoo, towels and a fluffy white robe. It'll have to do. I need to put myself back together and deal.

Only the first tear leaves a trail in the soot and general mess of my face. A second tear follows fast. Soon my vision wavers and I step into the shower, hiding the sound of my crying with the running water. It'd be great to be able to handle this, to stay strong. But first I apparently need a minute to let it all out. All of the anger, stress, and horror of the past few hours. All of my fear.

Because I'm trapped. That's what it comes down to in the end.

TWO

I
T'S LATE WHEN KNOCKING WAKES ME. HINTS OF DAWN LIGHT SLIP
past the curtain edges casting shadows across the plain white
walls. Being almost blown up, tortured, and interrogated
warrants a sleep-in. But apparently it's not going to happen.

I sit up slowly, pushing my hair out of my face, being
careful of the butterfly bandages on my forehead and other
assorted bruising. Meanwhile, Thom is already moving toward
the door, gun in hand. I didn't even realize he'd been in bed with
me. He wasn't there a few hours ago when a nightmare woke
me. It's bizarre, how comfortable he seems with the weapon,
as if it's merely an extension of him. His grip on it eases at the
sight of whoever's in the hallway, and he gives me a nod to say
it's okay.

Sleep hasn't solved anything. He still seems like a stranger
wearing Thom's face. More now than ever. I don't know if I'll
ever get used to looking into those hard blue eyes.

"Wolf." The man who enters is tall and lean, with black
hair and brown skin. Late twenties, I'd guess. He's got on a
sharp suit with a white shirt open at the collar and he's carrying
a wealth of shopping bags. Also, he's pretty. "And this must be
your beautiful fiancée."

I pull the collar of the robe closed over my ample cleavage
because hello.

"This is Crow," Thom says to me, tucking the gun into

the waistband of his jeans. His feet are bare and so is his upper body. The scars are once again on display.

He used to insist on having sex in the dark and always locked the bathroom door when he took a shower. I just figured he had the market cornered on inhibitions. Who hasn't got flaws? But after all of the excuses he used to keep me at a distance, to keep himself covered, it's strange to see them exposed. And it's a definite; I still want to hit him for all the lies and assorted bullshit he pedaled throughout the duration of our relationship.

He stands beside the bed, keeping his body partly between me and the stranger, despite saying, "He's a friend."

Crow smiles. "Didn't you once tell me there were no friends in this business?"

The edges of Thom's lips rise slightly in agreement.

"Hi," I say.

Crow drops the shopping bags on the end of the bed. The bulk of them appear to be labeled Neiman Marcus. "For you, Betty. Some clothes and so on. He gave me your measurements so everything should fit. It's a pleasure to meet you. I've been wanting to for a while now, but someone had you declared strictly off-limits."

"It was for her own good. And I said to pick up a few things," says Thom, sounding disgruntled. "Not empty the damn store."

"The personal shopper needed the commission and you can afford it. The replacement ring is in the little blue bag. I picked that one out myself."

Thom groans. "Do I even want to know?"

"Probably not." The man squats, sorting through the pile of bags with ease. And sure enough, a Tiffany-blue bag yields a ring box. "I suppose you should do the honors."

Without comment, Thom takes the box, sitting on the bed beside me. I can't read the expression in his eyes. But he grasps my hand lightly, sliding the rock onto my ring finger. The diamond is huge and it fits perfectly.

"I thought we weren't telling anyone about—" I start to say.

"You can trust Crow. If anyone asks, the story is that you took your old ring off while you were doing work around home yesterday morning. That's why you weren't wearing it when the explosion hit."

"I would have proposed properly, got down on one knee and done it right. A square-cut diamond of five carats with a platinum band," announces Crow. "What do you think, Betty?"

"Wow."

"I think she likes it," he says with a smile. "I have excellent taste."

Much irate grumbling from Thom. "You're buying her affections with my money. I'm supposed to be a low-level suit. How the hell would I have afforded that?"

"The only people that ring is meant to fool already know you're not just a low-level suit. Let her enjoy the rock."

"It's beautiful, Crow. Thank you."

The man gives me a brief smile. "You're very welcome, Betty."

"And thank you for picking up the clothes. I keep forgetting everything I owned has been blown up." The thought is both horrible and sobering, remembering exactly how much I've lost. Not that any of it was worth a lot. But the sentimental value... like my favorite T-shirts, for instance. Cherished books with cracked spines and worn pages. The beloved old record player and collection of vinyl I inherited from my grandfather. Just all the bits and pieces that made up my life. Though I know it's only stuff, and I am happy to be alive.

"You backed up your photos, right?" asks Thom.

I nod.

"That's something, at least."

"Yeah," I say, not quite convinced.

Crow clears his throat. "I take it you heard about Scorpion?"

Thom nods. "She was a good agent."

"I know you two were close. We have to find this bastard. Now."

"Badger's tracing access of any and all files relating to us. Anyone left kicking from jobs she and I did together. Someone who might hold a grudge."

"Whatever's out there, he'll find it," says Crow.

So Scorpion was a she, and she and Thom were close. Interesting. I'm not sure if I care if he cheated on me or not. No, I do. The mere thought stings.

I drag the closest bags over to me, pushing aside layers of wrapping to get to the goodies. Some basic makeup, skin care, hair stuff, and tampons. An assortment of clothes, such as jeans, T-shirts, and a warm jacket, along with a pair of sturdy yet fashionable boots. Very nice.

The fancy lingerie I could have done without, however. Nothing wrong with sensible, comfortable, unsexy grandma panties. Especially in my current predicament. Not that Thom is prone to getting carried away at the sight of me scantily clad. Another dead giveaway about the validity of our romance. I'm such a fool.

"So what, you're all ex-military or something?" I ask, in the hopes that information will make me less of an idiot. At least pertaining to this particular situation.

"We're recruited from all over the place. It's not really something we can talk about." Crow leans against the wall, arms crossed. "No one's attempted mixing real life and work before. You being here is quite a first."

"I don't know how *real* it was, considering Thom lied to me about everything," I say. "But this is your life? What happens later? Do they expect you to just disappear into retirement and never discuss what you've done or the things you've seen?"

"Pretty much. Though retirement's not usually an issue," he drawls. "Few of us live that long. Governments adore handing over the hard cases to people it deems expendable with complete deniability."

Thom's eyes tighten. "That's enough. You're scaring her."

"I'm not scared," I lie.

"Sorry," says Crow, heading for the door. "I'll give you two lovebirds some privacy."

"Thanks for all this, Crow."

"Anytime, Betty." He winks before slipping silently out the door.

The room goes quiet and it's just us again. It takes me a moment to find my voice. For my brain to make sense of all the new snippets of information.

"How many times did you nearly not make it home?" I ask, fussing with the tiny satin bow of a thong I'll never wear. "The truth, Thom."

"Often enough to be thankful every time I walked back through the door. Remember when I said the ceiling had caved in on me when I was doing a fire-damage assessment in Idaho?"

"I remember complaining when you were back at work in two days, before the stiches had even healed over."

"You should have seen the other guy." He shrugs. "But I'm good at what I do. Try not to worry."

"Easy for you to say."

"I should check in with Badger." Thom rises to follow Crow, grabbing a shirt off the floor. "I'll bring back some food and coffee."

"Okay."

He just stops for a moment, studies me.

"What?"

"You're handling this well."

I laugh. "Oh, really? Because inside my head, I'm basically alternating between this freaked-out, endless, high-pitched screaming noise and an all-consuming need to kill you for all the fucking lies."

"Huh. Well, it doesn't show too much so…good work." He just watches my face, his own impassive. But then, Thom's always been what you'd call detached. Another strike against our faux romance. "I know this is difficult, Betty, trusting me after everything. But I'm your best chance of getting out of this alive."

"And yet you're the reason I'm in this situation."

He says nothing.

"You're right; it's very hard to trust you."

A nod. "I'll be back soon."

As I told Spider, I met Thom in a bar downtown one particularly crappy Saturday night. The thing is, it was all my fault. Exactly how bad my day had been. A bride had smilingly asked what floral arrangements I'd have if it was my wedding. Just being friendly-like. With my usual unthinking need to please, my mouth opened and it all came out. Peony roses. Lily of the valley. Everything I'd ever wanted for myself. She leapt at my ideas and accordingly, I'd just spent the whole day making all of my dreams come true for someone else's wedding. And it looked more amazing than I'd ever imagined. Damn me for being good at my job.

A more reasonable person wouldn't have minded sharing. It was only some stupid bouquets and boutonnieres after all. Table arrangements and so on. But for some reason I minded. A lot.

I was twenty-five then, had never had what I would term a serious boyfriend, and felt like utter and complete shit. No amount of vodka and sodas was going to make it better, but I was willing to try. That's when Thom found me. And how he'd insinuated himself into my life with such minimal effort. Because on that particular day, I'd given up. I didn't truly believe I deserved any better than a half-hearted love with a nice-enough guy.

Melodramatic and drunk are never a good combination. Eventually I came to my senses, of course, and realized someone's clothes hanging alongside yours in the closet didn't a relationship make. That was about four or five weeks ago. A quick learner, I am not.

I dress in a pair of skinny blue jeans, knee-high boots, and a black tee. I tie back my hair in a low-slung ponytail. Loose enough so it doesn't irritate my headache and assorted wounds. Even if I'm not tough like Fox, at least I can appear mildly capable. Maybe.

Nothing I can do about the butterfly bandages, but concealer hides the worst of my bruising. The black winged eyeliner and mascara I apply make me feel a bit more normal even if my life is spinning out of control. When it comes to makeup, I don't tend to bother with the natural look. I prefer a 1960s vintage vibe. Give me Sophia Loren with her hips and tits espousing the glory of pasta and wine. She knew what was what. There are way more important things than having a tiny waist. Take loving yourself and enjoying life, for instance.

As for the rest of the shopping, I condense it into the duffel bag also provided and also designer. The tag says it was purchased for the bargain price of only three thousand dollars. Crow definitely enjoyed burning through some of Thom's money. At any rate, it feels good to get dressed and organized. Like I might actually have a little control in this insane situation.

Coffee doesn't arrive within a reasonable amount of time. Therefore, it's time to go in search of some. Thom would probably prefer I stay hidden away. But I hate having no idea what's going on out there. And with half a day's distance between me and the whole interrogation thing, I've built up enough courage to go exploring.

No sign of anyone in the hallway. Scuffed terracotta tiles lead off in both directions. The quiet rumblings of conversation are coming from the left, however, so that's where I go. Curiosity compels me to stick my head in any open doorways along the way. Only a bare mattress and some bedside tables in the next room. And the one after that. Still no pictures, personal items, or anything resembling actual signs of habitation.

Voices float down the hallway uninterrupted. I am totally creeping up on a bunch of spies. Go me in stealth mode.

Hang on. A suspicious-looking stain marks the beige carpeting outside a closet door in the second room. Someone's left their mark. With the curtains pulled, leaving the room in shadows, the stain appears black maybe. Or dark brown. But the closer I get, the less sure I am about that. A metallic tang fills the room, the rich scent of copper, and my stomach turns over queasily. I have a bad feeling about this.

Seems the closet hasn't been fully shut, the topmost edge of a boot is sticking out. I should call for Thom. Reverse thrust and get the hell away from this. Only, what if whoever it is bleeding out on the floor isn't dead yet and my delay is what kills them?

Oh, God.

With a shaking hand, I grab the handle, pulling the door open.

The body inside is dark and bloody and awful. Same goes for the knife sticking out of his chest. It stinks of all sorts of bodily fluids left to rot, and I swallow down bile. Puking again is not the answer. I've never seen a dead body before. My eyes can't look away while my brain doesn't know what the fuck to do with the awful information. Probably I should tell someone. Yes. Right. That makes sense.

"Thom?" I say, my voice weak and useless. I take a step back, followed by another. Not panicking, because panicking won't help. "Thom!"

Footsteps, more than one pair, race down the hallway. Then firm hands are grabbing my shoulders, pushing me gently out of the way.

Thom takes in the contents of the closet and sighs. "It's Spider."

Someone swears behind me.

"Should you, ah, check if he's alive?" I ask.

"No one loses that much blood and gets up again." He looks back, taking in those assembled. More people have apparently joined the party while I was sleeping. Fox and Badger are still here. But there's also a tall blond Thor-like individual and a woman with cool red hair.

"Wasn't me," says Fox. "He was alive and well, if somewhat unconscious, when I dumped him in the last bedroom down the hall yesterday. Wasn't there when I went to check on him later, so I figured he'd slunk off somewhere to get away from Wolf."

"Wolf and Spider got into it?" asks the redhead.

"I gave him a warning, that's all." Thom's jaw tightens. "This is not good."

"Roger that," says the big blond man.

Badger's eyes are red, his fingers constantly tapping against his side. God knows how long he's been going hard at it with his search engines and energy drinks. He's younger than the others, wiry and wired. "So I'm just going to come right out and say what we're all thinking. It's one of us."

"Possibly," says Thom. "Probably, even. If someone breached our perimeter, then they wouldn't have just taken out one of us. They would've kept going. At least, that's what I would have done. It feels like someone's picking us off for fun. Plus the security system on the house hasn't shown any sign of other entries."

The Thor dude turns to me, holding out a hand. "Hey. You must be the fiancée. I'm Bear."

"Betty."

His grasp is gentle, his gaze serious.

"I'm Hawk," says the redhead, wiggling her fingers at me with only vague interest. She's wearing a little green dress with a large knife strapped to her thigh. "With two down that still leaves six of us alive as possible suspects. Seven if we count Betty."

Thom takes up position standing in front of me, hiding me from view. Guess his protective instincts are real. Or at least they seem to be.

"This is real bad. Nothing against y'all, but I'm relocating until further notice." Badger shakes his head and wastes no time squeezing past Fox and Crow to get out the door.

"Try one more time to get that message through to HQ before you leave," orders Thom. "If they're cutting coms until this is sorted, we all need to know now."

Hawk frowns. "Those fuckers."

"Nothing like a little loyalty to let you know where you stand," says Bear.

No one seems to disagree with the sentiment.

"Complete deniability. It's safe to assume there'll be no help from on high." Thom gives me a quick glance over his shoulder. He doesn't seem worried exactly, but he's not happy either. "Let's not forget the job. We need to figure out whoever this is and stop them before we all wind up dead."

Fox rolls her eyes. "A rousing, spirit-raising speech as always, Wolf."

Instead of answering, he grabs my hand and leads us back to the room we'd been using. He points to the packed duffel sitting on the bed. "This everything?"

"Yes."

The duffel bag goes over his shoulder and he takes off in long strides down the hallway, leading me into an attached garage. Two vehicles sit waiting. A sleek Lamborghini and a bulky SUV. He, of course, bundles us into the SUV. No sexy sports car for me. A pity. I'd like to ride in something like that before I die.

Because it's feeling like that may not be so far off.

"I can put on my own seat belt." I smack his hands out of the way. "Jesus, Thom."

He deposits my bag in the back, withdrawing a jacket, pistol, and an extra magazine from some hidey-hole back there before closing the door. Every move he makes is swift, economical. Graceful in a way. The gun goes into the waistband of his jeans, the mag in a pocket, and the garage door starts rising. While doing something on his cell, he slips into the driver's seat and turns on the engine. Old Thom was shit at it, but this Thom can clearly multitask and then some. I bet he could juggle knives if I asked him.

"Are we going to die?" I ask, just making conversation.

Gaze on the rearview mirror, he backs out the vehicle. "You're not going to die."

"But you might?"

"Do you care?"

"Honestly, I don't know." I laugh.

Nothing from Thom.

"I need to call Jen and let her know I'm okay."

"Betty, it's not safe for you to be contacting anyone. Not right now. Not Jen. Not family. Not anyone."

"Everyone at work will be wondering where I am." I frown. Mom would tell me it causes way more wrinkles than smiling, but it seems to me that being forced to abandon your life and possibly face an early death is worth a line or two. "Surely we can at least get a message to them that I'm alive."

"Too risky."

"But they must be so worried." My throat tightens, my eyes burn. "God, this is insane."

"There's nothing we can do about it right now," he says, voice firm. "Just try and stay calm."

Easy for him to say. My mind won't stop racing. Fear apparently makes me chatty. Or maybe some part of me thinks more information will make this situation easier to get a grip on. "So you're in charge of the zoo? They all seem to look to you for direction, follow your orders."

"I'm the current most experienced operative."

"Who's Scorpion? Was she your real... Forget it. I don't want to know."

We speed away from the house on dirt roads, dust rising all around us and the sun beating down. No idea where we are. No idea what's going to happen. And the scent of blood still fills my lungs. The visual of Spider's corpse remains lodged inside my mind.

"Calm your breathing, Betty. I don't have time for you to have a panic attack right now."

The asshole's got a point. My chest is heaving. A sheen of sweat covers my whole body. He turns up the air-conditioning, blasting me with cold air. It helps a little. So does taking long, slow breaths.

"Never seen a dead body before," I say quietly.

"I know."

"Did you kill him?"

He glances over at me, his mouth a firm line. "No."

"All right." I nod. It probably makes me an idiot, but I believe him anyway. "Why am I still alive? I was asleep just a couple of rooms down, with no one between me and Spider. It would have been easy."

"The killer would have no reason to want you dead at this point. Whoever it is has probably marked you as a strategic liability, thinking it will be easier to deal with me if I need to focus on protecting you."

"Is that true? That I'm a liability?"

He swallows. "You're going to a place where I know you'll be safe. Then I'm going to go deal with this."

"You're dumping me somewhere?"

"I thought getting away from me was what you wanted."

"Really, you want to do this now?" I turn in my seat, all the better to face him. "Thom, you were never home. If it was your physical presence that pissed me off, all I had to do was stay right there. But it wasn't. Our relationship itself was complete and utter bullshit."

"In what way?" Now he sounds almost angry. This is quite possibly the most honest emotion that I've had from him in forever. "Because I had to travel for work? To earn a living?"

"Because even when you were home, you were never really with me. Mentally and emotionally, you were elsewhere."

"That's absurd."

"To be fair, this whole discussion is pretty absurd."

The dirt road ends and we turn onto something resembling civilization. More houses. Occasional people and other cars. Signs of life, normal life. People going about their mornings without their whole world turned upside down and the threat of imminent death hanging over their heads.

"How was I not with you?" he asks, definitely getting testy.

"Every time you wanted to bitch about some idiot at work or talk about who Jen was banging, I listened. Even when you were just repeating yourself, I was attentive and supportive."

"You know, I don't think you're as good at pretending to be interested in things as you think you are."

"I always let you pick what we watched on TV, let you decide what takeout we got."

"Is that all a relationship is to you?" I ask, any hint of a panic attack long forgotten. This insight into Thom's mind is fascinating. And somewhat disturbing.

"It wasn't all a lie, you know."

"Honestly?" I arched my eyebrows. "What part of it was real?

"I wasn't lying when I said I love you."

I laughed. Maybe I shouldn't have, but I couldn't help it. "Well that's ironic. Because that was the one thing you said to me that I didn't believe."

"Why not?" He scowls. "There was intimacy. We had sex."

At this, I scoff. I can't help it.

"What?"

"Our sex life was not amazing."

It takes him a moment to respond. "The average cohabitating couple has sex approximately fifty-one times a year. When you deduct time spent away due to work, we met the average."

"We met the average? Huh," I say. "How I aspire to always meet the average. It's my life goal, really."

"Bring on the sarcasm. What a surprise."

"Oh, yeah? How's this for sarcastic, Thom? More often than not the sex sucked—and not in the good way." So there. "I bought lingerie and read all of the stupid articles about tips for the bedroom. I tried to keep things interesting."

His fingers tighten around the steering wheel. "Most women

don't manage to climax every time they have intercourse with their partners. I'm sorry, but I had to maintain the median...the illusion of us being a normal couple."

I just blink.

"It's a well-known fact. Studies show that—"

"Wait a minute," I say, my brain on fire. "Are you actually saying you researched the average relationship, worked out how often we should be having sex, and then only occasionally bothered to give me an orgasm when it suited your purposes?"

"Not my purposes. Your purposes. I was trying to give you the relationship you wanted. Something safe. Normal."

"Give me your gun." I hold out my hand. "I'm going to shoot you."

"Betty—"

"Give me your gun."

"I'm not going to let you shoot me. Calm down."

"I don't want to calm down." So. Much. Rage. "Not only was the relationship fake, but you deliberately gave me bad sex! You're a monster."

He gives me a side glance. "I was trying to keep things realistic, believable. I was trying to meet what I thought were your expectations."

"Oh, yeah? Well, expect to be smothered if you ever try to sleep next to me again." I straighten in the seat, staring out the windshield. "I can't even...there's a special level of hell for you, buddy."

"I gave you what you wanted. You *said* that's what you wanted."

"What?" I felt like my head was about to explode. "When? When did I ever say to you that I would prefer the worst sex possible?"

"Not to me. To Jen. Before our first date. You said to her

that you were sick of pining for Prince Charming. That something safe and good and comfortable would do."

"You were tapping my phone? Listening to my private conversations?"

"I needed to know you weren't going to be a security risk."

There are no words. I just glare at him.

"I tried to be a good boyfriend to you. A good fiancé."

"No, you didn't. You did the least amount of work possible to keep me pacified. Big difference, Thom. Big. Huge." I will not cry. I refuse to show weakness. At least I didn't expect the truth to actually fix anything. Yay me for being less naive. "Thank God."

"What?"

"Thank God I raised my expectations high enough to realize I deserve better."

To this, he apparently again has nothing to say. Just as well.

"For so long, I thought it was me. That I wasn't pretty enough or smart enough or…just enough for you in general."

"Betty." His mouth opens, then closes again. "That's crazy."

Heart sore, I shake my head. "Just drive."

We drive north for hours. Thom is basically a machine. Like some killer robot sent from the future to fuck up my love life. Clearly the world would have been doomed if I orgasmed more than once a month, so the fate of humanity depended on this machine coming back and *not* getting the job done. Asshat.

His gaze is constantly moving between the road, the rearview mirror, me, and cars approaching on the driver's side. Guess he's watching to see if we're being followed. Also he may be slightly concerned I'm going to throw myself out of the moving vehicle in an attempt to get away from him. And I would;

I'm angry enough. But it probably wouldn't end well for me personally. After being thrown about by yesterday's explosion, I hurt enough without adding further injuries. So instead, I ignore him with all the pent-up rage I have in me and mostly nap.

We drive until refilling the tank necessitates a stop that afternoon somewhere in northern California. It's a small, desolate, off-the-highway gas station. Junk food, come to me. I haven't eaten in forever. We did stop about an hour back so I could pee behind a tree, since Thom's gone well beyond cautious and is sliding straight into outright paranoid territory when it comes to his concerns about people seeing us. Along with keeping up the constant vigilance, he swapped out the SIM card in his cell, crushing the old beneath his boot heel. Apparently his cell also has a program to check for trackers so he's sure the SUV is safe. And I know he's packing all sorts of weaponry beneath his clothes.

"Thank God; I'm starving." I move to open my car door, but before I can, Thom grabs my arm. "What?"

"Please stay in the car. I'll get you whatever you want."

"Why? There's no one else here but you, me, and the woman behind the counter. I highly doubt she's the least bit interested in us."

"Because even a dump like this is going to have security cameras that can be hacked and used to find us."

As much as I'd like to get out and stretch my legs, he's making sense again. Dammit. So I slump back against the seat. "Fine. Get me one of everything."

"Will do."

Thom grabs a baseball cap out of the back of the car and puts it on before stepping out. Head down, he avoids giving anyone or any camera a clear visual of his face. He skulks, yet makes it seem normal somehow. Just a man going about his business, nothing to see here. Inside, he fills up a basket before heading up to the counter to pay the bored-looking middle-aged lady at the register. Even then, he moves with an easy everyday swagger, behaving in as uninteresting a fashion as possible. It's quite the performance. The slouch in his back reducing his height and the slump of his shoulders declaring him another harmless slacker passing through.

No wonder he had me fooled for so long. This man is a veritable wolf in sheep's clothing.

"You're a natural," I say as he climbs back in the car, handing over my bag of junk food.

"Hmm?"

"The way you move and behave and everything. So sneaky."

He turns on the engine, reaching over to grab the bag of Swedish Fish.

"Where did you learn it?"

His glances at me. "I'm not supposed to talk about that, Betty."

"Yeah, but I figure if you're right about us being stuck together for the foreseeable future—"

"Which, unless you'd prefer being dead, I am."

"Let me finish talking," I say. "Once we get through this, if we survive, I'm sure you can figure out a way to pacify your bosses while ensuring we spend as little time in each other's company as possible. You're a clever and cunning dude. It comes with the job territory, right? So we get your organization off our backs and live separate lives. See other people. Have our emotional and sexual needs met elsewhere."

"You're planning on cheating on me?"

I shrug. "Is it really cheating, though?"

The look he gives me is flat and unfriendly.

"Or," I continue, "you can start talking."

"Me talking is going to fix things?"

"Not even remotely." My laughter is completely without humor. "But here and now, we could maybe get along just enough to almost be friendly."

"Remind me: What's in this for me again?"

"Are you actually telling me you want to resurrect our relationship in some form?" I cock my head. "Seriously?"

The smallest of shrugs.

"That's honestly the best you can manage? And you wonder why I was leaving you, with such stellar communication skills as that. Wow."

"C'mon, Betty—"

"You know, you're the one who dragged me into this mess," I say, well and truly cranky now. "Basically, you talking would be a start toward attaining a little forgiveness and building some small level of trust between us...assuming you're interested in that sort of thing."

Nothing from Thom. Perhaps he'll get sick of me and kill me himself. After all, what do I know about this man really?

"Isn't it nice, having me all compliant and agreeable?" I ask.

"Isn't it nice, riding in comfort instead of being bound and gagged in the trunk of the car?"

What an utter and absolute douche-canoe. And this is about when I see it. "Holy shit. A man is robbing the gas station."

"Is he?" Thom doesn't even turn to look. "Car's bulletproof. We're fine."

"Yes, but the woman behind the counter isn't. Oh my God, do something!"

He cocks his head. "Betty, we're trying to stay under the radar. Crimes like this happen all the time. She's handing over the money. He's not going to shoot her."

"You can't know that for sure."

"What I do know is, if I go in there and spook him, odds are someone gets hurt."

Inside the station, the woman is pushing the cash and packets of cigarettes across the counter. She's crying and shaking. The robber stuffs all of the assorted loot into the pockets of his sweatpants and hoodie.

"Oh, this is horrible."

"See, he's leaving without a shot being fired."

"That poor woman. She might lose her job. I wonder if she even has medical insurance. You'd have to get post-traumatic stress disorder from something like this, right?"

The heaviest of sighs comes from the man in the driver's seat. "Put your seat belt on," he orders. "Now."

I do as told.

Thom swears under his breath. His eyes are locked on mine, but suddenly the SUV jumps forward, tires screeching as he suddenly slams on the brake.

We don't hit the robber. Or at least, I didn't think we did, but he is on the ground screaming, so obviously something happened.

The driver's side door is flung open, hitting something with a dull thud. I think it was the gunman's head. Then Thom steps out, grabs the pistol out of the bad guy's hand, before settling himself back into the car.

"Is he dead?"

"No," says Thom. "I just ran over his foot and knocked him out. Couple of broken bones and a concussion. The lady at the counter is already calling the cops. She'll get the cash back, and he'll be fine. It'll be educational for him."

Huh.

With more squealing of wheels, we take off. Guess Thom wants as much distance between us and the gas station as possible.

"A couple of broken bones and a concussion?" My stomach turns queasily at the thought. "That's all?"

"Yes."

"Ouch," I say. "Still, thank you for not being a complete sociopath."

"You're welcome. But we can't save everyone, okay?"

"Okay."

In all honesty, I'm kind of stunned. He did a nice thing, sort of. Used his powers for good instead of evil. Maybe he's not too far removed from the basically kind and ethically moral person I thought he was. Only, there're still all the lies and bad sex to be considered. His willingness to waste my life on a fake relationship to keep his cover intact. So yeah, not very deep down, I kind of still hate his guts and want to shoot him.

"Like I told you, I came up in the foster system," he says, tossing a Swedish Fish into his mouth and chewing. "Spent most of my time running wild, getting into and out of trouble. Eventually they'd get sick of me and pass me on to the next foster home. No one really cared what I did."

I always figured this aspect of his background accounted for his being somewhat emotionally stunted. A loveless childhood is bound to leave its mark. And I hate thinking of him being alone. My family has its foibles, though there's affection there too. We care about each other. I tried to give this to Thom, but he proved remarkably resistant to any and all exchange of feelings. At least now I know why. Not only did his childhood suck, but he was probably trained to go without. I can only imagine that forging bonds, having actual feelings about people, makes it harder to disappear when the job is done. Had to make it harder to kill.

"Enlisted in the army first chance I got, turned out I was good at something after all. Kept myself out of trouble and worked hard," he continues. "Worked my way up to Ranger before I got tapped for this. Thought I was trying out for Delta, but it was not."

"You're not in the military anymore?"

"Nope. This is closer to what you'd call private-sector work. No government oversight. Private funding."

"What'd they do to you?"

"Put me through the damn wringer. Made the training I'd had up until then look like a joke."

I nod, turning all of the information over inside my head. "But you're the good guys, right? You're trying to make things better?"

"Yes, Betty. Trying."

"In what ways?"

Now he's really frowning. "All sorts of things. Stopping terrorists, dealing with hostage situations, trying to prevent genocides, tracing nukes, obstructing arms trades. Basically cutting the heads off snakes."

Sounds like he's fighting the good fight. But I still wish I could read him. I used to think I could, but now I know I don't have a clue. In this current situation, he has all the power. I'm pretty much along for a ride that might wind up killing me. One that I have no foreseeable way of getting out of. Being so dependent on someone sucks. But then, everything about this pretty much does. "And that's the truth…what you just told me?"

"Yes, that's the truth. We're not always successful, but we try."

The only thing I can do right now is wait and see. "Okay."

THREE

"SO YOU'VE BEEN TRAINED IN ESPIONAGE-TYPE STUFF?"

"Define stuff," he says.

"Obviously, you've got your Boy Scout badge for lying and manipulating."

"Obviously," he agrees. "Though we tend to call it establishing and maintaining cover. Executing surveillance. It sounds nicer that way. More polite."

"Hmm. What else have you earned badges in?" I ask, turning in the seat again. All the better to see him. Somehow he seems more alive to me now. Just more, in general. Maybe I'm finally dealing with the real Thom as opposed to a weak facsimile of the man.

"Ah, infiltration, identity theft...all of your usual types of trickery and deceit. The skillset is generally labeled combat and counterintelligence skills."

"And do you have gadgets? Do you carry, like, a bug out bag?"

He gives me side eyes.

"You know what I mean, Thom. What normal people have in case of a zombie apocalypse? Or in your case, being caught doing spy-type activities."

"Do normal people really prepare for a zombie apocalypse? That's the question..."

"Reality television says yes."

He makes a low humming noise. "To answer your question, I have an operational bag. But there are a few things I also always carry on me in case of emergencies."

"Such as?"

A slightly pained expression crosses his face. Information's a valued commodity in his world and here I am forcing him to hand it over for no payoff at all. I almost feel sorry for the guy. "A razor blade, handcuff key, bobby pin...stuff like that I've pretty much always got on me."

"Why a bobby pin? Emergency hair malfunction?"

"Sure, it could be used for that. Though I tend to utilize it more for getting out of zip ties."

"Huh. I know you love your man bag, but I've never actually seen you with any of those other things."

"That's because they're hidden in my clothing, the hem of my shirt or pants, tongue of my shoe, in my belt and such. Our operations are called clandestine for a reason."

I shake my head. "Wow. Your world is weird."

"I can see how it would seem that way to you. But it's pretty much all I've ever known."

Interesting. "I guess you can acclimatize to anything given enough time."

"Guess so."

Earlier, we stopped and swapped our license plates with some others stored in the back of the SUV, making it a little harder for anyone who heard about the scene at the gas station to trace us. My ass aches from sitting in the vehicle for so long. But at least I'm still in one piece.

Somewhere in the middle of nowhere, we turned off the highway. Now we're heading into the hills and wilderness and I don't know what. "Are you going to kill me and dump my body out here among all of this natural splendor?"

"Wasn't planning on it."

"Oh, good. Hang on, do you have any other fiancées or families I should know about?" I frown. Not a nice thought. Things are confusing enough as is. "Do you?"

"Of course not."

I narrow my eyes on him.

"I'm telling the truth," he says, sounding mildly put out at being questioned. Guess he's not used to it from me. He takes a deep breath, letting it out slowly. "Anyway, I couldn't even keep you convinced long term. How the hell would I have managed convincing others too? Relationships, real or otherwise, are apparently not my forte."

"But you've had girlfriends before me, right?"

This time he gives me a long look. Long enough to make me worry about us driving off the road and hitting a tree. But we don't. For all of his uselessness as a boyfriend, he handles the vehicle with precision.

"No," he finally answers. "I haven't."

"Boyfriends?"

"None of them either."

My brows rise. I can feel them inching up toward my hairline, about to disappear at any moment.

"Generally, I was doing my best not to get shot, stabbed, or blown up at home and abroad. My priorities were elsewhere," he says. "Wasn't in the right head space in high school, I didn't have time for relationships once I enlisted, and work has kept me busy and on the move since."

"But you got tired of having no one to come home to."

He nods. "That's what I said."

"Guess we have that in common. It's amazing, isn't it? We have this modern world where we're all so connected and yet we're all still so lonely." Social media does not happiness make. I know that much. "Didn't you want to get real with someone, though? Instead of just going through the motions?"

"I don't think telling someone you steal, lie, and kill for a living would go over so well on a first date."

"Yeah, but we were going to get married. That's a bit beyond first-date territory, Thom."

He sighs. "I was trying to protect you."

Outside the window, redwoods flash by. "If you haven't got honesty in a relationship then what the hell *do* you have? All of it was nothing more than a lie."

"A lie that kept you safe."

"Except it didn't, did it?"

He rolls his shoulders, cracks his neck.

"I find it hard to believe you've never been in any sort of romantic relationship before. Haven't you at least done the preliminaries? Taken someone on a date?" I ask. "Not as part of your work, but just for company?"

"Stopped for a drink or something first? Sure."

Amazing. The man is a real romantic. I tap my fingers against my thighs, thinking deep thoughts. "But weren't you trained in seduction and all that? How to get people to give you what you want in the course of carrying out your nefarious and underhanded schemes?"

"Yes."

"Then how did you mess us up so badly?"

A small line appears between his dark brows. "I'm still trying to figure that out."

"Maybe I'm just too high-maintenance for you. Or maybe you misread me and played the wrong character."

"Maybe I did," he agrees.

"That happens with bigger girls." I rest my head back, gazing out at all of the aforementioned natural splendor. "People tend to think we'll be happy to take the scraps."

He shoots me a look, but says nothing.

Up a seemingly endless winding path, we reach a decrepit wooden cabin. Still somewhere in northern California. The ground is muddy with occasional puddles and the air has a verdant scent similar to the moss we use at work. Guess it's rained a lot lately. Trees are alive with the most beautiful bright autumn colors, while the shack itself is half-covered in spider webs, dirt, and overgrown vines. One of the front windows is shattered and a broken rocking chair sits on the front porch. It looks like something out of a horror film. The type with ghosts and other assorted monsters lurking in the basement. Serial killers hiding in the bedroom. That sort of thing. Not even the soft hazy late-afternoon light can enhance this dump.

"I guess no one will think to look for us here," I say.

"Come on." He grabs my duffel bag out of the back and hoists it over his shoulder. "Lesson number one, never trust your eyes."

Bypassing the cabin, he heads straight for the falling-down woodshed or whatever it is at the side. It leans against the original structure at an odd angle, the door hanging on mostly by a thread, so far as I can see. But then he just said not to trust my eyes. The door creaks ominously and Thom steps inside the dark, dank shed.

I, however, hesitate. "We're going in there? I think if you're going to kill me, I'd prefer it happened out here. Have the last thing I see be blue sky and butterflies and pretty things like that."

He grabs my hand and tugs me in after him. The door swings shut and clicks into place. And then we wait.

"What are we waiting for?" I whisper for some reason.

"You'll see."

Somewhere between thirty seconds and forever later, I ask, "Are you sure about this?"

"Yes," growls Thom. "Henry, quit dicking around and let us in."

At this, the back wall of the shed swings open to reveal a set of metal stairs descending below ground. Small white lights are embedded in the concrete wall.

It's an honest-to-God underground bunker. Holy hell.

The crazy-ass survivalist owner in question sits below among long work benches loaded with computers, assorted weaponry, and ammunition. I thought people like this only existed on the Discovery Channel. But he's real, and about fifty or so, with silver hair and reading glasses perched on the end of his nose. "Wasn't expecting you."

"It's an emergency," says Thom. "This is my fiancée, Betty."

Henry's mouth drops open. "You're getting married? You?"

"No," I say just as Thom says, "Yes."

The man looks between us, expression bemused.

"We're still working out some issues." A solid compromise from Thom. Sort of. "She's going to stay here with you for a while."

"This have to do with a friend of yours getting hit in Prague?" asks Henry, crossing his arms.

Thom just blinks. "News travels fast. Yes, it does have to do with that."

"Thought as much. All right, then, boy. What do you need?"

"The works."

Henry whistles between his teeth. "It'll cost you."

"I'm aware. Also going to need a hacker. The best you can find."

"On-site?"

"No."

"It's going to take some time to organize."

"That's one thing I don't have a lot of." Thom sighs. "How soon can you have it ready?"

"Give me 'til midnight. One at the latest."

"Okay. The vehicle up top needs to disappear as well."

"Roger that." Slowly, Henry rises from his stool, giving me a looking over. "Betty, huh? You realize he's a certified a-hole who doesn't deserve you?"

"I do," I say.

"Good for you, honey. Break his spirit and make him crawl." Henry grins. "Take the room in the back and help yourself to the pot roast in the fridge. Made it myself yesterday."

While I seriously love this guy, Thom exudes an aura of less than impressed.

The bunker is all concrete and steel. Though the numerous racks of knives, guns, and other assorted things that go boom lining the walls give it a homey touch. If home is meant to be vaguely apocalyptic, that is. Holy shit.

"You okay?" asks Thom.

"Um, yeah." I wipe my sweaty palms on the side of my jeans. Anxiety is becoming a bad habit, but I don't see it ending anytime soon. "Is that a rocket launcher on that table?"

He turns, taking in the instrument of mass destruction in question. "Only a small one. Hey, what's wrong? You're not feeling agoraphobic, are you?"

"No, no." My attempt at a smile feels weak and sloppy. "Just...you know...trying to keep up with everything."

"You're doing great. C'mon."

He takes my hand once more, leading me down a hallway. We sure are holding hands a lot lately.

First there's a long, narrow room with a couple of those paper body outlines hanging at the end. Henry has his own underground shooting range, apparently. As you do. Next is a storage room with even more gear and weapons neatly sorted and stored. Then a small kitchen and dining area. A lounge room with an elderly TV, battered-looking La-Z-Boy, and a green plaid sofa. A couple of closed doors, a very minimal bathroom, and finally, a small room with a double bed made up with military precision. It's like Batman's lair but with more weaponry and less of a cave-like aesthetic.

I'm so far out of my element these days, it's not funny.

"Make yourself at home." Thom dumps my bag on the end of the bed. "I've got some things to do."

I nod.

"Betty."

I look up. "What?"

"Everything's going to be okay," he says, eyes as serious as they can get. "I promise."

"Who is he? How well do you know him?"

And there's the pause. The entrenched reluctance to withhold all information, to not give anything away. I just wait while he wages his internal battle. Eventually he swallows hard, licks his lips. "Met him when I joined the Rangers. Things went south on a mission in Afghanistan and he took the fall. Dumbass politics. He retired from active duty, but he got bored, and also he was a little upset at the government in general, so he decided to set up shop."

"So, what, he's like the underground Walmart of war now?"

He almost smiles. It's a close thing. "Basically. Only deals with a very select clientele. He owes me a favor. You'll be safe here. This place is basically impenetrable."

"Okay."

"I got to get to work."

"Sure. Go. I'll be fine."

Another pause, and his hand half reaches out, gaze going to my mouth. And I realize what he intended. Because this is what we always used to do when one of us went to work. Before he'd disappear off on a business trip, he'd take my hand and give me a kiss. Nothing overly dramatic or reeking of romance. Just a squeeze of the fingers and quick peck, really. Us going through the motions of being a couple. Him pretending to be my boy-friend.

But now he just stands there, frozen. Lips slightly parted, a faint frown in place. I don't think I've ever seen him look so un-sure.

"I'll be fine," I repeat, taking a small step back. Because I don't want him to kiss me. Not if he's only doing it because it's what we do. Not if it means nothing. Though I shouldn't want him kissing me at all. I shouldn't want him anywhere near me. God, this is confusing.

He gives me a slow nod.

"You won't leave without saying goodbye, will you?" I ask.

"No."

"Okay."

Then, without another word, he's gone.

Underground bunkers are surprisingly boring. Or not so sur-prisingly, depending on your point of view. I take a shower and change into a fresh set of jeans and a blue T-shirt. I eat some reheated pot roast and peruse the collection of DVDs. Lots of Clint Eastwood and John Wayne. Some Hong Kong gun fu, Jackie Chan, and Bruce Lee. No idea where Thom has gone, but Henry is back to leaning over a workbench. The same as he was when we arrived.

"What are you doing?" I ask, wandering closer.

"Making bullets."

"Can I help?"

"No thank you."

"So you've known Thom a long time, huh?"

"That I have."

With a hip leaned against the bench, I do my best just-hanging-out-and-taking-it-easy impression. I am the queen of subtlety. "You know all about his activities and his history and everything?"

With a smile, he sets his little tools and the weighing machine aside. "You have questions."

"Yes."

"I can't answer them for you."

Damn. "Well, how about you tell me about you, then?"

"Sorry, honey. That's classified." And he's serious. Very much so. "But if it makes you feel any better, I've never seen a woman make Thom nervous before."

"Me? Make him nervous?" I laugh. "You must be kidding. He certainly doesn't show it."

"Of course not; it's been trained out of him. Physical tells are a big no-no. Can't have targets reading your body language and figuring out what you're up to." Henry leans in closer, like he's selling state secrets. "Yet I've seen him slip a time or two around you already. It's quite entertaining."

"Huh."

"Why don't we talk about something I'm actually allowed to talk about?" he proposes. "Tell me, Betty, if someone attacked you, what would you do?"

"Scream."

"A good start. What next?"

I think it over. "I don't know. I guess I'd hit them or kick them or try to run away if possible."

"Mm-hmm." He crosses his arms. "Do you carry pepper spray?"

"I did, but I lost my handbag and everything when the condo blew up."

"What about a knife?"

"Do not give her a knife." Thom appears behind me, sunglasses resting on top of his head. I hate it when he sneaks up on me, which is often. Another giveaway for his true vocation. He's so stealthy, not making a sound. "Moved the SUV into the garage. Where'd you pick up the Cobra?"

"None of your business," says Henry. "And it's not for sale."

"Pity."

Meanwhile, there's me and my outrage to consider. "Hey, I'm a florist. I play with pretty flowers and sharp things all day. I can handle a knife."

Thom doesn't even blink. "Not fighting with one, you can't."

"All right. Then you need to teach me how to fire a gun so I can defend myself."

"You hate guns."

"More than I can possibly say. But we're being hunted here, Thom."

His jaw firms. "No."

"This is ridiculous," I say with just the right touch of petulance. "He just wants to hide me away, safe and sound."

"That's what people do with things they treasure." Henry rises to his feet, cracking his neck. He's pretty buff for an older guy, broad of shoulder, with a barrel chest. But he's way off on the treasure thing. Mostly I'm probably just a pain in the ass where Thom is concerned. But Henry doesn't know that.

"This is a lovely underground bunker." I paste a pleasant smile on my face. "But I'm not sure anywhere is completely safe right now. Isn't it better to be prepared?"

"She's got a point," says Henry. "Teach her how to shoot, Thom. You've got the time and facilities—use them."

"I don't want this shit touching her."

"Too late—it already has. If you wanted her to remain a

nice, normal girl from the suburbs, then you should never have gone near her."

"I'm aware of that."

"Then do something about it, clown-dick."

I snort. "Good one."

Thom, however, is not amused. "Back off, old man."

"You're just pissed because you know I'm right," returns Henry, nonplussed.

"Am I allowed to say something?" I ask.

"Of course you are, honey," says Henry. It's good to have someone on my side. Especially someone who makes Thom stop and listen.

"Neither of you can promise me safety. Not really. Things happen." I look Thom right in the eyes, face set. "If the last day and a half has taught me anything, it's that none of us are in complete control of this situation. There's a chance you may not be able to stop what's coming. Give me a fighting chance."

Thom's gaze is flat and unhappy.

"Oh, dear," whispers Henry. "He wanted to be your hero in shining armor and you've just gone and burst his bubble."

Both Thom and I frown.

"Of course, if they get past our boy here, we're probably all screwed." Henry gives me a warm smile. I think Thom's father figure just became mine as well.

"They don't know about you or this place," says Thom. "Why do you think I brought her here?"

"He doesn't have any connections to the zoo?" I ask.

"None."

"The zoo?" Henry laughs. "I love it. She's adorable. You should definitely marry her. But teach her how to kill first."

Turns out Henry is right about the physical tells. Thom has micro-expressions. A hint of furrowed brow, or a certain tightening of the eyes, like right now. Then there's my personal favorite, the ever-so-slight upward curl of one side of his lips. This is how he frowns, expresses anger, or smiles. In small ways. No wonder I thought him an emotionless automaton. Not only was he hiding everything from me, but I definitely wasn't reading him right. Until recently, that is.

Guess it isn't until you know someone's a liar that you know to really look. As he said, don't trust your eyes. They can deceive you far too easily.

Spies and so on in the movies are always rough and rugged or debonair and dashing. But Thom just sort of blends in. Slouches just enough that his height doesn't stand out. Medium build. Must be useful for his job. Of course, I thought him attractive. Or maybe what sealed the deal was his initial interest in me. The fact that someone wanted me. Everyone needs validation now and then.

Never again will I fall for that shit. I am woman, hear me roar. I do not need a man or a relationship or whatever it was I thought was so lacking from my life. I will stand on my own two feet and learn how to defend myself. Even if the thought of being violent sort of makes me want to hurl again.

"You all right?" asks Thom.

I raise my chin high. "I'm fine."

He just looks at me.

"I am."

"If you say so." His gaze seems to take in everything. He's not a classically handsome man, but there's something enticing about his angular features. The hard line of his jaw and fine lips, his clear blue eyes and high forehead. Then there's the nose that's been broken a time or two. He told me he'd broken it skateboarding as a child. Another lie, no doubt.

"C'mon." He tips his chin. As if that explains anything.

"Where are we going?"

"You wanted to learn how to handle a gun," he says, selecting one off the wall. "This is a single-stack nine millimeter."

"What's single stack mean?"

"Instead of two alternating lines of ammunition in the magazine, you've just got the one. So the grip is smaller and the gun is lighter. But you've got fewer rounds, okay?"

"Okay."

"It's a compact. Women usually like them."

"Ooh, does it come in pink?"

"Are you taking this seriously, Betty, or shall we not bother?" He gives me a look from under his brows. "I could happily do without you accidentally shooting yourself in the foot. Or me."

"If I shoot you it will not be an accident."

He just waits.

"Sorry," I say, chastened. "I am taking this seriously. Please proceed."

His hand moves over the piece. "If you're not using the gun, keep it pointed away toward the ground. If you're not prepared to fire it, don't draw it in the first place. Brandishing a weapon is pretty much guaranteed to escalate tension every time. Sometimes trying to talk your way out of a situation first is best. Got it?"

"Got it."

He nods toward the hallway. "Let's head into the shooting range."

We go inside the long room with the weird thick gray padding hanging on the walls and matching foam attached to the ceiling. At one end is a small desk with a couple of pairs of earmuffs. Far down the other end of the room is the traditional paper target with the outline of a body. Other people would use this space for a home theater or bowling lane. Not Henry.

Thom shows me the magazine with a neat stack of ammunition before slapping it back into the grip or butt or handle or whatever it's called. Then he runs his fingers over the top of the gun, indicating each piece. "Front sight, ejection port, slide, and rear sight."

I nod.

"And this here is your trigger," he says, passing the weapon to me. "Put your ear protection on."

With nerves beginning to kick in, I do as he says.

"Give it a go. See how it feels." He closes the door and puts on his own earmuffs. It makes our voices sound like they're underwater or something. Muted, but not completely silenced.

"How exactly do I hold it?" I ask, probably yelling.

He moves to stand behind me, putting his arms around me in an almost embrace. Then his fingers position mine in a solid grip on the gun. "Like that," he says in a deep voice beside my ear. "Hold it firmly, but don't throttle it. Not too tight."

"All right. I think I've got it."

His arms fall back to his sides, but he doesn't move. His breath is warm against my neck, the heat of his body at my back. It's all very distracting.

"You're going to stay there while I do this?" I ask.

"What's wrong, Betty? Don't trust me out of your line of sight?"

"Not really."

He chuckles. A rather nice sound, unfortunately. "Put your feet shoulder-width apart, knees slightly bent. That's right. One hand holds the gun while the other supports it. Arms extended, but not locked. Now line up the target. Nice, even breathing. And don't tug at the trigger; it's a gentle squeeze."

"Okay." I do as told. "Do I fire now?"

"Whenever you're ready."

My whole body is rigid with tension despite my best intensions. Maybe I just need to get the first one out of the way. Breathing hard, I line up the target, and squeeze.

The gun bucks in my hand and it is loud. Like crazy loud. "Where'd it go?"

"The roof," he says. "You're fighting the recoil. You're anticipating the gun going off and jerking your hand. That's what's throwing off your aim."

"All right. What's the cure?"

"Awareness and practice. Go again. Squeeze slowly and stay relaxed. Let it surprise you."

I try to calm my breathing, carefully lining up the target. Yet there's something about him being so close. In the good old days of our fake relationship, back in the beginning, he'd kiss my forehead, slide an arm around my waist, all those sorts of little touchy-feely couple things. Now, however, I'm way too aware of his proximity. "You're really going to stand there the whole time?"

"You're fine," he says. "C'mon. If you can't relax and fire with me near you, how are you going to manage in an actual situation?"

I just wait.

The man releases a pained sigh and takes a step back. "Happy?"

"Ecstatic." I fire again. This time I clip the corner of the paper target. "Yes!"

"Good job—you just mildly inconvenienced the enemy. Try again and actually hit him this time."

"You're not being very supportive."

"I never wanted to see a gun in your hand. Never wanted any of this to touch you." His voice is full of frustration, regret. It almost makes me not hate him quite so much. But then he manhandles my arms back into position, getting all up in my space again, and lining up the next target. "Aim for central body mass. That's what we want."

"Okay, okay. Give me some breathing room."

Once more, he steps back. "Sorry. Shoot."

This time, I hit the paper low in the bottom half. "How'd I do?"

"I think you clipped his groin, the poor bastard. Probably took out his left nut."

"Ha. That'll teach him to mess with me."

I smile, and he smiles, and for a brief moment everything's fine. Right up until I remember everything is most definitely not fine. Not even a little. My grin fades and so does Thom's. Only his disappears at a slower rate. We're most definitely not meant to be making any new and happy, if somewhat odd, memories here. We're weaponizing me because of the shit he's dragged me into. Best not to forget this salient fact.

"Go again," he says. "You're doing good, Betty. I'm proud of you."

Huh. I don't think he's ever said he's proud of me before. At least, not that I'm aware of. But they're just words. A small throwaway statement with little real meaning, most likely. Nothing worth having warm, fuzzy feelings over.

I fire the rest of the bullets in an angry rush. None of them hit.

"You were way off. What happened?" he asks, because the man isn't stupid. He's also not distant or absentminded like he used to be, unfortunately. "What are you thinking about?"

"I just…nothing." I sigh. "Let's go again."

He gives me a long look, then nods and hands over another magazine. "Okay. Take your time. I know you can do this."

A half-assed smile is the best I can manage. Practice. I'm going to need a lot of practice. At both firing the gun and ignoring the real Thom, apparently.

FOUR

"**W**HY ME?" I ASK, LYING ON THE BED LATER THAT NIGHT. "I can't have been the only desperate single at that particular moment in L.A."

Thom steps out of the bathroom on a cloud of steam. It's one of those bathrooms that has doors opening onto the hallway and the guest bedroom, so we get a little privacy. Though we don't particularly need any. The towel wrapped around his waist doesn't hide much, however. I don't mean to stare, but I'm pretty sure I do. While it's one thing to know his body by touch in the dark, it's quite another to see it backlit by the bathroom and highlighted by the bedside lamp. If anything, the scars just add an interesting element to the ridges and planes of his musculature. He's all lean and lethal. I don't know if I'll ever get used to the way he flaunts his form these days. Though I guess he's not flaunting it exactly. He's just not pathologically hiding it anymore.

Have I mentioned I don't like change?

"Do I have to answer this?" he asks.

"Yes."

He moves as if to cross his arms or similar, but stops himself mid-motion. Maybe Henry was right when he said I make Thom nervous. "You're going to hate me."

"Eh. Kind of already do."

"Good point," he says. "I actually spotted you a few weeks

before that at the taco place you like. You were with Jen and what's-his-face and Aiko from your work."

"Ethan. His name is Ethan. I don't know why you can never remember it."

"I remember it just fine. But he's a dick, and you kept making me socialize with him so I prefer to never have his name cross my lips."

"And that's not petty and dramatic at all." I raise my brows. "You said he was an okay guy."

"Yeah. I lied about that too."

I snort. "Of course you did. Continue."

"It's pretty straightforward." He makes the smallest of shrugs. "I liked your smile."

"That's it?"

"Yep. I liked your smile. End of story."

For a moment I pause. Digest. Then respond with, "Bullshit."

"What part?"

"You liked my 'smile.'" So I may have used air quotes. While it shouldn't be encouraged, it's not technically a crime. "Really?"

"Yes."

"That's such a lame line. I mean, you're saying you chose me out of all the single women in the city to lie and deceive because of my smile."

"I really did."

I narrow my eyes, but he doesn't even so much as blink. So my ability to intimidate the man is limited. Given he's probably faced down much scarier types than me, it's to be expected.

"Okay. Then what happened?" I ask.

"Then I may have done a bit of research before approaching you that night at the bar." He scratches his head, sets his hands on his hips. Maybe he's trying to divert my attention to his treasure trail or something. Throw me off base. I don't know. It won't work, though. I hardly ogle him at all.

"Research," I repeat. "Hang on...do you mean you stalked me?"

"I'd prefer to neither confirm nor deny that statement."

"Oh my God, you did. That's so wrong and gross, Thom. You creeped around sticking your nose into my life as if you had any right to."

He winces ever so slightly. "I never said that...exactly."

"But it's the truth, isn't it?"

"It's a harsh way to look at things," he says. "I saw a girl and I liked her smile, so I got to know her. What's wrong with that?"

"The part where I had no idea you were getting to know me?" I just can't with this man. His whole concept of legal and normal is lost somewhere in outer space. "You did a bit more than googling me, didn't you?"

"I just did some looking into your background," he says. "How else was I going to make sure you weren't crazy or related to someone in the FBI or something else that might complicate matters?"

"This is crazy."

"Had some concerns about your cousin Sara's husband. What with him being an undercover cop a while back."

"He was? I had no idea."

Thom nods. "But he's been banging one of their neighbors for years. Dude's got no credibility at all."

"He's been doing what?" My voice rises somewhat in volume. "Holy shit. Poor Sara. I have to tell her."

"And how exactly are you going to tell her you came by this information?" he asks, calm as can be.

"Good question. How did you happen to come by this information? Oh my God, did you peek through windows? Watch me and other assorted people with some long-range camera lens or something horrible like that?"

Nothing from him.

"Holy shit, Thom."

"Sorry. I'm sorry. But I didn't look at you naked or partially undressed or anything." The faint frown line between his brows is back. "What else can I say?"

"I don't know. Honestly, this is pretty messed up."

"I apologize. Again." He studies the ground. "Truth is, you seemed like a nice person, and I wanted to know if I had any competition or anything. We're trained to assess situations, prepare for any and all issues that may arise."

"Our whole relationship was like a mission to you. You assessed my life, inserted yourself into it, and then only worked within the parameters you were comfortable with."

"Is this about the orgasm thing again?"

If I had laser vision, I'd have smoked the man. Guaranteed.

Thom opens his mouth, then closes it. "Anything I say is just going to piss you off more right now, isn't it?"

"Probably." There's a crack in the ceiling high above my head. Fitting, given that there's an even bigger and even more destructive fault line running smack bam through my life. Move over, San Andreas, Thom Lange has you beat. "Are you actually sorry or are you just saying that because it's expected?"

His tongue plays behind his cheek. "Well, I don't like it when you're unhappy or angry. Especially not at me."

"All right."

"Was that the correct answer?"

"It wasn't a completely bad one, I guess. Though, honestly, the bar for any chance of you behaving like a normal, well-adjusted member of society has been set pretty damn low."

Despite my words, he nods, satisfied. "This is kind of

challenging, having a relationship where you're actually aware of who and what I am. It's interesting. Not something I thought I'd ever do, but…"

"A real growth experience, huh?"

"It is." His gaze is warm, fingers trailing along the top of his towel, over his flat stomach. It's almost like he wants to draw my attention to the bulge beneath the towel. What a showoff. He's all but feeling himself up. And he's totally doing this on purpose, trying to turn me on with his hot looks and hard body. Probably in an attempt to lure me into forgiving him or at least going easier. Either way, I'll give the man this much, he's perfected the art of the come-hither stare. Wonder if they gave him training in that too.

"Forget it," I say. "Garbage and recycling are on Tuesday, and you like your sex on a Saturday night if you're in town. It's not even the right day of the week, Thom…"

"Very funny. Just thought we could both do with a little stress release."

"Not happening."

"No?"

"Hell no. You just told me you stalked me, for goodness' sake. So stop it."

"Stop what?" One side of his lips rises. "What am I doing, Betty?"

"You know what you're doing." I laugh and it's a pained kind of sound. "The whole bedroom eyes and running your hands over your body and fumbling around with the tuck in your towel. This whole seduction thing you've got going on… just stop it. You disgust me."

"Is that why your nipples are hard?"

"Shut up and get dressed."

"No need for me to rush if you're enjoying the view," he

rumbles in a low, lusty voice. "If this life has taught me anything, it's to appreciate the quiet moments among the chaos. You have to enjoy yourself when you can."

"Save the philosophy. We are not having sex. I don't even like you."

"Oh, I think you like me a little bit. And you're bound to like me a lot more when I've got you naked beneath me, screaming my name."

Holy shit. I stare at him, dumbstruck. "You did not just say that to me."

"Want me to say it again?" he offers. "I can talk dirty to you in French if you'd like. Or Arabic, Spanish, Russian, Mandarin… lady's choice."

"Enough. You're not funny." My panties are not wet because of him. I just had a slight accident or something. Either that or my vagina is confused. And who could blame it? Meanwhile, heat is creeping up my neck, giving me away. Goddammit. I'm honestly not sure if I'm turned on, embarrassed, or a weird combination of both. If I had to categorize Thom and his penis previously, I'd say big but doesn't know what to do with it. The man standing before me, however, I'm pretty sure he knows exactly how to handle himself. "I mean it."

"No joke. Let me show you. I've got all sorts of skills you might find useful."

"Thom—"

"I'll give it to you right this time, I promise. Be the best you've ever had."

"N-no."

He cocks his head. "What's wrong, babe? You look like you're getting a little flustered. Not feeling a bit heated, are you?"

"I said we could maybe be friends. That's all."

"Sure. We could be friends who fuck, for a start."

"We are not…no." I take a deep breath. "Why are you even doing this?"

The man stares at me with the heat of a thousand suns and I am dead. My emotional walls, sense of self-preservation, and various other fortifications erected over the past twenty-six years are nothing but rubble. All that remains is a girl-shaped mess spread across the remarkably unattractive and scratchy khaki blanket.

Thom has won.

"I already told you," he says. "I like your smile."

Hard banging on the bedroom door, followed by Henry yelling, "Thom, got your hacker on the line ready to talk. Get out here."

"Be there in a minute." Thom reaches for his pants. Thank fuck.

Footsteps head back up the hall—Henry returning to his workbench, no doubt. Guess he's forgoing sleep, like Thom. I myself am in need of a nap and starting to get more than a little ragged. Worn out. And this scene hasn't helped. For some stupid reason, I'm all emotional, almost on the verge of tears again. This is not normal for me. Not even remotely. Sure, I may bawl my eyes out at the end of certain movies (looking at you, *Titanic*). But generally, I prefer descriptors such as stalwart and stoic. For all my somewhat bitchy mouth, I do tend to generally just deal with shit. Though, to be fair, I've never been in it this deep before. My resting heart rate may never return to normal. Let alone my overly busy mind, the tremors coming and going in my hands, and the excessive perspiration.

Forget about my nerves; this situation has my whole body highly strung.

"Got to go," says Thom, pulling a shirt over his head. "But we should talk about this some more later. Honest and open communication is important, right? Or at least, that's what they write in all those books on relationships."

"You want open and honest communication?" I bite out. "I trusted you with my body before and you let me down in more ways than I can count. I tried to love you and you hurt me."

He blinks.

"That's not happening again. So do not play with me. Is that understood?"

For a moment, he just stops. No motion or anything. The man is a statue. Then slowly he nods. "Understood. I'm sorry, Betty."

"You know, you keep saying that." I sniffle in as dignified a fashion as possible. "But I'm still not even sure you know what it means."

"I'm learning."

Once he's gone, I slump back on the bed in relief. Maybe I should just let our unknown nemesis kill me. Blow me to smithereens. Because, honestly, this is the worst breakup of a nonexistent relationship ever.

A wailing alarm wakes me at some horrible hour the next morning. The noise is deafening. Red light fills the room, and the bedroom door is thrown open a moment later. Thom rushes in, throwing back the bedcovers and grabbing my arm.

"On your feet," he yells, just as the siren shuts off. "Move, Betty."

I shake off the sleep, bare feet touching down on the cold floor. "What's going on?"

His face is all business. "Someone's on the mountain. We've got to go."

"What? Someone's found us?"

"Looks that way."

Mind reeling, I crouch down beside my duffel bag. Quickly, I grab a pair of jeans, another T-shirt. What does one wear when they're on the run? Thom is wearing sturdy hiking boots, jeans, and a flannel. All very practical.

"Just put your shoes on," says Thom, stuffing the clothes back into the bag. "We don't have time for you to get dressed."

"Okay." My butt hits the mattress and on go the boots, over my thermal pajama pants. They have unicorns with laser eyes printed on them and are quite possibly the coolest thing I've ever owned. Not all of the sleepwear Crow bought is sexy. Thankfully. Though if I die in this ensemble, I just might haunt his ass.

I get to my feet, hauling the strap of the bag over my shoulder. No one is separating me from my stuff again—small amount that I have.

Thom gives the duffel a look, lips tight. "You're going to have to leave it. We don't have time to check for trackers or any such shit in there."

"You said you trusted Crow."

"Betty, we don't have time for this."

It sucks, but I do as told, setting the duffel bag down. He takes my hand and leads me out into the hallway. The red light gives everything a weird postapocalyptic vibe. And instead of heading toward Henry's work area, we turn left, deeper into the subterranean complex.

"Where are we going?" I ask, half-running, trying to keep up with the man.

"Away from here."

Like this tells me anything.

"Plan B," he says. "You'll have to come with me for the time being."

Out of the gloom, Henry dashes toward us, breathing

heavily. "You're all set. Don't stray from the path. It'd be a shame if you got your asses blown to pieces."

"Thank you," says Thom. He has a gun in his other hand now.

Henry just tips his chin, turning to me. "Later, Betty. Keep your head down, okay?"

"Okay." My voice hardly quavers at all. "Thanks."

Then he's gone, moving past us. Thom leads me farther down the shadowy hall. It seems to go on forever.

"What's he going to do?" I ask, out of breath now too.

"Henry takes uninvited guests pretty seriously. He's got this mountain rigged with all sorts of shit. He'll probably just sit in front of a screen and watch 'em burn." Thom gives me a smile full of sharp teeth. "Or, if he's feeling frisky, he'll go out and have some fun with a sniper rifle."

"If this place is safe then why don't we stay put and wait them out?"

"Because I can't afford to be on lockdown in the bunker for days on end," he says. "As for you, I don't like how fast they found us and I don't know the extent of their resources. How much they're willing to throw at this. Might only be a one in a thousand chance they breach the place, but I'm not risking it. Until I know more, you're safer with me."

"All right. Makes sense. So you think Henry's going to kill them?"

Thom squeezes my hand. "Whoever these people are, they're not our friends. Friends don't sneak up on you wearing tactical gear, bulletproof vests, and carrying Uzis, while moving in an attack formation."

"How did they find us?"

"Good question. I'm still figuring that bit out."

Eventually, the hallway loses all pretense of sophistication and turns into more of a tunnel. Intermittent lights cast a scarlet glow from the sides of the walls and we duck our heads so we don't hit the ceiling. At the end, a steel ladder leads up to a generous-size hole.

Above us, the ground shakes. Dust sprinkling down on us. I don't even want to imagine what caused that mini-quake.

"It's all right," says Thom, slipping the gun into the back waistband of his jeans. If he accidentally shoots a butt cheek, he's going to be sorry. Though he does seem to know what he's doing. One of his front pockets bulges with extra ammunition. "Someone just stepped on one of Henry's traps. But they should be nowhere near us. I'll go up first and you follow straight behind me, okay?"

I nod.

"Soon as we're up top, you make for the passenger side of the vehicle. Get in and get your seat belt on. I'll do the rest." His gaze slides over my face, taking in my bitten lip and fear-filled eyes, no doubt. "Babe, I've got this. Just follow behind me and do as I say. You're going to be fine."

Another nod. I don't quite feel up to speaking for some reason. Shaking in my boots? Yes. Forming sentences? That's a hard no.

"Okay," he says. "Let's go."

"Wait. I want a gun."

He shakes his head. "You've spent about five minutes in your entire life with a gun in your hand. Shooting at a fixed target from a safe, stationary position."

"True. But I still want a gun. You said it yourself: anything could be waiting for us up there."

"It should be clear, at least until we're in the car, and then you'll need to keep your head down."

"The safe house should have been clear," I snapped. "Henry's should have been clear. They've—whoever *they* are—have been right on our tail at every turn. For all we know they're waiting for us right where that ladder comes out."

He glares at me. Then he reaches under his armpit to a holster. It's dark and compact, so I hadn't even noticed it. He hands me a small, snub-nosed piece. "When you're holding on to it, keep your finger away from the trigger and point it at the floor. You don't use it until you hear me say 'shoot.'"

"Understood."

"I mean it. Otherwise you're more likely to accidentally kill us both."

I nod and stuff the gun into the back of my pants, just like Thom did. Except of course my pants aren't combat ready like his. This is my life now, unicorns and rainbows and guns. Still, the elastic around the waist is strong enough to bear the weapon's weight without too much wobbling.

Thom moves swiftly up the rungs while I follow, my innate lack of physical prowess slowing me down some. At the top of the ladder, he punches numbers into a security panel. The lock on the round metal door above us clicks and he pushes it open. Up above, the light is equally dim and the air smells musty and earthy. Of course he climbs out all grace and athletic-like. I, on the other hand, clamber and stumble. Not that it matters at a time like this.

We're in a small, rickety barn, moonlight shining through the slats overhead. There are more woodpiles, a few bales of hay, and some tools. Along with an old, rusted Dodge Charger. I guess our SUV and the muscle car Thom mentioned are housed elsewhere.

Another explosion shakes the mountain, though this one sounds farther away. Henry is not playing around.

"Not the Cobra?" I whisper.

"Not the Cobra. Sorry. And not the SUV either, just to be safe."

Outside, a small light flickers in the distance. Then there's a sound. The rustling of dried leaves.

Thom immediately pushes me in the direction of the vehicle. His gun is back in his other hand. "Go."

We both dash for the car, Thom all but sliding on his ass across the hood à la a totally cool and smooth move. The passenger door might have been closer, but he still beats me into the car by a long shot.

"Seat belt," he says.

"Getting there." I wince at the louder-than-I-intended sound of my car door closing. "Sorry."

"Head down. I need you to stay out of sight as best you can. Make yourself as small a target as possible. And hold on to this for me." He hands me another gun from out of his ankle holster. The man's a walking armory. "Don't use it. Just hand it to me when I ask for it."

"Okay, okay."

Thom rolls his window almost all the way down, and reaches for the ignition. He glances at me. For a moment, he looks like I feel, rattled with more than a touch of afraid. Then his jaw sets and his eyes go hard. "Get down farther, as far as you can."

He starts the engine, the car roaring to life. All pretense of quietly escaping the mountain disappears as he throws the car into gear, and we rush out of the barn in a cloud of dust.

Bullets ping off the side of the vehicle, freaking me right the fuck out. Thom, however, returns fire while singlehandedly driving the car along the bumpy dirt road. No idea how he can actually aim the gun to hit anything. Also, the noise of the gun firing is deafening.

What with my head down, I have no real idea what's going on. We're going fast, however. Damn fast. The motion of the car throwing me this way and that, with the seat belt digging into my middle. I'm leaning so far down that the top part of the belt can't grip me properly at all. I can only trust Thom knows what he's doing.

Something breaks above my head. I look up to see a small hole in the windscreen, glass splintering into a myriad of spider-web patterns. Any farther over and the bullet might have hit Thom's head. Cold air whistles through the bullet hole in a freaky fashion.

"Holy shit," I squeak. "We're going to die."

"We're not going to die."

I do not believe him.

"Everything's going to be fine. Try and stay calm and focus on your breathing for me."

"Fuck my breathing." My heart hammers inside my chest. "Just in case we are, I accept your apology for lying to me about everything."

He pauses, the gun in his hand ceasing its crazy noise. "Do you actually mean that?"

"God. I don't know," I say, my voice still unnaturally high. There's a good chance I'm about to pee my pants. "Forty-nine percent, maybe?"

"Awesome," he says flatly. "Do me a favor and keep your head down."

"We're going to hit a tree."

"We are not going to hit a tree."

"Can you even see to drive?"

"Yes," he says. "Now let me concentrate."

We bounce over the rough road, my head hitting the dashboard. Which is painful. Like I didn't have enough bruises already. I brace one hand straight in front of me against the glove compartment. I also try not to think about death. Though it would have been nice to hear Mom's voice one last time. To tell my parents I love them. Due to the condo going boom with boxes of my stuff still inside, my browser history and vibrators are already dealt with, at least.

Not knowing what's going on is killing me, so I take a peek.

Thom fires another couple of shots. "Swap guns with me."

I grab the empty one he's shoving at me, handing him the fully loaded backup weapon. Just in time, as it turns out. Because a shadowy figure steps out onto the road ahead of us, wearing a balaclava and brandishing some sort of automatic weapon, I think. Whatever it is, it's big and scary.

Before he can turn us into Swiss cheese, Thom mows him down. Or rather, sends him flying. Because the body crashes against the top of the windshield before continuing up and over. A bang on the roof of the Charger, then the body disappears into the darkness behind us.

"Oh my God, Thom."

"Get down, Betty."

And I do. But apparently that was the last of the bad guys on our trail. Because the sounds of shots being fired at us comes to an end. Hallelujah. I turn my head to see Thom place the gun in his lap and put both hands on the wheel, thank you, baby Jesus. Really rather not drive off the side of the mountain and all.

Now that we're no longer being shot at, I cling to the interior of the car and concentrate on breathing. All I can hear is blood rushing behind my ears. My ex-fiancé or whatever he is really likes hitting people with cars. It's a concern. Old Thom was an excruciatingly safe and slow driver and always behaved like such a pacifist. Though the people involved in this particular violent instance were definitely deserving of getting hit, so there's that.

"Just a bit longer, then you can sit up," he says, shifting down a gear as he takes a sharp corner. "We should be clear soon."

"Okay."

"Most of them were sneaking up the other side of the mountain. Those two just got lucky, I think." His tone of voice is scarily calm and matter-of-fact, now that we're clear of the action. "Doesn't really bother me so much if they fire at me. That seems fair enough, you know? Not that I actually want to get hit because it hurts like a bitch."

"I bet it does."

"Seriously pisses me off when they fire at *you*, though. I kind of take that personally."

"Ah…thanks?"

"No problem." Then he chuckles. "So it takes a near-death experience to get you to accept my apologies. I must remember that. Though it wasn't a particularly sincere acceptance."

"It wasn't completely insincere," I protest. "I'm trying, all right. Just didn't want to have all of this anger between us. Not if there was a chance we were about to go down in flames."

He sighs. "You could just accept my apology one hundred percent, you know? That would be nice."

"I'll think about it."

He just looks at me.

"What you did was pretty damn awful, Thom. I would first have to be convinced you understand how messed up it all was. And that you sincerely repented your asshole ways and were never going to lie to me again so help you God."

"You sound like a foul-mouthed priest."

I don't dignify his statement with a response.

"Cute jammies, by the way."

"Thanks. Not the kind of thing I'd have expected from Crow."

His lips skew slightly. "I told him you like unicorns."

"I don't keep any figurines or anything around. How did you know?"

"Just remembered you put up a picture on social media once. Given the somewhat stressful situation we're in, thought they might make you smile."

"Huh."

We keep going for miles and miles along dirt roads barely deserving of the title. Somehow Thom manages driving with the splintered windshield. With dawn rising in shades of violet and gray over the hills, he pulls up next to a hatchback left on the side of the road with a For Sale sign in the window near the highway. The Charger's battered windscreen faces away from the road, the worst of the damage hidden from any passing motorists.

God. It's taken just about the entirety of the drive for my heartbeat and breathing to return to normal. And I thought the panic of making a floral delivery on time was intense. Thom has to be an adrenaline junkie or something.

"This is our new ride," he says.

"We're stealing this car?"

He stops, glances at me. "Betty, priorities please. We're on the run from dangerous people. People who want us dead. We need a change of vehicle and our options are not good. Come on."

Still, I hesitate. I can't help it. Mom and Dad raised me to try and see both sides of any situation. While the hatchback is admittedly old and crappy, it still belongs to someone. A person who probably needs the money from the sale of the vehicle. I've never actively broken the law before (apart from the occasional bit of speeding or jaywalking, which don't count). Though I don't actually want to die. It's a conundrum.

"Give me strength." He lifts up his shirt, displaying an elastic-type band halfway up his chest. It's about the width of his hand and comprised of pockets, and is apparently the stealthy version of Batman's utility belt. From one of the pockets, he pulls out a wad of cash and throws it on the seat of the bullet-hole-riddled Dodge Charger. Then he marches over to the hatchback, pulling out a small kit from another pocket. Lockpicking tools, apparently. "Come get the For Sale sign. Quickly. Stick it in the Charger's window."

"Thank you."

A snort of amusement from him.

In no time at all, with the help of the straightened wire, he has the hatchback open. Next, he sets to work hotwiring the engine. It splutters before catching on, a far cry from the roar of the Charger. Yet I highly doubt anyone will be looking for us in this vehicle.

I put the sign in the Dodge's back windshield before climbing into the new car. The interior is tiny. It's like one of those little cars out of Europe. Perfect for the inner city and not much else. Country and Western blasts out of the tinny stereo. Thom surprisingly turns it up. Guess he's a Dolly Parton fan. I approve of this entirely.

Next, he does the traditional killing of the SIM card before getting out to place his cell under one of the front tires. Guess he ran out of time earlier due to the gunman sneaking up on us. To destroy the entire phone, he must be seriously concerned about us getting tracked down. Understandably.

"We overpaid," he says. "You know, the bad guys are probably going to find the Charger and the money long before the owners of this piece of shit do."

"At least we tried."

A grunt.

"Not screwing over people is important."

"If you say so," he says.

"Your empathy levels are of concern to me."

He gets us onto the highway and on our way before answering. "Guess I'm not used to having many people to care about. Most of my life it's been everyone for themselves and sacrificing anyone for the greater good. Keeps things simple."

"And yet you came looking for me."

"Yes, I did."

"So you were ready for complicated."

A small line appears between his brows. "Didn't think it would get *this* complicated."

"Relationships. What can you do? Emotions won't stay confined in neat little boxes just because that's what works for you." I try to get comfortable. But the size of my ass versus the width of the seat makes it hard. Thom's head brushes against the roof; his elbow bumps the driver's side door. I'm not alone in this quandary. "So what comes next?"

"You want to talk about having children?" he says, sounding a little surprised. "I'm not totally against the idea."

"No, Thom," I say slowly. "I mean, what's next in Operation Don't Get Killed?"

"Oh. We're heading to a small airfield to rendezvous with a charter flight to New York. Time to get out of here. You're going to hole up in a safe house I have in the city while I go and get some answers."

"Answers from who?"

"People who run the zoo." His gaze shifts from the road to me and back again. "You know, we could talk about the future if you want."

I frown. "Still not convinced we have one."

"A couple of kids would probably be all right."

"I'm sorry, Thommy Junior. Daddy's going to miss your school play because he's off dusting a dirty politician this week."

"No." He gives a brisk shake of the head. "Politicians are usually pretty soft targets. You can often just blackmail them into early retirement. Don't have to resort to wet work. Much less mess, so long as it sticks."

"What a relief."

"My job really bothers you," he says, as if this is somehow news. "I mean, I knew you weren't crazy about the odd hours and time I had to spend away. But I didn't think you hated it."

"Your work hours did irk me. But again, that wasn't why I left. And also, Thom, that was when I thought you were an insurance assessor. Now I find out you're some weird vigilante assassin ninja super-spy, I don't even know what exactly."

"Just 'operative' is fine. Fits onto a business card easier."

I lean back against the headrest. "Honestly, I have no idea how I feel. Give me the spare magazine so I can reload this gun for you just in case we need it sooner rather than later."

He shifts in the seat, slipping his hand into his pants pocket to retrieve the ammunition as requested. "Thanks."

"Sure."

"See?" He smiles. "We work well together."

I say nothing. I don't know what to say. The hope and enthusiasm he has for our faux relationship throws me. Though to be fair, the last few days have been real. Strange and hellish in parts, but genuine.

Without too much trouble, I remove the empty clip and slide in the new one. My aim may not be the best, but I don't totally suck at guns. And his enthusiasm over us doesn't weird me out due to my not believing I'm worthy of a loving and honest relationship. Or that having someone fight for me is such an out-there notion. Just to clarify, by "fight" I didn't mean guns blazing, et cetera. But a person willing to stick by my side through good times and bad. A best friend. Maybe even a soul mate. All we have is a bundle of lies to build on. Where would a rational and sensible person stuck in this particular situation even start? I mean, seriously.

"Babe," says Thom. "I realize you're thinking deep thoughts. But please don't tap the gun against your thigh like that."

"Oh." I place the loaded weapon into the mostly empty glove compartment alongside a small half-used packet of Kleenex and an out-of-date protein bar. Nice and safe.

He gives me a nod, satisfied with the precautions. The other gun disappeared back into his ankle holster earlier. If necessary, he can get his hands on one or the other relatively quickly. Now that we're on the move once more, on a busy-ish highway, he's back to darting his eyes from the road to all the mirrors and back again. Making sure we aren't being followed. Yet he's also obviously watching me too.

"How did you know I was thinking deep thoughts?" I ask, curious.

"You're always overthinking something. It's pretty much your S.O.P."

"And you don't?"

"Wouldn't have stayed alive long if my thoughts drifted when I'm on missions," he says. "I've been trained to collect the data and crunch it. Decide upon a plan and carry it out."

"You never change your mind?"

"If factors alter, of course I do. You have to be willing to be flexible."

"So why haven't you changed your mind about us?"

"I see no reason to change my mind about us."

"Even though I know your secret now and all the parameters you set on this relationship have been shot to hell?"

He glances my way. "I figure if anything, Betty, you knowing should make our relationship better. In the long-term. Once we get through this somewhat rocky period."

"Only you would describe being on the run for our lives as a *somewhat rocky period.*"

"Only you would make me pay for this piece-of-shit car."

I laugh. Apparently fear makes me giggly sometimes. Go figure.

We pull off the highway, taking a one-lane road deep into some different woods. These are on flat ground.

"I'm still not going to kill you and bury your lovely body among all of this natural splendor, just in case you were wondering," he says.

"I wasn't. I know you're not."

The smile he gives me is kind of glorious. The way it reaches his eyes. Old Thom's grins kind of left me unmoved a lot of the time. Unsure about his true intentions or feelings. They were perfunctory things. Now I know why, of course. But also, now I'm seeing something so much better. It's even a little tummy fluttering and knee weakening. Damn him.

"You do trust me," he says.

"Eh. Maybe."

He smiles some more as we pull into a small airfield. There's one large hangar and a sleek white private jet waiting on the tarmac. We might be on the run for our lives, though if I'm not much mistaken, Thom is actually starting to relax around me. To be himself. I don't know how I feel about this. It is harder to sustain the anger when he's being all charming and protective and so on. But maybe our relationship or lack thereof doesn't require an emotional status update. Maybe I can just let it be.

Bear comes down the little jet's steps, the big man lifting a hand in welcome. With his long blond hair neatly tied back, he's dressed to impress. In a pilot's uniform, by the look.

"You think he's safe?" I ask.

"Yeah." Thom nods and we pull to a stop near the jet. "He was the first to be cleared by our new hacker friend. She's pretty efficient at searching for offshore accounts and so on. Any possible dodgy or coded communications that might coincide with recent events. We can't be a hundred percent certain of anyone, but I've known Bear a long time. Switching sides isn't his style."

"Your hacker works fast."

"She does. Charges a fortune too," he says. "But you get what you pay for. Can't afford any more mistakes with this. Whoever is involved needs to be found. You hop out here and I'll go stash this thing around back, out of sight."

"Okay."

Bear opens my door, giving me a hand out. What a gentleman. "Nice ride."

"Fuck off," replies Thom without heat. "Wheels up in five."

"On it." Bear tucks my hand around his elbow, leading me toward the plane. "There's fresh clothes for you onboard. We need to get rid of everything you're wearing, okay?"

"Is this about possible beacons or tracers or whatever?" I ask.

"Got it in one."

"Can I keep my gun?"

Bear's brows rise. "Thom gave you a gun?"

I nod.

"If it's one of his, then sure, you can keep it."

"Wait, will there be airport security when we land?"

The man just smiles and ushers me up the steps. I guess airport security isn't a thing in the circles these guys move.

Inside is all white leather and charcoal-gray carpeting. Big comfortable-looking seats and discreet lighting. It's the sort of thing billionaires and celebrities ride around in, no doubt. Wonder where they got it from. I'm probably better off not knowing.

"Bathroom's at the back," says Bear. "Your outfit's hanging up inside. Try and be quick, all right?"

I nod.

The facilities aren't much bigger than on a regular plane. But there's a tiny sink trimmed in marble and an impressive, if small, shower unit. Hanging on the back of the door encased in clear plastic is a navy pants suit in my size, complete with a white knit crew neck. The brand is all Escada. I'm certainly dressing fancier since Thom got outed as an operative, that's for sure. As per Bear's instructions, I hurry. Behind the suit is a bag with all of the necessary underwear. No shoes, however, so I head out barefoot.

"Where do you want them?" I ask, old clothes bundled up in one hand and boots in the other. "Do I keep the same shoes or what, because they don't really—"

And I stop ever so slightly dead.

Thom is standing in the aisle pulling on a pair of dark boxer briefs. His arms flexing and junk hanging free. There's just so much skin to see. Take the ridges of his spine and strong planes of his back muscles leading to the dimples above his ass, for instance. The sadness and almost indifference of the days prior to my leaving him have been replaced by a horrid hyperawareness of him, which is growing by the moment. And it's dangerous.

My gaze cannot be averted fast enough. Why the hell can't the man keep his clothes on? I feel personally attacked.

"Give me a second," he says, reaching for a pair of black suit pants. Then he, too, stops. "Why do you have your angry face on?"

"I'm not angry; I'm fine."

Nothing from him.

"Can you please get dressed? We're in a hurry, right?"

"Huh. I find it fascinating that seeing me naked messes with you to this degree."

"Thom," I growl.

The side of his mouth kicks up. Smirking bastard. "Dump them anywhere. I'll deal with them. Your shoes and coat are on the chair there."

I don't throw my clothes on the ground because it would be juvenile and possibly confirm his bullshit theory about me being frazzled by his bare ass. He's right, but he doesn't need to know this. Also, I really did dig these unicorn jammies. Instead, I place my load gently on a plush white leather seat and turn to inspect the rest of my goodies. Not thinking about the thickness of his thighs or anything along those lines. Though I may need some private time soon. All of this restless (possibly slightly sexual in nature) energy is amassing inside of me. It can't be healthy. Maybe it's been brought on by all of the ongoing fear and tension from almost being killed, et cetera. Couldn't be anything to do with him. Or it *shouldn't* have anything to do with him.

Yeah, right.

Regardless, I don't look at Thom again. It's nice to know I have at least this much restraint. Meanwhile, Bear is in the cockpit, doing whatever pilots do before takeoff. My shoes are a pointy pair of gray leather high-heeled booties that I'll quite possible break an ankle in. Though they are lovely. I'd kill for some make-up, but never mind. A woolen coat, pair of big sunglasses, and a Chloé handbag complete the outfit. Nothing is actually in the bag, but you can't have it all.

"If you make me dump this outfit somewhere, I just might have to hurt you," I say. "I look good in it."

"You look good in everything, and I will buy you more unicorn-patterned items. Promise."

I ignore the compliment. It's safer that way. Yet when I dare a peek from under my lashes, it's hard to say if I'm relieved or disappointed at his full state of dress. He, too, is wearing designer, by the look of things. A beautifully cut black suit with a plain white shirt. No tie. Shiny black shoes and hair slicked back. They say a man in a suit is like a woman in lingerie. Now I understand why.

"So what's the occasion?" I ask.

"Another couple of rich assholes hitting New York for some shopping and a couple of shows shouldn't raise any interest."

"Let's hope not."

Thom gathers up the old clothes, tossing them out the plane's still-open door. Such a waste. Hopefully whoever uses the airfield next will put them to use. My parents would be appalled. They don't get rid of anything until it's half-past dead, and even then, it's inevitably somehow recycled.

Thom and I, on the other hand, are leaving a trail of abandoned cars and clothes across the country. Something tells me such things don't concern operatives. Further evidence of my fiancé and me having nothing in common. I'll have to donate to a charity on both our behalfs to erase the karmic debt so I'll be able to look my parents in the eye come Christmas. Damn guilt complex. Of course, we have to live that long first. They must be so worried about me. I hate not being able to contact them, let them know I'm still breathing.

Thom hits a button and the stairs fold up, the door slowly closing. "Put your belt on, please."

We could both catch a bullet at just about any time and yet he's always so safety conscious in these little ways. It's interesting. I do as asked. "How did you organize all of this stuff so quickly, the outfits and plane and everything?"

"I have my tricks." Of course he'd be secretive. It's second nature to the man. He takes the seat beside me, settling in and closing his eyes. The plane engine hums and we start to move, taxiing down the runway.

"Or you could give me a straight answer," I suggest.

He gives a slight shrug. "Contacts. Ground crew. People for hire. Take your pick."

"And you trust them to know where we're going?"

"I trust people who are completely removed from this situation with small amounts of information."

"But you thought Henry was completely removed from the situation too."

"Yeah." The little line appears between his brows. "We were traced. I'm not happy about that."

Not a pleasant thought for me either. But not one I wish to dwell on right now. "I've never been to New York."

"No?" he asks. "Oh, you'll love it, even though you're not going to get to experience any of it because you're going to be tucked away nice and safe while I sort shit out."

"I'm supposed to love it through a window?"

"Exactly," he says, eyes still closed. "You'll watch a stupid amount of television, eat a dazzling array of delivery cuisine, and catch up on your R and R."

"Speaking of which, I need a holster for my gun. Preferably something that doesn't interfere with the lines of my new look."

A heavy sigh. "Can you at least give me a few hours while we're in the air to reconcile myself to my fiancée being permanently armed? Just to pretend I have a choice in the matter before I eventually give in?"

"All right. Thank you."

"Try and relax. We're safe for a little while," he says. "It's not like anyone is going to blow us out of the sky."

"You know, it hadn't even occurred to me that was a possibility until you said it just now."

"Oops."

"How do you get used to people wanting to kill you all the time?"

His brows lift slightly. "Well…usually it's not all the time. But yeah, it's not easy."

"No kidding." I rub at my chest with the heel of my hand. "I feel like I'm constantly on the verge of having a heart attack."

"And it's all my fault. I dragged you into this mess and I'm sorry." His face is deadly serious. "You're going to be fine, Betty. I'm going to make sure you're fine."

I attempt a smile, but it doesn't quite work. It's a delicate balance, blaming him for this situation, while still being glad he's here beside me to help deal with things.

Thom picks up my hand, lacing his fingers with mine. Without asking or anything. And I let him. That's the kick of it—I just let him. Not because I need comfort. Hell no. But it seems only polite after he agreed to give me a gun. One of the flimsiest and oddest pretexts for letting a guy hold my hand ever. I should take a stand and insist on a little space between us. Affectionate gestures like this just confuse things. My speech should probably also include a request for him to remain fully clothed in my presence.

But I digress. We both need to be focusing on staying alive as opposed to sorting out the eternal mystery that is our relationship. I don't want to die. I also don't want him to die. And killers are on our trail. Before I can attempt to extract myself, however, his hold slightly tightens while his breathing evens out. He's either fast asleep or on his way there.

I can't disturb him now. No. I'll just have to hold his hand.

FIVE

"**Y**OU'RE TRYING TOO HARD."

"What?" I pause, caught somewhere between a swagger and a dash as we cross the tarmac. My hair is being blown apart by a wind cold enough to chap a snowman's ass. But my outfit remains fabulous just the same.

"Relax," says Thom, steering me toward a parking lot. "Car's over here."

"You said two rich assholes hitting New York. I'm just trying to live up to the designer suit and everything." And the gun. It's a slight weight to the side beneath my jacket, nestled against my boob, and sticking into my side. The power to take a person's life is sitting right there. Or at least the power to seriously inconvenience them and quite possibly cause immense pain. Only I don't mention the gun because Thom's probably still not happy about me having it.

Like mine, his face is also partly covered by sunglasses, and he keeps his head angled down. Probably insufficient for throwing off facial-recognition-type software stuff. But he obviously doesn't believe the government is the threat. Still, it never occurred to me how thoroughly security cameras have infiltrated our lives. Of course, I never tried to avoid them before.

"Best way not to attract attention is to not act suspicious." His hand hovers at my lower back, ready to move me if the need arises. "Or like you're someone important that everyone should notice. Rich folk get killed the same as poor people."

"Okay. Sorry. I got carried away."

"Remember, you're on a missing persons list. We do not need any attention. Just try and act natural."

"There's nothing natural about wearing five-inch heels," I scoff.

The side of his mouth quirks.

Bear is stowing the jet or whatever it is you do with those things when they're not in use. I thought I had an idea of what my life with and without Thom would be like. But it's all changing so fast I can barely keep up. I'd thought maybe I'd feel better once I was away from stifling safe houses and creepy cabins in the woods and back in public, among people again. But instead it turns out that being out in the open sucks. Paranoia is once again running rife, the back of my neck itching with the feel of being in somebody's crosshairs. Thom moves us at a good pace, though we're definitely not running for cover. Guess it means we're okay for now.

He draws a fob out of his pocket and the lights of a new black sedan flash once. I'm ushered into the passenger side while he moves around the front of the car to take the driver's seat.

"Are we waiting for Bear?" I ask, doing up my seat belt.

"He'll catch up with us later. There's a cell in the glove compartment—do you mind getting it out?" The engine purrs to life and we're on our way, out of the parking lot and onto the streets in a built-up industrial-looking area.

"Sure."

"It's not locked. I need you to key in some contacts for me, please."

My thumbs move over the screen.

"Contact one, ready?" he asks.

"Go for it."

He rattles off a string of numbers. "Now text to them the word *report*. Just that. Nothing else."

"Done."

The exact same process is repeated no less than nine times, with Thom reciting the numbers off the top of his head. Me remembering my own number is a minor miracle. But he has no problem, never hesitating, never getting a digit wrong. Again, the question of how intensive his training was and what it covered makes me wonder. I know he's dangerous. I also know he says he's on my side. I think I trust him. But none of this really helps answer the fundamental question: Who the hell have I been sleeping with?

"Contact two says Fox is clear," I report. "I take it that's your hacker doing checks to see if there's any online trace of backstabbing and murder?"

The skin tightens around his eyes. "Yeah."

"Hey, you gave me the cell."

"I know."

"You're just not used to me being all up in your business."

His lips flatline. "I don't want you in any more danger than you already are."

Another alert flashes across the screen. "Contact one says 'The Thornbrook.' What is that, a hotel or something?"

"Yeah. Upscale. Good security." He's frowning, so maybe The Thornbrook isn't our new safe house, but something else entirely.

"How are you going to get inside?" I ask. "I assume that's what you need to do."

He takes his time answering, gaze switching from the road to me and back again. "The less you know, the better. I'll think of something."

"So you're not going to tell me who you're going to meet there either, huh?"

"No, I'm not."

I set the cell in my lap, thinking deep thoughts. It's way too late to keep me safe by keeping me in the dark. The man is an idiot. So what if I'm constantly terrified and freaked out over all of this? I need to know what we're dealing with so I can be better prepared. Already, people have tried to blow me up, interrogate me, and I've been in my first gunfight. Fact is, the sooner he sorts out this mess, the better. So I can tell my friends and family that I'm okay. Get back to my normal life and find out if I still have a job. Put all of this crazy behind me. No idea if this will mean saying goodbye to Thom. No idea how I even feel about that. Probably best to deal with one impossible situation at a time.

"You're checking all of your work pals out via the hacker you hired since they're the most obvious suspects and there's a high probability of this being an inside job," I say, putting all of the pieces together inside my head. "You said earlier that Bear was the first to be cleared by our new hacker friend. I assume Fox is the second. No bad guys outed among the group so far. So no leads on that front."

A big loud nothing from Thom. Meaning I'm probably on the right track.

"You said something to Badger about having trouble getting a message through to the bosses. Guess they either don't want to be caught up in this, or they're the ones responsible."

A muscle pops in the side of his jaw.

"You're going to make contact with one of them, aren't you? One of the bosses?"

"How did you figure that out?" he growls. "Did another text come in?"

"No." I raise my chin. "I used my brain."

He glances at me.

"Also, I watch thrillers and spy movies. I know stuff," I say. "And I manage a successful, high-volume inner-city florist with a multimillion-dollar turnover. Every day I deal with impossible deadlines and frantic brides. I organize things and solve problems. Well, I used to, before I became a fugitive. Point being, I'm not stupid."

"Betty, I know you're not stupid. But these people are dangerous."

"Everything right now is dangerous," I say. The man is seriously unhappy. I almost feel bad for him since he's only trying to protect me. When he holds out a hand, I pass him the cell without further comment.

For the longest moment, he says nothing. "You're right. I need to find out what's going on with the bosses, learn what they know."

I nod.

"Sorry. I'm not used to sharing this sort of stuff with anyone. Even with Bear and Fox, it's a need-to-know policy."

"You didn't share it with me. I guessed." I turn to watch the pedestrians out braving the bad weather. "Why did you crush your cell before we left California? Why not just kill the SIM like you usually do?"

"Someone could have been tracking us through a program loaded onto the cell. It's not easy to do and they probably would've had to physically access the phone sometime in the past to do it. So we ditched it. Wasn't worth the risk."

Outside, the traffic thickens as we draw closer to the city. The daylight turns into little more than haze this late in the afternoon, streetlights glowing in the wet conditions. We circle a block twice before finding a place to park. Thank goodness for the thick coat and leather gloves. As awesome as it is, a designer handbag is no defense against the cold.

Thom leads me over to the sidewalk, keeping his body between mine and the street. Constantly surveying the area, we head toward an old brick building three stories high. Nothing fancy or anything, though it does seem clean and well-maintained. The elevator smells vaguely of Thai food and makes a few suspicious mechanical-type groaning noises as we ride up.

He stops at a door on the top floor in the corner position, unlocks it, and turns off the alarm. "In you go."

"Does this place belong to you or the zoo?"

"Me. Wait here a moment, please." He ducks his head into several small rooms, scanning them quickly. "We're fine. Come on through."

An exposed brick wall runs the length of the loft-type space. First I see a small walk-in closet, a small, clean white bathroom, followed by the main open area. There's a clean white kitchen, a large bed made up with sheets and blankets, a wooden table with two stools by the window, and a two-seater sofa and TV hanging on the wall.

"Cozy," I say, hanging my coat over the back of a chair. I place my handbag and gloves on top of the table. It seems wrong to invade the space with stuff, given the perfect minimal look of the place, but that's life. The apartment has a lot in common with the ranch safe house back in California. No pictures. No personal belongings. At least, none I can see.

Thom just shrugs. "Not somewhere I spend much time."

"Where do you spend your time?"

"When I'm not working, I'm home with you." He empties his pockets onto the table. The car fob, the new cell, his gun and spare magazine...you know, the usual. "Guess we're going to need a new place to live."

No comment from me.

"I've got a few properties around L.A. you can take a look

at. See which one you like best. Or we can get something new, though I'd prefer to avoid any large financial transfers if possible. Makes it harder to stay off people's radars."

"How many places do you own exactly, and what is your bank account balance?"

"My job pays okay." He cracks his neck. "And in this line of work, it's wise to have a few safe houses."

"In case your cover gets blown."

"That's right. I stop by each of them now and then, collect any mail and check on security. Make sure nothing has been tampered with and see to any basic maintenance."

"Your world is interesting, I'll give it that." I rub at the back of my own neck, trying to relieve the bunched-up muscles. Stress always winds me up tight. And I don't think I've ever been as stressed as I am these days. Even being a florist on Valentine's or Mother's Day has nothing on running for your life. On being hunted.

"Let me," says Thom, standing in front of me. Much closer than necessary.

"You don't need to—"

"I know I don't need to. But I want to." Strong fingers dig into my sore muscles, turning me into mush. Then he makes a disgruntled noise and undoes the buttons on the front of my suit jacket. His hands are sure, certain of my submission. His warm palms skim over the knit shirt, slide the jacket off my shoulders and down my arms before placing it on the table. My gun and holster are next and Thom does not look sorry to see them gone. "That's better."

I'm not so sure. The sensible part of my brain suggests I need all the armor I can get when it comes to this man. Though it feels good, the kneading pressure of his hands. It also feels a whole lot like seduction.

Warning bells once again ring inside my head. "What are you doing?"

"Working on the knots in your neck. What are you doing besides overthinking everything?"

"You'd like it if I just stopped using my brain and didn't ask questions, wouldn't you?"

The edge of his lips quirk up. "Now that you mention it, it would make things simpler."

"Ha. Keep dreaming. Speaking of overthinking things, how are you going to get the bosses to help you?"

A sigh.

"I'm serious. What's the plan?"

"You're not going to let this go, are you?"

"Not a chance." I gave him my very best fake smile. The one that's so blatantly obvious it's like a slap across the face. Never say sarcasm can't be a superpower. "I know all about your bullshit now, sweetheart. May as well answer my questions because there's no way I'm just going to go along quietly with whatever you want. Consider us partners in this whole staying-alive thing."

"Well, that sucks. Though I must say, you're particularly hot when you're being all stubborn and demanding, telling me off like that."

I look to heaven. "Just answer the question."

"There's a few ways to go about obtaining someone's assistance or compliance in a situation," he says. "Start by trying to appeal to their principles or feelings of patriotism. I know you haven't seen much of it so far, but the zoo actually does a lot of good in the world. If neither of those work, then you move on to their ego. Sometimes it takes a mix of all three. Last resort is usually blackmail or threat, because once you try that, there's no putting it back in the box. The key is finding an incentive that hooks them on a personal level. Even if you're paying them, they need to feel emotionally invested so there's less chance they'll turn on you. Especially if you need them to act against their own interests or just not do what's easiest for them. People are lazy as all hell, and ninety-nine percent of the time, they'll choose the path of least resistance."

"But you're not going to be paying them."

He shakes his head. "No. These people have the sort of wealth that makes billionaires look low-key."

"And standing back and letting you all get killed would be easier for them."

"Absolutely. No one's irreplaceable," he says, voice matter-of-fact. "I imagine they're pretty busy covering their own hides right about now."

"You need to convince them to come out and play." It makes sense. Whoever these people are, they obviously have serious power and resources. But maybe we can still get out of this without anyone else dying. If we can get them to help us.

"I'd rather convince *you* to play with me."

"This is serious."

"I'm being very serious, Elizabeth."

"No, you're not, Thomas."

"Gonna have to respectfully disagree with you there," he says. "After all, I answered your question. Don't I get a reward?"

"You get the warm, fuzzy feeling that comes with telling your fiancée the truth for a change."

His eyes light up. "My fiancée, is it? That means we're still together. We're going to get married and have babies and drive a minivan and live in a—"

"Wait. No."

"You said it." He grins. "There's no taking it back now."

"Oh my God, what are you? Eight?"

"Thirty-four."

"You lied about your age too? Holy shit. Is there anything you didn't lie to me about?"

The mirth disappears from his face. "I wasn't lying when I said I love you."

"That seems ironic. Seeing as it's the one thing you told me that I'd definitely worked out was a lie."

"Let me convince you."

"Prioritize, please," I snap. "People are trying to kill us. There are bigger things to focus on here."

"Yeah. But what if we died without having makeup sex? That'd be a tragedy."

Give me strength. "A tragedy, huh?"

"Absolutely. But I've got to say, I do like how instead of giving in to panic, you're trying to figure things out."

I just shrug. "It helps distract me."

He smiles. He has a really great smile.

"Why are you so hell-bent on us staying together? Answer me that."

His fingers move up to my scalp, working their magic. "Pretty sure I've answered you that about a dozen times already. I like your smile. Hell, I like every damn inch of you. And I like who I am when I'm around you. The way I don't have to be on edge all the time. Especially now that I don't need to pretend to be someone else. Now that you know all my secrets."

"Hmm." My eyelids slide closed. I can't help it. Nothing like a good massage to render you helpless. Without a doubt, his knowledge of anatomy is top notch. Probably makes him a better killer. My knees turn to water at the thought. The ever-present threat of a panic attack turning my insides to jelly.

But then he moves closer, lips skimming over my cheek, my jawline. He's with me. I'm not alone. However, I should put a stop to this. Any minute now. "I highly doubt I know all of your secrets."

"More than pretty much anyone else alive."

"Maybe."

"Definitely. You do more than just give me a home. You let me feel things like a normal person. You make me human."

That might be the saddest, loneliest thing I've ever heard. "Thom…"

"Most of the time it feels like I've been at war my whole damn life. But not with you. With you, even the fighting is fun. Touch me, Betty."

His lips graze the side of my neck as he speaks. His hands and his mouth are perfection, messing with my mind. The heat of his body pressed up against mine. Thom never used to be particularly tactile when it came to sex. Though I guess keeping me from feeling his scars made things complicated. Now, however, everything seems to have changed.

"Put your hands on me."

My hands are fisted at my sides.

"Let me distract you for a little while. Let me please you."

"You're seriously persuasive, do you know that? What is this, the full secret agent treatment?"

"Fuck, I love how soft you are."

"I-I'm not sure about this," I stutter, my breath coming heavy.

He rests his forehead against mine with a sigh. "It's up to you. Tell me to stop and I will."

Only I'm not sure I want that either. I'm frozen. Confused. "You will?"

"Of course. I'm not taking anything else from you that you're not willing to give. We'll do whatever you want." His lips press gently against mine. "You already know what I want."

"The hard-on pressing into my stomach kind of gives it away."

"I bet it does. But I can wait." His chuckle is this deep and harsh sound sending a shiver straight down my spine. His warm mouth on mine delivers light, sweet kisses that go straight to my head. And he smells good. Like some awesome warm and woodsy aftershave and him.

Still, I hesitate.

"Want me to take my hands off you, take a step back?"

Problem is, somewhere along the line, he's become the balm to all my fears. I've never met anyone less like a teddy bear, and yet I want to hold him tight until the monsters under the bed go away.

"No."

"All right, then," he says, doubtless pondering the confusion that is my chaotic state of mind. I almost pity the man. "I know... How about once we get this mess sorted, we just go get married? Get on a plane to Vegas and just get the job done. No more discussion. What do you say?"

"What?!" My jaw falls open in surprise, and he's right there. Tongue sliding into my mouth, rubbing against mine. I was absolutely about to hit rant mode. To tell him he can't be serious. But now it's much too late. The man is kissing me stupid. It was all a trick, damn him. And I fell for it.

With his demanding mouth on mine, there's no mayhem or death or anything outside of this moment. Just me and him connecting on a new level. Never in my life has someone kissed me like this. Like touching me, being here with me, is his sole reason for existing. I know, given our history, there's every chance it isn't real. Yet right now, I'm finding it hard to care. Thom and I suddenly have serious chemistry. Like off-the-charts, breath stealing, blazing heat and lust. If he's faking it, I might just have to kill him. The man makes my heart feel cumbersome. Just generally big and confused and…I don't know. Pretty sure I need a feelings warning whenever he's around. That would be useful.

My fingers fist in the fine cotton of his button-down shirt. While his big hand slides down my back to grab ahold of one of my ass cheeks. He's grinding his hard cock into me, turning us both on, no doubt. Dry humping has never been so exciting. Our teeth knock together and he all but eats at my mouth. Nothing about this is sweet or slow. The cool and calm operator is nowhere to be seen. It's good to know I'm not in this alone.

We need to be skin to skin. This is all that matters right now. However, my hands are trembling over the buttons on his shirt. It's frustrating as all hell.

Thom kisses me once, twice, then pulls away.

"Hang on, babe." He grips the back of his shirt, tugging it over his head. Buttons go flying. Oh well. Next, he grabs the hem of my knit top, pulling it up and over my breasts. I lift my arms and he gently eases it over my head. "God, I love your tits. Have I ever told you that?"

"I don't think so."

"No?" he asks, voice husky. "Shit. Sorry. You have the most magnificent fucking breasts I've ever seen."

I tug at his belt, getting it undone and out of the way. Then the button and zip on his pants. Thom quite helpfully toes off his shiny shoes, trying to kiss me all the while. Coordinated, we are not. Though we sure make up for it with dedication to the cause. In a frenzy of motion and need, our clothing disappears piece by piece. It sits pooled at our feet, soon kicked aside. Turns out I couldn't care less about looking after designer goods when getting naked with Thom is on the line.

Soon, we're both standing there in our underwear. Or at

least I am. He pushes down his boxer briefs, the hard length of his cock jutting out, pointing straight at me.

"Don't get shy on me now," he says with a smile. There's something hesitant about it, and a softness to his gaze I haven't seen before. Like I'm not the only one feeling things here. As if getting real with me is a big step for him too. God, I hope I'm not misinterpreting this. Not projecting or imagining things.

I swallow past my dry throat. "I-I'm not."

"So beautiful."

His hands slip around my sides to undo my bra. A gentle touch slides the straps off my shoulders, tugs the underwired cups away from my body. Then, it, too, is on the floor. Eyes heated, he takes the weight of my breasts in his hands, thumbs flicking over my nipples. Electricity shoots through me. My panties are the only thing standing between us now. A damp thong that doesn't stand a chance.

"Babe. Jesus. Look at you. This is what I missed out on in the dark, huh? I'm a damn moron."

"Yeah."

He laughs and kisses me slow and deep. A sensual exploration of my mouth that doesn't stop until he's got my head spinning. And all the while, he's maneuvering me onto the bed, getting me beneath him. Without breaking the kiss even once. He has skills.

Clever fingers glide down my chest, between my breasts and over my belly. Then he's cupping my sex in his hand, grinding the heel of his palm against my clit.

"Oh," I gasp.

"You don't usually get this hot and wet for me." He rests his forehead against mine, rubbing the side of my nose with his own. It's weirdly intimate, having our faces this close together. Gazing into his eyes.

"You don't usually care this much."

"I'm an asshole."

I smile. "Yeah, that too."

Fingers part my labia, sliding inside while his thumb plays over my clit. My eyes just about roll back into my head. Everything between my thighs is dripping wet. Swollen and oh-so-sensitive. He gently thrusts two fingers into me, building my need into something out of control.

"But I'm *your* asshole, if you'll have me," he says, licking over first one hard nipple and then the other. "Betty, will you have me?"

"I need…"

"I know what you need."

Every muscle in me goes tense, on edge. My hips squirm against the mattress. It's all too much and yet not quite enough. I tug on his hair as he sucks on one nipple, teasing it with both his tongue and teeth. Holy hell. He definitely knows things. Doing this for myself usually takes much longer and some serious mind porn. But the things he's doing to me…I can't keep up. Total body overload. My heart's pounding, every nerve ending rioting. It's a little scary, feeling this much.

"And I'm the man who'll give it you," he says, voice rough. "Every time without fail."

His hot mouth on my breasts grows more insistent. The prickle of his stubble against my skin is verging on painful. Then he works a sweet spot inside of me. No hesitation, he really does know exactly what I need and where I need it. Like all his previous explorations were just investigations, marking out the terrain for the moment when it would all matter.

Hands tangled in his hair, I climb higher and higher, reaching for bliss. My whole body is strung tight until it breaks and splinters and falls apart. Pretty sure I officially no longer exist. It's too much. All of this light rushing through me. Just a mess of molecules are left lying on the bed in a vaguely womanlike shape.

R.I.P. me. She died happy.

Before I finish coming down, he thrusts into me with a groan. His thick length sets off even more aftershocks. Kneeling between my legs, Thom looks down the length of my body, gaze possessive in a way I've never seen before.

Hands wrap around my thighs, his grip unbreakable. Again he shows no hesitation. Just keeps thrusting in deep and forcefully, as if he's branding me for all time. While he might be mine—it's still open to question—in this moment, I'm undoubtedly his. Because this certainly isn't lovemaking. But it isn't just rough sex. His body demands and mine gives. Each sigh and moan I make, he owns. The sweat and fever of us fucking. The chaos of emotions.

It could never be like this with someone else. Whatever happens, I have the worst feeling he's ruining me for anyone else. Dammit.

"Your pussy feels fucking perfect," he says. "So wet and hot. Made just for me."

"Watch your ego."

In response, he changes his angle slightly, hitting something wonderful inside. I can't come again so soon. Not possible. But he obviously doesn't agree. The man has something to prove. So he stirs that big cock of his deep inside of me, setting off all sorts of shakes and shivers. Everything below my waist is being worked into a frenzy. Way overexcited. Meanwhile, his fingers dig into my thighs, doubtless leaving marks. Jerking my body onto his cock time and again. Making me take him deeper. I clamp my legs tight around him, because my body knows the facts even if my mind isn't quite sure. I want more. I need more. And he's the one who's going to give it to me.

"You're going to come again," he says.

I just nod. When Thom said he knew things, he wasn't kidding. And the bastard held out on me all this time.

His hard body is slick with sweat, the man looking like some sort of god of procreation towering above me. The strength in his thighs and the set of his wide shoulders. All of the rippling going on in his chest region. The intense raw look on his face. It's a whole lot of shock and awe. Meanwhile, as wonderful as I am, I'm no petite doll. As much as I hate it, I can't help but wonder sometimes what he sees when he looks at me. And there goes that insecurity. Nearly everyone has parts that jiggle or wobble. I will not allow stupid stray doubts to get me down. They can fuck right off. I am a curvy goddess.

"Your mind is wandering," he mutters. "That won't do. Come back to me, babe."

He does some swivel-type move with his pelvis before proceeding to pound into me. Holy shit, it feels good. So good. My mouth falls open on a gasp and the heat is coursing through my bloodstream, building shockingly fast inside of me once more. Muscles tightening, electricity running up and down my spine. Someone is whimpering, and I have the worst feeling it's me.

Then it hits me and it just doesn't stop. Wave after wave of light and sensation. The orgasm just goes on and on. My vision blanks, my mind empty. Every part of me goes weak.

Thom groans, thrusting into me once, twice more. His cock jerking deep inside of me. Shoulders slumped, panting, he remains kneeling between my legs. Damp tendrils of hair hang in his face. Meanwhile, the throbbing between my legs persists. All of those delicate inner muscles still fluttering around his half-hard cock.

All of a sudden, I feel horribly exposed, lying naked on the bed. Not just my flushed, sweaty body is on display, but it feels like all of my emotions are too. My heart and mind are lying open for his perusal. And I'm not sure it's safe. I need armor immediately. Emotional walls at least ten feet deep.

I open my mouth, close it, and open it again. "That was—"

"That was what? Where's the snappy, irreverent comment, hmm?" He pushes back his hair, inspecting me. "Oh shit. Betty, don't freak out. Everything's fine. Well...everything's not fine. But here, you and me, we're good. Okay?"

I have nothing.

Gently, he pulls out of me, and lies down at my side. One arm slips beneath my head, the other sliding over my hip and gathering me up against him. We're cuddling. Only Thom doesn't cuddle. Normally, it's an all-out race to the shower to wash off any body fluids or evidence of possible intimacy. And the bathroom door is shut firmly against me every time. My presence neither required nor requested.

The Thom of here and now presses a soft kiss to my forehead, the tip of my nose, a final one on my lips. Quite a change from all the finesse and fury of hammering me with his cock a minute ago. Now he's all sensitive and sweet. I can't keep up.

Oh man. Am I going to have hot rough-sex-with-Thom flashbacks when I masturbate? I am. I know it. He's doomed me for all time.

"Please don't cry, or I'll have to cry too," he says, tightening his hold on me.

I snort.

"It's okay if you want to cry. Pretty normal after coming, actually. Your muscles relax, all of the tension you're carrying in them gets released. And with all of the stress and shit you've been through lately..."

"I'm fine."

"You sure as hell are."

I try not to smile. It doesn't quite work. "Stop trying to make me laugh. You're not funny."

"Sorry," he says, not repentant in the least.

For a while, we just lie there, legs tangled together. His fingers draw circles on my back, trace the curve of my spine. It has been a beyond-crazy few days. That's the only reason I'm indulging in this weakness with him. My nemesis—intelligent, wise, and together Betty—would be getting her ass into the shower, locking *him* out for a change. Pay him back for all of those extra Kegel exercises, expensive sex toys, and the sheer embarrassment of suggesting we do it in weirder and weirder positions in an effort to fix things in the bedroom.

Only I don't want to move away from him. Not right now. So instead, I lean in and fix my lips to his collarbone, digging my teeth into his flesh. Just because. And I don't stop until I taste blood.

"Ow, babe."

"That's for all of those months of fumbling and shitty sex," I say. "Making me think there's something wrong with me when you were deliberately sabotaging things between us."

He growls low in his throat. "There's never been anything wrong with you, and I will happily spend the rest of my life proving it to you. Or being tortured by your vicious, gorgeous self if that's what's required. Your choice."

I frown, resting my head on his shoulder. Silence fills the apartment. The distant sounds of the street are muffled by the snow. We could be the only two people in the whole wide world. That would be nice.

"If you want, we can just disappear," he offers, somewhat hesitant. "I can get us out of the country easy enough and we've got money. We could settle somewhere quiet. Off the grid. No guarantees we wouldn't have to move around periodically, though."

"You mean we'd be on the run for the rest of our lives."

"Most likely." He swallows. "I can't make any promises until I know more about who's trying to kill us."

"I'd never be able to see my family or friends ever again."

"No, you wouldn't. Or at least, not for a while," he says. "But we'd be together, if that's what you want."

I listen to his heart beating harder beneath my ear. Feel the slight tensing of his hold. As if he's afraid, maybe. The super-spy who's been all over the world killing bad guys and righting wrongs is worried about losing me.

It's a big leap to trust this man. He did me wrong and then some. And yet…my heart might be confused and wary due to our history, but it's also all soft and mushy at the idea of him. Despite the biting. Which he totally deserved. I want more of his scent, his touch, the sound of his voice. I need it.

So I guess the truth is, I don't want to leave him anymore.

"I have no idea if this is going to work or not," I say. "But, yes, I want us to try and stay together."

He exhales hard in relief. "Okay. Good."

"But no more lying. I mean it." I rise up on one elbow, giving him my best, most serious face. "And we're not going to run. We're not going to live like that, always looking over our shoulders. We're going to stay. We're going to fight and we're going to fix this."

SIX

"**T**HIS IS NOT GOOD."

When I get out of the shower, Bear has arrived. He and Thom stand in front of the TV, gazes glued to the screen. It's a news report about an English lord's death, his body found only hours ago in a mansion in London. Their complete focus on the news report, combined with their utter stillness, gives the room an edgy vibe.

I clutch at the towel around me, wet hair hanging down my back. There's no blow dryer, so I'll just braid it and hope for the best. "He had a heart attack?"

"That's how I would have done it. Easy enough to fake or induce." Thom's already showered and is dressed in black slacks, a turtleneck, and boots. Sensible for the weather yet still displaying much of his quiet hotness. Or maybe I'm still heated from the sexing. At least if we die, we've had the makeup sex. Though, this is no real comfort. My anxiety roars back to life easy as that. But I do my best not to show it; Thom has enough to handle without me adding to his woes.

"You're sure he was one of them?" asks Bear, arms crossed.

Thom nods. "Yeah. He's one of the three bosses. I've known about him a few years now."

"So it's not just operatives someone's trying to kill," I say. "They're taking out the head honchos as well."

Thom turns, taking in my disheveled appearance. His gaze

warms for a moment at the sight of me, steamy and wet, wearing nothing but a towel. Then he does a quick turnaround, realizing he and I are not alone to enjoy this state of affairs.

Pretty sure Bear has seen women in various stages of undress before, but cleared of suspicion or not, Thom still stands between me and our guest, the same way he did with Crow. It's like having my own personal protection detail.

He tips his chin toward the table. "Come get some fresh clothes, babe."

Several shopping bags sit on the floor, along with a laptop and some other techy-type stuff on the table. Listening devices, maybe. I don't know.

"Might as well put on something comfortable, since you're staying in," he says. "Are you hungry? I ordered pizza. It should be here soon. But I can get you something else if you want."

"Pizza sounds good."

"Wolf, who takes over with this boss-guy dead?" asks Bear.

"His son inherits his share of things," answers Thom. "Typical rich kid living his best life in Ibiza, from what I know. I don't have a lot of int on him, actually. I didn't dare get too close, in case someone in-house followed my trail to him."

"Okay. Sounds bad. What do you know about the other two?"

"Only Helene Sinclair matters to us right now. She's the most accessible of the remaining bosses, from what I've been able to find out."

Bear frowns. "I know that name. U.N., right?"

"Among other things. Connected like you wouldn't believe, fingers in plenty of pies," says Thom, lips a flat line. His expression grim. "Enough money to help fund an operation like ours with the resources to stop any possible shit from flying in her direction if we got exposed."

"What exactly are you going to do?" I ask.

"The less you know, the better," responds my idiot fiancé. "In fact, cover your ears, please."

As if. I just shake my head.

"What about recce on the hotel?" asks Bear.

"We'll sweep the surrounding area and case the place before attempting entry. I don't want to risk delaying too long."

"She going to be up for a chat?"

"Good question. We have no idea who axed communication when things went south. If it was her…"

"We're fucked."

I watch the two with interest. "Int? Recce? What is this language you're speaking?"

"Intelligence. Reconnaissance." Thom looks me over. "Weren't you getting dressed? I thought you were getting dressed."

"Well, I can't cover my ears and get dressed at the same time."

"Yeah," he says. "But you're not doing either."

"How rude of me. I didn't properly say hello," says Bear, leaning to the side to see me around Thom. Considering Bear saw me earlier on the plane, this politeness feels unnecessary, to say the least. Yet the man seems determined. "How you doing, Betty?"

"Fine, thanks."

"Great to see you again."

Thom's gaze hardens.

Whatever game they're playing, they can play it without me. I go over to examine the bags. The first two bags are full of men's clothing. Second bag is women's wear and intimate apparel. Much better. "Everything we got is black?"

"Yep," says Bear. "It's just practical. Only color that really hides blood."

"What about red?" I ask, curious.

"Blood dries a darker reddish brown and becomes visible." Bear shakes his head. "You don't want your enemies knowing if or where you're wounded. Also makes it harder to mix in with the general public if you're trying to make a swift getaway. Basic escape and evasion, you got to blend in."

"Clever." Makes sense, now that I think of it—he does own a lot of dark colors.

"Not that you're going anywhere and risking the chance of getting hurt," adds Thom. "Don't freak her out, man."

"I asked, and I'm not freaked out," I say. "Well, no more than the normal current level of oh my God, we're all probably going to die horrible, violent deaths. But you know, I'm almost getting used to that. It's harder to sustain a state of constant terror than you'd think."

Thom stands with his arms crossed, face a careful blank, watching his friend. Or the dude I think is maybe his friend. You wouldn't know it, however, from the current look in his eyes.

Meanwhile, Bear is grinning for all he's worth. "See? She's not freaked out."

Nothing from Thom.

"I'm excited to try real New York pizza," I say as my stomach rumbles and I ignore their dumbass staring competition. "What did you get? Because I kind of wouldn't mind a pepperoni, but on the other hand, I could devour a ham and pineapple right now. Or something different like meatballs could be nice."

Still nothing from Thom.

Bear's grin, however, only widens. At this point, it's taking up his whole damn face. He's like a toothpaste commercial for people with excessive facial hair.

"Basically, anything you give me I will eat at this point in time, I'm so hungry," I say. "But you're not actually listening to me, so I'm going to stop talking now."

"Huh?" says Thom, glancing at me over his shoulder. "Shit. Sorry, babe. What'd you say?"

"My apologies, Betty." Bear laughs. "He was too busy silently communicating to me that if I kept looking at you in your current state of déshabillé, he'll murder me slowly. Make it hurt. Cut me into pieces and hide my bits in the woods. That sort of thing."

"He managed to communicate all of that with just a look?" I ask.

"It was more like a really intense glare. He put a lot of effort into it."

"Ah," I say with much wisdom. "Stop winding him up, please. We have enough to worry about without shenanigans."

Bear sighs. "Sorry. But Crow was right, Wolf. You are one possessive, overprotective son of a bitch when it comes to her."

Pretty sure Thom is grinding his teeth. Something has to be making the noise.

"This is why I don't do relationships," says Bear, keeping his gaze fixed on the TV. Both gallant and wise of him. "Messes with your head. You need to be sharp to stay on top in this game. Ready to go on a moment's notice, not worried about leaving someone behind."

Thom just gives him a look.

"Not exactly fair for them, either. Being away for long periods of time, often out of contact, no idea if you're dead or alive. And even when you're home, it's not like you can talk about what you do. My dad was a SEAL, and let me tell you, it was hell on my mother." Bear heads for the couch, making himself comfortable. He's ditched the pilot's uniform in favor of jeans, a dark hoodie, and sneakers. It fits more with his bearded hipster aesthetic. "Same goes for friends and family. If they're not ex-services, they don't really get it."

"Sounds lonely," I say.

"Nuh." Bear smiles affably. "Easy enough to go to a bar, chat with someone about whatever game is on the TV, maybe find a friend for a little adult playtime."

"You realize none of those things actually equals a real relationship."

"Exactly. Now you're getting it."

Thom snorts at Bear's words. "You're wrong. We need to stay in touch with all the things we're fighting to protect. Love. Family. Life. The moment we lose those, we're just mercenaries."

"*Well-paid* mercenaries," says Bear, correcting him with a smile.

I shake my head. "Right. Well, I think you're all adrenaline junkies with intimacy issues. But you do you."

Thom turns and gives *me* a look this time. His heated gaze takes in my face before sliding down my neck to linger on the sliver of cleavage visible just above the towel. It's a look that says we've been plenty intimate, and quite recently too. Smart-ass.

Heat gathers in my cheeks and I duck my head, concentrating on gathering up some clothes. A pair of black skinny jeans, a long-sleeved black thermal, and socks, and so on. "Sure, traveling the world and doing all of these exciting things may have its moments. But you're actively putting yourselves in danger all the time."

"We're not so different from cops or firefighters," says Bear. "Someone's got to stop the bad guys, rescue kittens out of trees, and save the day."

The man has a point. I just wish the person doing dangerous stuff didn't have to be someone I might possibly have intense feelings for. A selfish sentiment, but there you have it. If we do stay together, I'm just going to have to pull up my big girl panties and deal with Thom being away often, saving the world. I'm half proud and half terrified. It's a precarious balance. But possibly he should have gone for someone less neurotic and with a shitty imagination. Because imagining Thom getting hurt makes *me* hurt.

Oh God, I cannot be falling for him again, not after all this time. So we had good sex once. Us, our history and everything, is beyond complicated and will require more than a few orgasms to set things right. Though they were seriously great orgasms.

"You okay?" Thom rubs my shoulder. I kind of want to lean into him, increase the contact. But I don't. It's too soon. Of course, if we die it'll be too late. Like I said, complicated.

"Um, yeah. Fine."

"Remind me to teach you how to lie convincingly sometime," he says. "Now go get dressed before you get cold. And don't worry about my work; I'm good at what I do."

"He's one of the best," confirms Bear, his gaze still set on the TV. "After me, of course."

"Of course." I paste on a smile before heading to the bathroom. My life really only has room for one meltdown at a time. First, get this target off our backs. Then figure out the next fifty or so years.

Excellent. I have a plan.

Once I'm dressed, I come out to find Thom squatting in the hallway sliding money underneath the front door. Weird and mysterious. Then, on a small security camera screen embedded in the wall at around eye level, he watches the pizza delivery guy pick up the money and leave a box on the floor in the hallway before walking away. Thom waits for a while longer, monitoring the empty space. Finally, he turns the dead bolt, opens the door, and collects the food.

Nothing in our life is simple anymore. Not even pizza.

"You never open the door for anyone but me, okay?" he says. "Slide the money underneath and make sure they're gone before you undo the locks."

"Got it."

The pizza is deposited on the kitchen counter and yes, pepperoni it is. Awesome.

Something beeps and Thom pulls out his cell, reading the screen. "Shit."

"What?" Bear sits upright.

"They got Badger. Looks like his house exploded. They're calling it a gas leak. Body found on site." His fingers tap against the screen. "Hawk is down too. Caught in the crossfire of a robbery at a liquor store, apparently."

"Like hell she was."

"Got a copy of the crime scene pics from a reliable source. It's the same detective who's slowing down the case looking into your disappearance." Thom gives me a look. "Having the ambulance you were riding in disappear did not make our lives easy."

I shake my head in frustration. "They must be so worried and frustrated. Let me call Jen and Mom and tell them I'm okay. Explain to them that I just needed some me time or something."

"A couple more days, babe," says Thom. "Just let me talk to Sinclair and get a better feel for the situation."

I am not convinced.

"Their phones and computers are being monitored; I can guarantee it. We cannot afford to be traced again. You know what happened last time. If anything, you'd just be putting them in danger by making contact with them."

The man has a point. Doesn't mean I like it. "All right. But only a couple more days."

"Thank you." His gaze returns to the cell in his hands. "Jesus. Half of Hawk's face is missing, but it's definitely her."

Bear swears up a storm.

"That leaves you, Bear, Crow, and Fox," I say. "Crow is the only one who hasn't been cleared."

Thom stares out the window into the dark. "Let's not jump to conclusions. We don't know anything for sure yet. That might not even have been Badger's body in that house. Until we have DNA or dental confirmation on the corpse, we wait and see."

"True," grumbles Bear. "Has Crow reported in?"

"No, he hasn't." Thom tips his head back and stares at the ceiling. "He could be our leak. It makes a certain sense. He was the one who organized supplies for Betty. Could have easily placed some tracers among all that stuff."

I frown. "Really? But he seemed so nice. He said he was your friend."

"Like I said, there are no friends in this business, babe."

"If it is him, I'm going to kill the fucker," growls Bear.

"We need to locate him first," says Thom, heading into the kitchen. He opens several cupboards and starts pulling out glasses and mugs, bowls and plates. They're all set aside on the counter, out of the way. "Find evidence we can take to command. Something definite. In the meantime, our hacker says the target is apparently holed up in the penthouse suite at The Thornbrook. She's got meetings with a variety of business and political types for the next two days along with attending a charity event at the Met tomorrow night."

"What are you doing?" I ask, curious about him carrying on with the crockery.

"We need supplies."

Once the cupboards are empty, he fiddles with something inside one of them. A false back rises to reveal a selection of shiny knives embedded in a black foamlike surface. The next cupboard has several handguns with extra magazines. The third contains yet more lethal toys.

"Help yourself," he tells Bear, slipping a magazine into a pistol. The two of them get busy secreting various weapons on themselves. Getting ready to go to war. "Rifles and bigger stuff are in a hidden safe in the walk-in closet, but I'm thinking we stick with more compact gear for this."

"Agreed," says Bear.

I square my shoulders. "So what's next?"

"We're going to go check out the setup of the place, see if there's been any increases or changes in security since the last time I visited. Then we'll figure out our approach." Thom rattles off the details, ignoring the slight look of surprise on Bear's face. Guess for an operative, my fiancé is being super open with the facts. "There's a couple of events happening at the hotel tonight, so it shouldn't be too hard to blend in with the crowd."

"Okay."

"For you, however," says Thom, "there is staying here, putting your feet up, relaxing, and eating."

"There's nothing I can do to help?"

"The best thing you can do is stay here and stay safe so I don't have to worry about you," he says, his expression serious. "Can you do that for me, babe?"

"Sure," I say. And I mean it at the time. I really do.

SEVEN

THE HOURS PASS SLOWLY AFTER BEAR AND THOM LEAVE. I didn't feel particularly safe sitting on the sofa all alone in the loft apartment. Security might be tight here, but the few bites of pizza I managed to eat still churn in my stomach. Every muffled noise from other apartments, the hallway, the street beyond, makes me jump. It's nothing; everything is fine.

So fine that I get my gun out and make sure the ammunition magazine is full, even though I checked it just under an hour ago. I'm pretty sure I haven't shot at anyone in the meantime. It seems like the sort of thing I would remember.

Thom gave me a quick lesson on cleaning the gun earlier today, and my fingers itch to go through the process again. Just to be doing something. But the piece is brand-new and gleaming. If I try cleaning it, I'd probably just make it grimy. Dammit.

For a while, I debate where to put the weapon. Cradling it in my lap isn't a viable alternative. My nerves are so fried that a knock on the door would have me firing a bullet through the TV. Leaving the gun on the coffee table just seems too out of place. Like I'd need a nice little pile of white powder and a stack of money beside it to pull off the gangster look properly. Perhaps I could put on my shoulder holster.

In the end, I tuck it into the couch cushions beside me. Ready for action, but out of sight.

On the TV, Wonder Woman kicks the bad guy's ass and then some. I try to feel the empowerment, but it's just not working for me.

It's not that I'm terrified of Thom not being here to protect me. Though, come to think of it, I am a little. But it's the fact he's out there with an unknown quantity wanting him dead that has me on edge. Bear is with him, sure. And yet…this must be what it's like for people with family in the service. All of the not knowing and waiting to hear. As if a part of your life is permanently on pause and all of the fear and love forms a tight ball of unease deep inside you, which never quite goes away. I guess you learn to ignore the thing. Cover it up with everyday life and wait for them to come home one way or another. Talk about bravery and sacrifice.

Not that I *love* Thom. Whoa there. Let's not go throwing the L word around all crazy-like. So we had good (great) sex for once. He's being honest with me and showing some emotions. These are all nice things. But it's still early days. Any attempt at dissecting our relationship is bound to just leave me more confused and it's definitely too early to get carried away, envisioning shiny happy futures.

The sad truth is, no matter how much I dig Wonder Woman, this movie is not holding my interest. And flicking between the news channels isn't getting me anywhere either. Since it'll be a while before I hear from the menfolk, I need to be doing something more useful than just staring at a screen.

Or maybe not.

In movies and TV shows with detectives and stuff, they're always using CCTV and such to track people down. To figure out their movements. Of course, I don't have access to that sort of thing. But the internet is everywhere. People are constantly attached to their cell phones. Sure, it's a little farfetched. I'm probably clutching at straws. Though it's not like I have anything more pressing to do with my time.

I switch over to the cell Thom left me in case of an emergency. Easy enough to search #thornbrook and let social media give me an update on Thom and Bear's whereabouts. Instagram seems the easiest to access without actually logging into an account. Or at least it comes up first. Helpful that the place Thom and Bear are checking out is so popular. There's a PR pic of a bellboy wearing a black uniform with shiny gold buttons, busy at work with a broad smile. Another of the hotel florist grinning maniacally as she places an arrangement on the front desk. It's tagged #MollysFlowers and #lovemyjob. Her enthusiasm seems a little hard to take. Floristry's not a bad job; don't get me wrong. About the worst part of it is washing buckets and dealing with difficult customers. But no florist I've ever met has ever been quite this ecstatic. Maybe she's on drugs.

Next is two women taking a selfie in a cool-looking bathroom with a Jacuzzi. A nighttime view from a window with the lights of New York. So pretty. Two men beaming at the camera dressed in tuxedos. I tap on this one. It says "Holy matrimony, guys!" and is also tagged #SteveandDae. Here we go. Plenty of pictures of the two grooms with and without assorted family and friends, all looking delighted. Except for the woman caught shoving a giant shrimp into her mouth. Awkward timing. Don't get me wrong; seafood is great. But I wouldn't be down with this particular shot being spread about the interwebs. A three-tier wedding cake, plain red-rose boutonnieres, and elegant table centerpieces in autumn colors. I approve. Lots and lots of delighted guests.

I study each of the pictures, yet nothing stands out. It was an interesting idea, but this isn't going to work. Insert heavy sigh here. There's no sign of Thom or Bear since the bulk of the shots are taken inside a ballroom. Everything else recent and tagged with #thornbrook is either older than tonight or about an organic farm in New Zealand or a men's shoe designer.

Time to get more specific. I move on to #thornbrookhotel, and yes, we have a winner. A conference is in full swing and the attendees are apparently filling the bar to overflowing. Bonus points for them being addicted to social media. According to the hotel website's map, the Uptown Bar opens onto the huge, extravagant marble lobby/reception area. Plush red velvet seating, crystal chandeliers, and lots of people coming and going.

I study every shot, enlarging them to the point where the pixels go fuzzy. No sign of Thom or…wait. Maybe one of them is in the back of this shot. Yes, there's Bear. Or at least I'm pretty sure it's him. The height kind of gives him away. In all likelihood they're trying to avoid getting caught on camera. Though I'm guessing they'd be more worried about the hotel security system than someone taking a happy snap. After all, it's hard to be on the lookout for everyone all of the time.

The shot was posted an hour and a half ago. Perhaps Bear wandered in, sat down with a drink or something, checked out the situation, and reported to his partner. At least, it's what I'd do if I were an international person of mystery.

But what the hell do I know about doing reconnaissance ("recce," I remind myself)? Nada. Hence why I'm here fiddling on Instagram.

Still no message from Thom on the new clean and secure cell phone he gave me. Of course, it's only for emergencies. Like someone knocking on the door or a bomb going off. The man even made me pinky promise not to call anyone. As tempting as it is to shoot Mom or Jen a text (which wouldn't be breaking my word, strictly speaking, because it would be a text, not a call), I don't.

After examining dozens of pictures for further signs of my fiancé's continued existence, I'm about ready to give up. Go back to surfing the news channels or attempt another movie. Maybe just stare dejectedly at the apartment walls. Sounds like fun.

I reload the screen one more time for good luck. Three new pictures have been posted. It's a busy night at The Thornbrook Hotel. An expensive bottle of champagne resting in a bucket of ice. Very fancy. An older couple posing in their hotel room, arms around each other's waists. They look so happy. I wonder if Thom and I would be all loved-up and gracious if we were still together in fifty years. Though who knows if we'll even be together next week.

And the final pic is a couple of dudes hanging out in the lobby. On their way to a concert, apparently. Lots of people wandering past in the background of this one. Along with a figure who seems oddly familiar. Lanky body, sloped shoulders, hands stuffed into his jean pockets. There's a certain air of skulking. Much nefariousness. His clothes are dark and damp from the rain, hoodie pulled up to cover his head. But his head is turned as he looks over his shoulder. Most likely to check he's not being followed, or to avoid the security cameras at the entrance to the hotel. Whatever his reasons, he's almost full-on facing the camera.

It's Badger. The supposedly recently *deceased* Badger.

"Holy shit. He's the bad guy!"

A doorman in one of those black uniforms with shiny gold buttons opens the taxi door as soon as the car pulls up outside the hotel. Despite the crap weather, there are plenty of people coming and going. I stride into the lobby, a woman on a mission. This isn't a job for the Escada suit, despite the opulent surroundings. I stuck with black jeans, a black T-shirt, and a leather jacket. Along with lots of mascara and winged eyeliner for confidence and good luck, of course. Cell phone and some cash are stuck in my back pocket. I try Thom on my cell one more time, just in case. No answer, and no indication that he's read my message.

It's not my fault I broke almost all the rules and left the apartment. Thom needs to be told. If Badger shoots him in the back because he didn't get warned the guy was still alive and kicking, I'll never forgive myself. I can't stay hidden away while Thom's in danger. So I'm just going to have to be very brave and get this done despite being shit-scared and way out of my depth.

I do a discreet wander around the main lobby area, searching for a familiar face or two. Music streams out of the crowded bar. A jazz pianist, by the sounds of things. How cool. But there's no sign of Bear or Thom anywhere. The only thing I know for certain is that they were scouting out this hotel and planning a meet with Helene Sinclair. If the scouting section of the mission is finished, then there's only one thing for me to do. I need to get up to the penthouse suite and locate Thom there. Hopefully.

Three people stand behind the reception counter and only a couple are waiting to be served, or checked in, or whatever. Luggage sits at their feet. No one at the concierge desk right now, and this suits me fine. I pick my prey carefully. He's the youngest one on duty. The newest member of staff, most likely. Also, he seems slightly flustered, frowning at the screen in front of him. Of course, what I'm about to attempt could all backfire spectacularly. Odds are probably about even. But at least I'll have tried.

"Hi, I'm supposed to fix the arrangements in Helene Sinclair's room," I say, sliding him the business card I picked up from Molly's Flowers and moving the bunch of white roses that I bought from the shop up in my arms a little. I've got a whole bullshit presentation thing happening here.

The young man, whose name tag says "Cory," just blinks.

"She's staying in the penthouse, apparently."

Now he frowns.

"Sorry." I give him a brief smile. "I'm Liz from Molly's Flowers. Guess I should have led with that. Anyway, Molly sent me in since she's at a thing right now and can't get away." That part of my story was at least somewhat true. Molly's enthusiasm for Instagram made her frighteningly easy to stalk. "Apparently your guest has severe allergies, but someone forgot to notify us about it. It's a disaster. So I need to remove the white oriental lilies and fix things up as best I can, since they can't get an actual replacement arrangement here until the morning, after we've gotten our delivery from the markets. You know how it is."

"Oh," he says, just a dash of panic in his gaze. "Ah..."

"I know right? Such a pain in the rear." I sigh. "Can you give me a card to quickly pop up there and get this done, or will you need to escort me? How do we do this?"

"You work with Molly?" he asks.

"She's my boss. You've met her? Isn't she great?" At least she looked nice enough on her website. My smile is all things friendly and inviting as I lean closer. "I'm new there. I guess that's why I've been assigned this task. Everyone has to pay their dues, huh?"

"Yeah. Tell me about it." His posture relaxes as he shoots his coworkers farther down the counter disgruntled looks. However, both seem oblivious to his inner pain.

"The concierge must be off running an errand, and I really can't wait around."

"Just give me a minute." He picks up the phone and dials Sinclair's room. For a moment, he just listens. "No answer."

"Thank goodness. That means she's not back yet, and we can get those lilies out before she gets anywhere near the pollen.

It'd probably be all our asses on the line if she wakes up tomorrow covered in hives. Moll said she's some bigwig at the U.N. It'd be a PR disaster if we hadn't caught this in time. We just dodged a bullet, you and I." I raise my brows in a *phew*-type fashion.

"Okay…um, listen," he says, also leaning in closer and lowering his voice. "I'm due to go on my break, but I can escort you up there first. That should be fine."

"Really? That would be so great."

"Sure."

"Thanks so much, Cory. I really appreciate it." I was prepared to try and bluff the manager if I had to, but this is ideal.

There's a discreet swagger to his step as we head for the row of elevators. I've made him feel important. Stroked his ego a little. Now I must find Thom before this all blows up in my face. Inside the exclusive elevator just for the penthouse suite, everything is mirrored and trimmed with gold. Soft music does little to soothe my jagged nerves. My hands are once again shaking and I'm sweating my butt off. But the stupid smile stays plastered on my face. Even when I bust Cory checking out my cleavage. The kid is not subtle. And while using him doesn't feel good, it is necessary. Lives could very well be on the line here.

I make good use of his distraction by slipping my gun out, keeping it covered by the roses. Eventually the elevator doors open.

Time comes to such a sudden stop that I almost get whiplash. In slow motion, my mind makes a whole bunch of useless observations. A large art-deco style room with white walls and luxurious furnishings. A black grand piano. A wall of windows looking out onto the lights of New York. But it's all just background noise to the shocking scene in front of me.

There are two dead bodies dressed in suits and leaking blood. Strangers. No one I know. And six people holding guns on each other. Some of them wearing balaclavas. One of them is noticeably smaller than the others. A woman, perhaps.

On the opposite side of the room, facing toward me, are Thom and Bear, and I can just glimpse another smaller figure, sheltered behind Bear's huge frame. Probably the boss-lady they're here to protect. Then there are three men standing with their backs to Cory and me, like maybe they were waiting for the elevator to make their escape. Everyone has weapons out, leveled at each other. Guess it's a stalemate.

Thom steals a glance at me, his jawline shifting in apparent anger. But Bear ignores our arrival entirely, keeping his focus on the scene. Then one of the men standing in front of us turns, and it's Badger.

All of these details go through my mind in a moment. There's no time to think them over. No time to assess the situation. I just drop the flowers, aim my weapon at Badger's center mass and fire. *Boom.*

And it begins.

"What the f—" It's as far as Cory gets before something pops and a red bloom spreads across his chest and he falls.

Meanwhile, Badger drops to his knees, gun still pointed at Cory. Then he topples over, dead before he hits the floor.

"Betty, get down!" yells Thom.

I do as told and hit the floor as all hell breaks loose. The popping noise of guns with silencers versus the louder thunderclap of your regular pistols. Something I know care of watching too many action movies in my youth.

Realizing they're trapped between two sides, Badger's accomplices dive off to my right, firing as they do. Oh fuck me. I crouch down against the elevator wall, hands covering my ears. The doors try again and again to close but Cory's body blocks them. Blood is everywhere.

"Get her out of here!" yells Thom, squatting behind a couch.

Bear hustles the lady toward me and the elevator. A porcelain vase shatters on a nearby pedestal. White flowers scatter all around us. Chips of the marble flooring fly through the air as one of the balaclava people sprays bullets in our direction. Bits of stuffing from the couches explode out as bullets fly from Thom returning fire.

One of the bad guys trying to dart to the side wasn't fast enough. Whoever it is wearing the balaclava in front of the elevator doors lets out a pained grunt and stumbles. Black really does hide the blood. He seems to be falling in slow motion when another bullet hits him in the head. Blood and brains and bone spew out of the exit wound. There's no hiding *that*.

Bear arrives and pushes the woman into the opposite corner of the elevator, covering her with his body. She has gray hair, and she looks elegant, even amid all the carnage. Someone's shouting. I can't hear what. Thom jumps out from behind a wingback chair, sprinting across the room as the last living bad guy keeps shooting. I cringe as Bear pushes Cory out of the way. He takes no care with the young man's body. Not that it matters to Cory anymore.

But I did that. I got him killed.

Thom finally joins us, sliding in the blood, almost losing his footing. Slowly, oh-so-slowly, the elevator doors close on the scene. Bullets ping off the metal. One thunks into the wall above my head. All I can smell is gunpowder, dust, and blood. Also, my mind is spiraling. Definitely not keeping up with current events. I notice blood on the white roses. Even discarded and half-trampled, the red speckles on the white petals look kind of pretty.

"Stay down," orders Thom. "What the hell are you doing here, Betty?"

I try to find the words. They're just kin of, sort of not there right now. Finally we begin to descend. We're all in there: me, Bear, Thom, and the lady. Safe for the moment. Oh my God.

"Why did you leave the apartment?" he growls.

"Had to tell you Badger is alive," I say, voice choked for some reason. "I saw him in the back of a photo, and I thought he might be the bad guy and might try to kill you and...yeah."

He swears softly.

"That was really scary," I say, exhaling slowly.

Thom kneels beside me, holding me tight against him. Then he swears some more. Apparently he's in a super-sweary mood. I can relate.

"I shot someone." The information doesn't quite compute. Guess my brain still isn't working right. Mostly I just feel numb. "Killed them."

"We'll talk about it later. Right now, you need to get that gun out of sight."

"Right. Okay." I do as told.

Bear, meanwhile, has been busy on his cell phone. "Your car is being brought around right now, ma'am."

"We're taking you out the front door," Thom says to her. "If they got to you up here, it's likely the underground exit is already compromised."

The elegant older woman nods and pats down her hair, pulling herself back together. "My security are dead. I trust you're available to temporarily replace them starting immediately."

"Yes, ma'am." Thom swallows. "Everyone on their feet. We're going to make our way through the lobby as calmly and quickly as possible. Bear, you take the lead. Mrs. Sinclair, please follow closely behind him. Betty and I will take up the back."

As soon as the elevator doors open onto the lobby, Bear is stepping out, confronting the anxious-looking security guards waiting to go up, likely to check out all the noise coming from the suite. Guns are loud. Even the silenced ones aren't actually silent. Then there's all of the blood splattered around the elevator.

"FBI," says Bear, flashing some doubtless fake I.D. "Step back, please. Keep out of the way."

Surprise flickers across the two men's faces. But they do as told. The nearest one says, "Agent—"

"Establish a cordon. Allow no one up to the penthouse suite. More agents will be along shortly to handle the situation."

"Y-yes, sir."

We hustle through the space, moving double -time as ordered. The side of my jeans are clinging to my leg, wet with Cory's blood. All of the marble and crystal and beauty of the place is lost on me. In my mouth there's an off, sort of sour taste. Violence taints everything. We cut through the crowd, not slowing down for anyone or anything.

A big black luxury sedan with tinted windows waits for us out front. They weren't kidding about the car being brought around right away. Though if you can afford to stay in the penthouse suite, you're probably used to such service.

Bear pushes aside the porter holding open the rear door of the vehicle. Then he sticks his head inside, checking out the interior. Mrs. Sinclair climbs into the car.

"Betty, get in the back," says Thom, giving me a gentle push.

Meanwhile, Bear drags the driver out of the vehicle, flashing his I.D. once more. The man sputters, wearing the same startled expression as the hotel security dudes. Thom then climbs into the passenger side, doors slam shut, and we're on our way, pulling out into traffic.

Safe for the moment. At least, I hope we are.

"Glass is bulletproof?" asks Thom.

"Yes." Mrs. Sinclair nods. "I have a property several hours away on the Hudson. We'll go there."

"Ma'am, it wouldn't be safe to—"

"It's safe. It cannot be traced to me." Her chin rises. "Believe me, young man, I fully realize the gravity of this situation. I've been involved in this business longer than you've been alive."

Thom turns in his seat, assessing the woman with his serious eyes.

"Secret or not, many enemies have been made by the members of the committee over the years. I was not blind to the eventuality of just such an attempt on my life."

He nods. "We'll go to the estate."

Helene rattles off the address.

"You know who that was up there who got away?" asks Bear.

"I know." Thom's voice is hard with anger. "Scorpion's still alive."

"You recognized her even with the balaclava?" I ask.

"She spoke just before you came in. Wanted us to know it was her. Guess she was only wearing the balaclava for the sake of any cameras. Now we just have to figure out who the hell she's working with."

"At least Badger's appearance upstairs confirms why comms were down," says Helene. "I've been trying to contact you for days."

"Nice to know you hadn't abandoned us."

"Abandoned you? After all the money we've poured into each of you and this venture? Don't be ridiculous."

"Speaking of which, someone's got to be funding this bullshit," says Bear.

"That would be the late Lord Blackmead's son, Archer. Lord Blackmead is...*was* on the director's board with me." Helene takes a deep, steadying breath. "Archie approached me several weeks ago with a proposition to make assets available to the private sector…for the right price. I tried to warn his lordship about his heir apparent, but he wouldn't listen."

Thom turns in his seat. "Archie wants to sell our services on the open market?"

"Oh yes," says Helene. "Has all sorts of grand plans for turning you into his own private army for hire, and making a good deal of money while he'ss at it. None of which were in keeping with the organization's original objective."

"So he had shares already or just inherited them?"

Helen shakes her head. "There are no actual shares. This is more in the way of a philanthropic venture," she says. "But he's now inherited his father's place and obviously plans to undermine us and all we've done."

"What did you tell him?"

"I said no, of course. This morning I offered to buy his newly inherited seat at the table. Recompense him for the sum total of his father's financial involvement in the organization over the years. He didn't take it well."

"What about Charles Adisa?"

"So you know about him too, hmm? You have been busy. Nice to know all my money has been well-spent. Yes, Charles is the third and final member of the committee that runs the organization you're both employed by." Helene crosses her legs, smoothing down the skirt of her black dress. She seems way more together than I am. Perhaps she's been in the middle of a shootout before. Looked death in the eye and lived to see another day.

"Charles was no more receptive to that little shit's nonsense than I was. We are not here to turn a profit. This organization was started by our families not long after World War II. All three of the founding members had lost children on the battlefield. So they strove to monitor hostile situations on an international level and hopefully deal with them before they escalated beyond control. We're not always successful, but that will never stop us from trying."

No one says anything.

"Then what?" asks Thom, jaw gritted. "He approached the operatives most likely to go along with him or willing to sell out, and then set about killing the rest?"

Bear exhales. "Sure sounds that way. Asshole."

"Scorpion's morals have always been flexible, but I never thought she'd screw us over like this."

"I'm not."

Thom's brows rise ever so slightly.

"It's the truth," says Bear. "You two might have gotten along once upon a time. But there was never any loyalty there. And Badger was always a dubious little shit. Can't entirely blame them. I mean, sometimes it's nice to save the world. But it can be even nicer to get paid lots of money."

Thom grunts. "Yeah? So why are you here?"

"Me?" Bear laughs. "I try not to be a raging asshole whenever possible. It's a lifestyle choice. Besides, I like to think of us as friends...sort of."

"Right. Would have thought Spider'd be up for selling us out."

"Guess he said no, otherwise he wouldn't be deceased, same as Hawk. Nice to know people can still surprise us."

"Think I've had about enough surprises for now." Thom pulls out his cell. No doubt seeing he's missed about fifty calls and text messages from me, along with other updates. Though the stiffness in his shoulders eases some at whatever news he's reading. "Crow is cleared."

"Makes sense, or he would have been in on this hit with Scorpion. We're going to need all the backup we can get."

"Roger that. Sending them coordinates."

"Locating Archie won't be easy," says Helene. "Now that he's taking control of his father's estate, his resources will be innumerable. We need to reel him in, however, and the sooner the better."

Thom says nothing, still busy on his cell phone.

"I trust you have access to a secure line? Give it to me, please." The woman holds out her hand, her polish immaculate. Unlike mine, her hand is steady. Though she didn't kill anyone, only dodged bullets. What a day.

Without hesitation, Thom hands over his cell. "You can get a warning to Mr. Adisa?"

"I can try. But I have a feeling this is going to get much worse before it gets better."

EIGHT

O F COURSE, HELENE'S IDEA OF A SAFE HOUSE IS A LARGE, renovated English-style cottage with a widow's walk on top sitting on tons of acreage on the Hudson River. It's not dirty, just a little dusty. As if no one's been here for a while.

In the basement, there's an operations room. Lots of computers and stuff. It's the only room in the place that has clearly received constant attention and cleaning. No dust, and the tech looks like it just rolled off the shelves. There's also a large walk-in weapons locker and a security system that could rival a Swiss bank's. The woman is obviously prepared for just about anything.

Bear sits at one of the consoles, tapping away on the keyboard. "Fox and Crow are on their way. ETA for Fox is an hour and a half. But Crow is going to be longer."

Not a surprise. The sun is rising since it took us forever to get here with Bear staying off main roads and often doubling back on himself. No one could have possibly managed to follow us. Though we've thought this before, and been unpleasantly surprised. After all, traffic and security cameras would have been able to monitor us for at least some of the way. And Helene's car is a Rolls Royce. Very distinctive.

Thom pulls a collection of weapons out of the locker, lining them up on a table. Night-vision headset thingies. Fully automatic rifles. You name it, we've got it. Even Henry would be impressed.

"I can call in backup from the security firm I use," says Helene, watching the screen over Bear's shoulder.

Thom shakes his head. "We don't know who Archer's gotten to, except that he's likely already penetrated the group once. Scorpion and her people had inside knowledge of your movements and security detail, Helene. I'd bet my life on it. They knew exactly when and where to attack to get their best shot at taking you out. If Bear and I hadn't shown up, you'd be dead."

"Very well. I'm going to rest while I have the opportunity. Alert me to any changes."

"Yes, ma'am."

Helene ascends the stairs like a queen, with her head held high. Not a sign of anxiety, despite the recent assassination attempt. Meanwhile, I'm sitting on a chair to the side, mentally running through song lyrics from a few decades ago. Because I'm practical like that. And I'd rather think about Janis Joplin and her general awesomeness than death in general, or actually dying sometime soon. Mostly it keeps my mind occupied and away from things best not pondered. Like bodies and blood and brains on the wall. Me killing someone. The surprised look on Badger's face. White roses with red specks.

Maybe I'm in shock. I feel cold and the real world seems distant. Like any moment now I might wake up from this horrible dream.

"Babe." Thom holds out his hand. "C'mon upstairs and lie down. Nothing's going to happen for a while."

I take his hand, letting him pull me out of the chair and lead me upstairs. There's plaid wallpaper and chunky brown leather furniture. Walnut kitchen cupboards and stainless steel appliances.

"Are you hungry?" asks Thom. "There's nothing fresh, but the freezer is apparently full of frozen meals."

Just the thought of food turns my stomach. "No. Thank you."

Thom ushers me into the closest room, a tan-colored bedroom with a large sleigh bed made up with forest-green sheets. The curtains are drawn against the morning light. Like the rest of the house, the room is only a little dusty. Guess a cleaner comes once a month or so. The gardens might be basic, but they'd still need looking after. Perhaps she pays the people through a shell company so no one knows who they're actually working for. Not that any of it particularly matters.

We're safe for the moment. I should feel safe. I should be able to breathe easy for a little while. But I can't. I'm just waiting for the next disaster to befall us. Which sounds like I have nil respect for Thom's abilities. Though that's not true. I'm just...damn. I don't know what I am. I can still feel the gun bucking in my hand when I squeezed the trigger. Hear the sound of bullets entering flesh and pinging off metal. It's as if a part of me is still standing in that elevator, watching all hell break loose.

And there's a bathroom attached to this room, which is mighty handy given how my night turned out and what a mess I am. "I might just—"

"Let's get you out of those bloody clothes." Thom shuts the door and turns the lock. He inspects my face. A whole lot of too-pale skin with dark circles under the eyes, no doubt. It's been a hard few days. A tough night.

"I convinced that kid to take me up to the penthouse," I say. Just needing to hear it out loud. The cold hard fact of the matter. I am culpable. There is blood on my hands. "Cory. His name was Cory. He'd just finished his shift. He was doing me a favor."

"You had no idea about what was going on up there." Thom kneels at my feet, unties my boots. "Sometimes innocent people get caught up in bad things. If you want to blame someone, blame the person who shot him in cold blood. Sit on the bed, babe."

I do as asked. "I shot someone too. I killed Badger."

"Yeah. But he was a bad person who needed shooting." He tugs off a boot, followed by a sock. Then moves on to the other foot. "You were defending yourself, Betty. He would have killed you. He'd already tried to kill us before by leaking our address to set up the bomb in our house."

"Mm."

"He was a hired mercenary, fully prepared to take out innocent people for no reason other than money." He lifts the hem of my tee, giving me a brief smile. "Arms up."

With my arms in the air, I say, "I don't think anyone's undressed me since I was a child."

"I undress you constantly in my mind, if that counts. Stand up." He tugs on my hand and I let him draw me back onto my feet. Next he deals with the button and zip on my black jeans, easing them down my legs. The fabric is stiff with blood below the knee. It's a relief to get out of them. "Lift your leg."

"I don't have anything else to wear."

Both of us ignore the red-brown stain of another person's blood on my shin. I stand there in my underwear, too dazed to feel exposed. Besides, he's seen it all before. "I'll get them washed for you. Don't worry."

Next he leads me into the bathroom, turning on the shower, testing the water with his hand. No previous lovers, or other such types have looked after me this way. Tended to me. Is this love? The need to look after your chosen person? The desire to be close to them? I guess so. At least, it's got to be close to resembling the sentiment. Maybe he wasn't lying about his feelings all this time. Maybe I'm lying about mine now.

135

"Let's get this off you," he says, reaching around to undo my black bra.

"I know there's work to do, but can you stay with me for a little while?" I fist my hands in his shirt, needing the contact. Right now, he has a much better grip on the world than I. I'm spiraling. Free falling.

"Sure."

"Thank you. I just...I don't know."

He doesn't say anything, but nods in understanding.

Once my underwear is gone, he tears off his own shirt, toes off his shoes. He gets naked much faster than I could ever manage. Another one of his useful skills. He takes my hand and backs into the shower, water sliding over his skin. "Come on in here so you don't get cold."

The spray of water wakes me a little, breathes a bit of life back into me. How is it I'd killed someone, yet feel like a part of myself has died? A bit of my innocence maybe. I'm not quite sure if I'm a good person anymore. Or maybe I'm someone who, when pushed, can go to extremes I never imagined possible. I can kill someone who's not a stranger. Can cross lines and fight back. Maybe good and bad aren't as straightforward as I thought.

My hand sits on his shoulder as he kneels down to wash the blood off my leg. Pink water swirls down the drain. His skin is hot and alive. Everything I need right now. He's so beautiful with his scars and his hardness. How gentle his hands are on me, despite the things they're capable of.

I'm the one who starts the kissing, my mouth pressed against the side of his neck. Even with the water, I can still catch the warm scent of him. The taste of salt on his skin. It's all so perfectly Thom.

"Babe," he mutters. "You okay?"

"Absolutely not." I kiss him again. Harder.

"Whatever you need." His hands skim down my back, comforting as opposed to sexy-times exploring. The muscles in his arms flex as he holds me tighter and tighter. "I thought I was going to lose you today. I've never been so fucking scared in my life. The elevator doors opened and there you stood. Then that asshole turned and aimed his gun and..."

"I'm right here."

"You almost weren't."

I don't know what to say to that.

"Jesus. If he had harmed you, I would not have given him a quick death." The fire in his eyes, the stark way his cheekbones stand out...this man is a lot overwhelming. Especially in this moment. "I know you don't want to hear that sort of thing, but it's the truth."

"I understand." And I do. The thought of anyone hurting him makes me stabby too.

"You'll never come after me again. Promise me."

"But you needed to know—"

"Nothing is worth you getting hurt. Shit! You almost got killed. Tell me you understand that, Betty."

Problem is, I don't exactly agree. "Did you know about Badger?"

"As a matter of fact, I found out a moment or two before you made your entrance."

"So me killing him—"

Thom groans. "It helped. I'll admit it. But we would have managed."

"You would have been cornered, waiting for the elevator to arrive. Admit it."

But apparently he has no interest in further debate right now.

His kiss is gentle at first. Firm lips pressing against mine, again and again. As if he's just reassuring himself I'm still here and alive. I'm the one who pushes for more. My mouth opening, tongue teasing. And Thom doesn't hold back at all. Not once he knows I want it. Hell, that I need it. His body hard against mine, his fingers possessive on my flesh. After today, we both crave this physical confirmation of being alive and together. There's no doubt.

My spine hits the tiled shower wall, his hand cradling the back of my head. He kisses me hard and deep. It's a soul kiss. Like nothing I've ever had before. His tongue caressing mine, his lips molded to my mouth. With all of the death we've been facing, he's breathing life back into me and I can't get enough.

One hand grabs my breast, kneading and playing. And it all feels so good. Someone apparently turned my sensitivity levels up to eleven. Because even with the shower water, I'm wetter than I've ever been. It's almost embarrassing. Normally these things take time. A certain care is usually required to turn me on. But apparently Thom even existing in my general vicinity works just fine these days.

When he gets to his knees, pressing his face against my mound, kissing the sensitive flesh below, my brain goes offline entirely. Worries, cares, concerns, none of these things exist. There's only here and now.

A strong hand hitches my leg over his shoulder, opening me to his attentions. In days of yore, he'd kind of fumble around down there for a moment or two. He'd pretend he cared then move straight on to the next thing. Now the man eats me like it's his life's mission. Tongue dragging through my cleft before circling my clit. Fingers easing into my body, pumping slowly. It's not enough though.

Rest assured, I'm not shy about expressing as much by

pulling on his hair. The muffled laughter in response all but drives me insane. However, he does as instructed and starts sucking on my clit, hooking his fingers to rub the back of it deep inside of me. Further confirmation the man knows anatomy and then some. He licks me and finger-fucks me and the noise of the shower and my heavy breathing fill the wet space. I'm close. So damn close.

Yet he does the unthinkable and stops. The bastard actually eases my leg from over his shoulder and rises to his feet. What the ever-loving hell?

"Thom," I snarl.

"You come with me in you. I want to feel that. I need it."

"But—"

"Now, babe."

Not a bad idea, as ideas go. Though I'm still kind of whiny about him stopping. He lifts my leg over his hip and the head of his cock teases my entrance. I'm so primed after the display of his excellent oral abilities. This might be the shortest round of sex ever. But who the hell has time to mess around when I can have him inside of me?

No slowing down, he slams his thick, rigid cock into my body. The shock of it jars me and yet feeds the fire building within. Every nerve ending in me is singing.

"Christ. Thom."

"I really do like the way you say my name." He withdraws before plunging back in. All of that thick, hard flesh stretching me inside in the best way possible. The top of his dick rubs against me in all the right places and I'm panting once more. And yet...

"It's definitely your real name?"

"Elizabeth." He keeps right on pumping into me, hard and fast. "Keep your mind on the job."

Hopefully my only job right now is to come. Because all I can do is hang on, my arms wrapped tight around his shoulders. We fit together so perfectly. Like we were born for this. No killing or chaos or any of those things. Just being together, he and I.

The man not so delicately, but with much talent, fucks me into a stupor. His magnificent cock lights me up from the inside. A wave of sensation rises inside of me, pushing me up onto my toes. I can't get close enough. And I'm so damn greedy for more and more. Except right then my body draws tight, the wave crashing. Every muscle in my cunt spasms, trying to hold him deep within. I tremble and shake, and it's sublime.

Thom swears low and fierce while I just float. Thank goodness he's holding me up. Also, lucky we're already in the shower, given the exchange of bodily fluids going on. Coming on him is pretty damn spectacular. Feeling him empty inside of me. Just being this close.

One thing is for certain, it's good to be alive.

"A bomb killed three of Mr. Adisa's staff this morning."

"That's unfortunate," says a man's voice. British and posh.

The cell sits on the table, everyone gathered around in the basement room to listen. And everyone now includes Fox and Crow. I descend the steps quietly, trying not to interrupt. It's early afternoon. Not much later than lunchtime. But after the mother of all nightmares, I know I won't be getting any more sleep. My freshly laundered clothes sat on the end of the bed. Just as Thom promised. But back to the phone call…

"Oh, it's a good deal more than that," corrects Helene. "On top of the kill squad you sent to my hotel room, Archie, I'd have to say your message has been well and truly received."

"I did try to sort this out peacefully first. Remember that, old girl."

Helene's lips settle into a flat, furious line. "So I assume from all of this that you're unwilling to back down from your insane plan to monetize the organization?"

"You're finally understanding."

"Very well. It's obvious we can't sway you, and I have little interest in having assassins sent after me. So I'm charged to act on behalf of Charles and myself as we both retire and leave things in your hands." Helene's chin rose. "Is that agreeable to you?"

Archer cleared his throat. "It is. This is most…unexpected. I didn't think either of you would be willing…at any rate. Yes, that's very agreeable to me."

"Charles and I are both getting older, and I have no heir apparent. We both feel that with the good work we've done over the years, bowing out now is not entirely intolerable. The responsibility for the committee's new direction will therefore be yours alone."

"I'm delighted to hear you've come to your senses."

"Indeed. I trust you've had the documentation prepared to handle the transfer of power?"

"Yes, I have," the man all but purred. "Where are you now? I'd be delighted to hand-deliver them myself. There's no need for more of this dreadful hostility between us."

Helene sat back in her chair, crossing her legs. "Oh, Archie. You can't believe I'm going to make it quite that easy. You always were rather spoiled. Now I may be willing to bow out, but it was only last night that you were trying to kill me. It was all rather upsetting. Forgive me my foibles; pettiness is such an ugly emotion. And yet, I do believe I'll allow you to locate me on your own. If you can…"

He laughed. "Very well. Let's decide now on the amount of security to accompany each of us to this event, hmm? I'd hate for there to be any last-minute misunderstandings."

"Send three of your people to deliver the papers, and I'll have two of mine here. But you don't get to come, Archie." Her voice hardens. "That's my condition. If I must sign over my life's work, I will not suffer through your gloating while I do it. At this point, I'll count it as a victory if I never have to see your face again."

"There's no need to take this so personally, Helene."

"Do you agree to my terms?"

A soft laugh echoes through the line. "Of course. My people will be in touch."

The line went dead.

"I feel like I'm dealing with a fucking Bond villain," Helene says, and sighs. "Honestly, to have it all come to this."

"You don't honestly believe this fucker, do you?" asks Bear.

"Not in the slightest. Make no mistake, he'll be coming in hard for all of us with a small army and lots of guns."

Fox crosses her arms, leaning against the wall. "Then why the games?"

"Why did I just prick that massive blowhard's ego? Tell him I'd count it as a victory if I never see him again? Because now he has to put the bullet in me himself. He won't settle for anything less than looking me in the eyes as he pulls the trigger," says Helene. "After his people have cleared the way, of course. This is the best chance we have to get a shot at him and put an end to all of this."

Thoughtful silence met her pronouncement. Not that I contributed to the general thoughtfulness. I was basically just a lot scared and doing my best to hide this fact.

"Wolf, how long would you guess we have?" she asks eventually.

My fiancé straightens. "Hard to say. A few hours at least. Or they could string us out, try and wear us down a little. They've got superior numbers and can choose the timing. So maybe they'll wait until well after midnight and try to catch us tired or with our guard down."

"If Scorpion's in charge?" asks Crow.

"Then she'll want to settle in and see what we're up to before making a move. She's cautious; it's what's kept her alive so long, made her such a good operator," says Thom. "We got lucky last night, stumbling into her hit like that. Doubt we'll get the drop on her a second time."

The sinking feeling in my stomach turns into an endless void. Thom's gaze meets mine across the room, and I try for a smile. Given the grim look on his face, my lips have failed me big-time.

Fox looks to heaven with a sigh. "Shit's going to hit the fan again, yadda yadda. We all know it. So what's the plan? Because I'm done with these assholes taking potshots at us."

"First up, clear all of the weapons out of the safe room and then, Helene, you and Betty are in there until it's safe to come out."

Their boss beats me to "oh hell no" by like half a second.

"No, I'm not," she says. "You need all the shooters you can get, and I'll have you know I was quite the markswoman in my day. If I can take a duck on the wing at two hundred yards, then I'm quite capable of putting a bullet through Archie's smug face."

"What she said," I add. "Apart from the markswoman thing. But I can point and shoot. You all saw that much."

Thom's lips thin, the man clearly unhappy and about to argue with us hardcore.

"This isn't up for discussion, Wolf," snaps Helene. "If I'm not visible then Archie won't bother risking himself and entering the firefight, which is our one chance of surviving this. None of this goes away until he's dead. Charles is safe from all of this for now. He's your backup plan in case anything happens to me." Her chin gets higher and higher. I don't think she's used to anyone so much as attempting to tell her what to do. "While I appreciate your wish to keep me alive and kicking, stopping that little prick comes first."

He sighs. "Fine. However, you're both down in the basement until we've got the initial assault under control. Then I'll reassess the situation. But only once we've downed the bulk of their force will we make our play. Crow, you're our expert on the long gun. I want you up on the widow's walk picking off everything you can. Bear, you take the road approach. Fox, you've got the waterfront."

Crow raises his hand. "I brought claymores."

"Love me some explosives. Good work. Knew I liked you for a reason," says Thom. "All right, let's get busy."

Everyone disperses, off to do who knows what home protection work. Fox starts grilling Helene about the security system, the location of any hardware including gardening tools, and the location of any and all access points. Given this isn't a place Helene spends quality time, they then go off on a tour of the house. Bear and Crow, meanwhile, start unpacking and prepping enough guns and knives to kill an army.

"I can still get you out of here." Thom stands at my side. "I'm serious, Betty."

"Don't. I'm not going anywhere." I sigh. "What can I do to help?"

His face is somber. "Make sure all the windows are locked and curtains drawn. We need this place locked down tight."

"Okay. What gun should I take?"

He picks up a small pistol, placing it in my hand with a grim expression. "Helene will be right beside you. Follow her lead.

Don't point your gun until she does. Don't pull the trigger until she does."

"Okay."

"I mean it," he says. "Otherwise the chances are you'll accidentally hit one of us. I'd rather die in your arms than in your crosshairs."

"Fair enough."

"So you stay in the basement, safe and sound." He tucks a strand of hair behind my ear. It's a tender, sweet thing for him to do. In fact, this whole moment fits that description, despite the weaponry.

My lungs feel leaden all of a sudden; my heart beats double time. The look in his eyes as he gazes down at me is everything I could have asked for. Everything I'd given up hoping I'd ever get from this man. And now here he is, giving it to me in spades. I do my best to memorize this, to commit it to memory for all time. Because, the truth is, we may very well not have many of these moments left, care of Archie and his goon squad.

"Pretty sure you said the same thing when you left me to go to Helene's hotel," I say in my ever so slightly sarcastic tone of voice. "Just F.Y.I.."

"Let's not have a repeat of last night." He kisses my forehead. "Hand to God, babe, you nearly gave me a heart attack."

Nearly gave myself a heart attack too. But I don't say that.

"Promise me you'll keep your badass self in the basement for now, out of sight, okay?"

"Okay. Fine." I shrug. "You're going to be careful, aren't you?"

"I'm always careful. I love you, you know?"

"You keep saying that."

He gives me the smallest of smiles. "Just making sure you believe me this time around."

And I don't know what to say. Especially not when he's

looking at me this way. The subtle shift of his features leaves me with no doubt that he knows all about the war going on inside me. Heart versus head and all that. My feelings for him are far from simple, but I'm not quite sure they're what he wants from me yet—assuming he wants me to say the same to him in return, as is tradition. "Thom…"

He blinks. "I better get to work."

And the blink is the only indication that I've struck a nerve, and hurt him by delaying saying it back. And wounding Thom in any way pretty much feels like driving a knife through my own heart.

I'm honestly stunned. It's a revelation. If this doesn't answer the do-I-or-don't-I-love-him question then nothing ever will.

Only he's already gone.

I'm just standing there staring after him like an absolute certified idiot. One who wants to kick herself for not saying it back right away, for not taking the risk and jumping, trusting he'd catch me. Now he's in a deep discussion with Bear, words like "perimeter" and "defense" being thrown around.

The moment's gone and, like everyone else, I guess I have a job to do. Or I could be honest and admit that I don't have the guts to pull him aside right now or just cut the shit and say it in front of other people. To wear my heart on my sleeve in front of an audience of operatives. Regardless of us potentially facing a messy and violent death soon, deep down, I'm apparently still an emotional scaredy-cat. This is beyond disappointing.

But if Thom can be brave enough to put his heart on the line, then so can I. He deserves nothing less.

Shoulders back, tits out. After being labeled a badass, the least I can do is rise to the occasion emotions-wise. I'll get another chance alone with him to 'fess up before everything hits the fan. Hell, I'll move heaven and earth to make sure of it.

NINE

"**T**HOM?"

He turns away from one of the living room windows. Behind him, a dazzling golden sunset lights up the yard. It casts the kind of perfect lighting that only comes along every once and a while. At his feet, an equally dazzling and dangerous array of firepower awaits, spread out on the Oriental rug. "Babe. Hey. You okay?"

"Yes. I um…" I cocked my head, taking in the weird tool in his hand. "What are you doing?"

"Cutting holes in the glass to fire through," he explains. "Less obvious and messy than breaking the windows."

"You think it'll make a difference?"

"Everything we can do to come out on top is worth trying. If this gives us an extra moment or two before they know where we're firing from, then, yeah, it could make a difference."

I nod. "That makes sense."

"Glad you approve."

Oh. My. God. He's making a tiny smirk and it's the absolute cutest. Man, I have it bad. My stomach does some intense swooping thing. Like my nerves needed any more help. I rub my sweaty palms on the sides of my jeans. Pretty sure I had more game in middle school than I have now.

Inside, the house is all shadows. Only a few lights strategically placed down low are on. If you didn't know better, you'd think the place was deserted. Which is exactly the image we're going for. We've been reorganizing the furniture to cover exits or slow down anyone trying to gain entrance via the doors and windows.

All of us have done our best to help turn the cottage into a fort. And while movie montages involving prep for battle are usually exciting, I'm here to tell you they're not. There was no dynamic music for starters, and my back hurts from lugging a jade coffee table into position. In truth, the whole getting-organized-before-the-big-action-scene thing is actually just really hard work.

"What's wrong?" he asks. "You haven't changed your mind about being here, have you?"

"Huh? No, not at all."

He exhales in relief. Guess getting me out this late in the day would be a big problem. I am, however, sticking by his side.

"But I, ah…I have something to tell you," I say.

At this, he sets down the tool, giving me his complete attention. And not that this isn't an important moment and all, but I can't help be distracted by how he looks. Thom wears a black long-sleeved Henley under a bulletproof vest like nobody's business. All of the rippling of muscles in his arms, care of the way the fabric lovingly molds to his body, is awe inspiring. My hormones do a giddy dance. I basically just want to plant my face in the middle of his chest and hide for a while. Maybe forever. But I'm a woman on a mission.

"Okay." He crosses his arms. "I'm listening. Then, after you've said your thing, you need to go put on your vest and stay in the basement with Helene."

"Right, I'll do that. But what I wanted to say is…" Honest to God, I'm about to tell him. About to say the big L word to someone outside of my immediate friends and family for the very first time.

Only, then I see a little black thingy discreetly tucked into his ear.

"Thom, can other people hear this conversation?"

"They're not interested in listening to us."

"That's not what I asked."

Just then, his gaze shoots to heaven and he holds a hand up to his ear. "Shut up, Bear. Go shit in the woods or something."

Chuckles drift down through the hole in the window. I think they're coming from a northerly direction. As in, above our heads. "Is that Crow up on top of the house?"

"Yeah. We're getting into position just in case."

"Can you possibly turn that thing off for a minute?"

"Sorry, babe. Just a sec." He does the slightly furrowed brow thing well too. "Thank you, Fox. I'm aware there's no time for fornicating just now. But I do appreciate your feedback."

"Fornicating?"

Thom shakes his head. For all his "there's no friends in this business" rhetoric, the man clearly enjoys having people he trusts and likes at his back. Which is nice. "Sorry. Apparently we're all reverting to twelve-year-old humor to alleviate tension. What were you going to say?"

And I have an audience. A big fucking audience for my big fucking feelings. My stomach pretty much falls through the floor. "Oh. Um. Later is fine."

"Are you sure?"

"Yeah. It can wait." Because as much as I like his friends, there's no way I'm vowing my eternal love to him under these conditions. Especially with them all in such a comedic mood. Nope. Not going to happen. The coward in me rises, once again victorious. Ugh.

Suddenly, there's the *pop pop pop* of gunfire.

The window where Thom was standing shatters. He's already in motion. His arm swings out to tackle me, taking us both to the ground. Holy hell.

"Confirmed contact, I know," he responds to whoever is talking to him through the earpiece. "Tell me you've got eyes on them…multiple hostiles. Roger that."

He quiets and listens, his body half on top of mine and his arm around me tight. From overhead comes the sound of Crow returning fire. And from one of the kitchen windows facing the waterfront, Fox does the same. Bear is outside somewhere, no doubt doing his part. But it would sure as hell seem they've got us surrounded.

"Crawl toward the stairs on your elbows and knees, babe," says Thom, picking up a rifle. "Stay low. I want you in the basement with the bulletproof vest on now. Go."

Shards of glass cut into my arms through my long-sleeved T-shirt, but I do my best to ignore them and hustle my ass out of there. The thought of leaving Thom sucks. I 100 percent hate it. However, I follow orders like a good recruit/fiancée.

As I crawl along there's more blasts and bangs and other assorted noises from various weapons coming from both inside and outside the house. People are damn well shooting at us. Again. And it's way worse than the time in the hotel room. It deafening, like hail is pelting the house or we're caught up in a tornado or something. People are actually trying to wipe us off the face of the earth and I'm terrified they're going to succeed. My blood is pounding in my ears, adrenaline pouring through my body. But we are not going to die. Everything is going to be fine. At least, I really fucking hope so.

My hope lasts exactly until the wall next to me explodes.

I'm flung across the room screaming, dust and rocks raining down. At least when I land, I hit the back of a sofa first and it sort of cushions my fall. Though everything hurts like hell anyway. There's also a bell or something ringing in my ears. Holy shit. This is insane.

"Thom?" I slowly rise just a little. Just enough to look around the room. "Oh God, please be alive!"

A hand reaches out of the dust storm, urging me back down. Blood drips from the side of his face where shrapnel or something cut him, but otherwise he seems all right. "Babe, it's okay. Are you hurt?"

"I love you."

The man doesn't even blink. "I know. But are you hurt?"

"No, I don't think so." I cough up a lung or two as the air slowly clears. His dismissal of my mind-bogglingly big statement would be weird if we weren't fighting for our lives, so I let it slide. "Did they launch a rocket at us?"

"Rocket-propelled grenade, yes."

"Are you injured?"

"Just bruised like you. But there's a hole in the wall now, so I'd really appreciate if you got your gorgeous ass downstairs pronto." He pauses, watching said hole. Someone's obviously talking to him via the ear thingy again. "On it, Crow. Bear is on his way in."

Sure enough, the gunfire outside intensifies as Bear comes limping in through the kitchen door. Fox swiftly moves to position an upended table in front of the entrance, using the available rubble to lock it into place. Assuming I'm going to do as told, Thom takes cover beside the new hole in the wall, leaning out to fire at bad guys every so often.

And I could run and hide as instructed. Or I could actually be helpful. I try to dart to my feet, but it's more like a zombie-style stagger over to where Bear and Fox are positioned behind the central granite kitchen island. Blood is dribbling out of a wound in Bear's calf, another wetting the sleeve of his black T-shirt. They're barely visible in the low lighting.

"Hey, Betty," says Bear, busy reloading a pistol. "Shouldn't you be in the basement? Wolf is going to freak if he finds out you're still up here."

Out of nowhere, someone grabs a handful of my hair. My head swivels around hard, and Fox's face is just inches away, her eyes drilling into mine. First one, then the other, as if she could look straight into my skull or my soul, or something.

"She's clear for duty. We need all the help we can get." She turns back to the firefight. "First-aid kit, by the door."

"On it," I say, scrabbling over on all fours through the dust and the glass to retrieve it.

"She shouldn't be here," Bear grumbles as I crawl back over to him.

"I said she's clear," Fox snaps. "You keep your eyes on our six, and let her get that bleeding under control."

"I'm going to need you to stop moving," I order. The cut on his arm is deep, but not too long. More like a stab wound. "Do I just wrap this?"

"Yep. There'll be clotting gauze in there too. Let's get my arm under control, then we'll wrap the bullet wound in my calf." Bear's doing as he's told, his eyes fixed on the windows to our side and the door behind us, gun cradled in his hands.

I fossick through the box until I come up with the goods. There're some bacterial wipes too. I clean the wound on his arm as best I can but the blood is flowing fast. Too fast.

Bear glances down. Amazingly, he smiles, looking almost relieved. Maybe the fact that my face isn't currently being painted with his life's blood at least means the bullet that went through his leg didn't hit a vein or artery or whatever. Or maybe he just likes being horribly injured. I don't know. People are weird.

Either way, he rests the gun in his lap and takes some thick squares of dressing, holding them onto the front and back of his calf while I deal with his arm.

"Go for it," he says. "Nice and tight."

"Okay." I take a deep breath, trying to keep my cool. Honest to God, my heart's beating so hard I think my ribs are about to break. I place the gauze over the wound and start wrapping a bandage around it with the other hand. Given the situation, my lack of any actual medical skills is evident. The cut does, however, get bound.

"Good job. Now grab one of the bandage rolls out of there." Bear nods toward the first-aid kit. "Bullet went straight through so we're just going to wrap it up tight to slow down blood flow, same as you did with my arm. I'll keep the gauze in place as much as I can."

It's awkward. The floor beside him is slippery from blood, and bullets are flying over our heads. Crockery, glass, and chunks of plaster and dust from the wall are all around us. There's nothing I can do about how bad my hands are shaking, so I just ignore them as best I can. Try to tune out the loud blasts and sounds of war. There's no time to be terrified. No time for sweating and panting and shaking, though I'm doing all three anyway.

"How many are out there?" I ask.

"Enough."

Crow comes racing out of the library. It's the room with the old spiral staircase leading up to the widow's walk. Guess it got too dangerous up top. He's abandoned his sniper rifle already. Without hesitation, he takes up position across from Thom, drawing a pistol from a holster on his thigh.

It doesn't particularly surprise me when Helene appears at my side with a rifle and a bag in one hand, and my bulletproof vest in the other. There's no real point in either of us hiding down in the basement. Archie's coming at us with everything he's got. Everyone needs to be up here helping if we're to stand a chance of coming out of this alive. Even if it's just wrapping wounds and shooting in the bad guys' general direction.

"You forgot this." She drops the vest beside me.

"Thanks."

Carefully, Helene raises her head just enough to check on the view out the kitchen window. "There're dead bodies all over my lawn."

"There's also a hole in your living room wall," I say.

"Whatever will the neighbors think? Make that bandage tighter, Betty." She watches my hands closely, finally shaking her head once more at the chaos all around us. The woman is calm with a touch of irritated. Like someone interrupted her tea party or something. "Not that I'm surprised by all this. Archie always did have a habit of taking things too far. Not a subtle bone in his body. Also, he's afraid of us. We've proven rather difficult to kill up until now."

An explosion shakes the left side of the house where the bedrooms are. Thankfully, all the windows were boarded earlier. Another roar comes from the same direction a moment later. Guess the claymores are doing their job.

How a neighbor hasn't heard and called the local police, I have no idea. Perhaps the cops will scare off the attackers. A girl can only hope. But the most likely scenario is Archie and his gang killing innocent people before concentrating on attacking us once again.

"Sounds like a few someones tried to approach through one of your rose gardens." Bear smiles. Even in the low lighting, his face is pale from blood loss and pain. "Good work surrounding the house with thorny things, by the way. Always useful for slowing people down."

Helene just nods, checking over her rifle. The bag she brought up with her is full of weaponry. You can't say the woman didn't come prepared. The bang of various pistols is overtaken by the ongoing bark of the submachine gun Fox is wielding. It's loud as all hell. Makes it almost impossible to hear a damn thing apart from a long, suspended tone in my ears.

"Okay, all finished." I have to almost shout for Bear to hear, even though he's right beside me.

Bear pulls himself up into a crouch, immediately putting weight on the leg. Testing it, I guess. He grimaces, then nods. We're done here.

I wipe my bloody hands on my jeans before struggling into the vest. At least a small percentage of me is now bulletproof. Truth is, it's no easier being in a firefight for a second time than it was the first time. All of the noise and action and fear of death are as bad as they ever were. God, I hope we don't all die. A metallic taste fills my mouth, dust and gunpowder everywhere.

"Time to get back to work," says Bear. "Pick a position that covers you with as much wall as possible and keep your heads down whenever you're not shooting."

Then, with those words of wisdom, he's gone.

"Betty, follow me," yells Helene over the sounds of war, crawling toward the kitchen door with its shattered glass and upended kitchen table blocking half of the view and providing us with cover. As per Bear's instructions, there's solid wall on either side of the entrance for us to also hide behind and Fox is alone holding off this side of the house. The woman has chosen well. "You take the other side. We can cover for each other when we have to reload."

It's also a solid plan, which is more than I have to offer. I summon up the will to peek around the wall, taking in the back garden.

For a moment, it's hard to make out anything in the fading light, until a muzzle flashes like a tiny firefly in the dark, bullets whining around me. More adrenaline floods my system, the fight-or-flight mechanism setting off all my internal alarms. I want to huddle into a ball and hide. Hell, I want to run. But I refuse to give in to the fear.

Still, I'm back behind the bricks before any thought of shooting even crosses my mind. The gun's shaking in my hands. But we have to win this. Everything has to be all right. And while I know logically Thom can look after himself, not being able to see him scares the crap out of me. He has to be okay. I'm not up for dealing with anything else.

I focus on keeping my elbows steady. A trick an old florist once taught me on my first day of real paid work, when my hands were shaking from nerves. Different stakes back then, but it worked then, and it works now. A bit, at least. Enough for me to lean out and fire a volley of shots in the general direction of the muzzle flash. There's no time for guilt or any of that bullshit. If I kill someone, so be it; they came at me first.

Helene and I take turns shooting at anything moving out in the twilight. Not sure I hit any actual people; my aim isn't that great. But we have to be slowing them down, at least.

As my eyes adjust to the gloom, I can see she wasn't lying about all the bodies littering her lawn. With all of the rose bushes and ornate hedges, it's like a garden party gone wrong. Psychotically so. Archie apparently brought a small army with him, and bit by bit we're mowing them down. In the gray-and-violet sky, the first star twinkles. With something so everyday ordinary in sight, it's hard to keep a grip on how we all got into this mess.

We don't bother to reload. Instead, we grab fresh weapons out of her bag of tricks sitting between us.

Fox dives for the floor. "Fire in the—"

The whole building shakes once again and all three of us hit the ground. Everything becomes smoke-filled chaos. More rocket-propelled things must be coming at us, because there's a hole where the kitchen window used to be and the cupboards behind us are now on fire. It's not a big fire—yet, but still…we're now in a war zone.

Ever so slowly, Fox pulls herself up off the floor. Glass has slashed her cheek; dust coats her dark hair. "Fuck a duck."

"I'll put out the fire," I yell, after getting my coughing under control. Fox and Helene are the better shots, so me dealing with the flames makes sense.

Helene nods and gets back into position with a huge, shiny revolver. The sort of thing you'd see in a Western. Though, honestly, I think even John Wayne would be wary of something this size.

"I hate to make it personal, but these people are seriously starting to piss me off." Moving somewhat slower now, Fox grits her teeth and draws the pistol attached to her thigh. There's no stopping. No time to rest, let alone recuperate. "Scorpion is going to pay for this shit if she's still alive."

A small fire extinguisher hangs on the wall by the stove. Helene really did think of everything. Though, bulletproof glass would have been nice. Of all the things to skimp on. If we make it out of this in one piece, I'll have words with her about it for certain.

I try to keep my head down, but this fire isn't going to put itself out. So I reach up, angling the nozzle at the flames. Safe to say Helene's expensive cabinetry is screwed. Same goes for all the fancy plates and crystal that have been blown to smithereens.

And it's while I'm thinking these truly useless, stupid thoughts that two somethings hammer me in the back—making me gasp.

My whole rib cage clenches up. Next comes a red-hot line of fire slicing across my upper arm. The extinguisher falls from my suddenly numb hands and all I can do is try and breathe through the pain. It's excruciating.

"Get down!" shouts Fox.

Excellent advice. If about five seconds too late.

My ass hits the floor, my hand covering the bloody trail the bullet left across my arm. *Ohmanholyfuckingcrap*. I squeeze my eyes shut for a second, taking a moment. At least the red stuff isn't gushing. It just hurts like hell. Also, I think a rib might be broken, care of the bullets hitting the back of my vest, because every breath is pure agony.

In movies, when people get shot, they just tough it out. What utter and complete bullshit. My body is shaking and tears are streaming down my face. Still, at least I got the fire extinguished. The cabinet is just a smoking mess of foam and carnage. Too bad I'm crying and ruining my badass status.

"I've had about enough of this nonsense," snarls Helene, setting down the revolver and pulling out her cell. Next, she shoves the first-aid box in my general direction, scowling heavily. Like I got shot on purpose or something.

The noise of various weapons going off seems to have calmed some. Not a lot, but a little. Instead of a constant barrage, it's more of an intermittent rain of violence. Hopefully the bad guys are running out of people to throw at us. That would be nice.

Meanwhile, the pain is so bad, I kind of want to yell for Thom. But I grab the first-aid kit and find those antiseptic wipes Bear used on his wound. The best I can do is dab at the injury with my teeth gritted.

"Cease fire! Cease fire!" Once the command is acknowledged, Helene holds her cell up to her ear, taking a deep breath. "Archie…let's talk."

"This is a mistake," mutters Thom, soon after.

Helene, of course, takes no notice.

"Using yourself as bait is unwise."

"I heard you the first time, Wolf. The decision's made. Do stop harping on about it."

"Yes, ma'am."

"I've lived a good life, giving most of it to this organization. If I have to make the final sacrifice to save it and take this abhorrent bastard out in the process, then I'll count it a victory." She sighs heavily. "Besides, I don't see any of us getting out of here any other way. We have no idea how many people he's brought with him or how well they're equipped. What we *do* know is that we're going to run out of ammunition, not to mention people to fire the weapons, in the near future. At least this way, there's a chance."

No one disagrees. It's more than a little scary.

"I always rather wondered what it would be like to be on the front lines, actually tackling these sort of situations head-on." Her smile is grim. "Think I've handled myself rather well, given everything."

"Yes, ma'am, you have." He passes her something, and she slips it into her right hand. It's too small for me to see, but he doesn't look happy about any of this. Not one bit.

We don't have an actual white flag to wave around, but at least temporary truce talks are about to happen. The kitchen doorway has been cleared, open for one and all. Or for Archie and some of his people. And they walk in like they own the place. The head douche canoe is wearing a striped three-piece suit. To a gunfight. Jesus fucking Christ. He has glossy black hair and a thin, pallid face. If you didn't know better, you'd think he was a banker or stockbroker.

Not so much the people accompanying him, however. Most

of them are big, buff, dressed in black with tactical vests on, and weird goggle-type things sitting on top of their heads. Night vision or heat sensing or something like that. A variety of submachine guns and pistols are in their hands. Just like us, they came more than prepared. But no one's pointing their weapons at anyone just yet. Everyone's pretending to play nice.

I'm sitting on my butt beside the destroyed kitchen cabinets, but almost everyone else is strategically spread out around Helene. She stands in the large opening to the living room at the back of the open combined kitchen/dining area, putting some space between her and our visitors. And the dining area to the right when you first walk in the door is mostly cleared, tables and chairs pushed aside. Only Fox is with me in the actual kitchen area to the left of the doorway. Everybody is ready to jump into action at any time, no doubt. You could honest-to-God choke on the tension in the air. And the damn smoke still drifting around.

"Scorpion." Thom's voice is low and furious, his gaze set on one of the women. I've never seen him so pissed off. "Good to see you."

How he managed to recognize her among the rest of them, and beneath all the badass black commando gear, I'll never know. But she pulls back her goggles to meet his eyes.

"Wolf." The blonde's grin is all teeth, the way she looks at him purely predatory. Even with the manic expression, she's pretty. "Hey. You know it's not too late. Sure you don't want to change sides? There's better money to be made here. Not to mention, your longevity of life would far exceed current expectations."

"Hmm. I'm good." Thom's gun is in hand, but like the rest of our team, pointing at the floor for now. "Thanks."

Scorpion pretends to pout. "Sorry to hear that. Spider and

Hawk felt the same way, unfortunately for them. Look how *that* worked out. So sad."

Thom says nothing.

Scorpion's gaze wanders over the rest of those assembled, finishing finally with me, off to the side. I'm under strict orders to look harmless and civilian, but I refuse to back down from this woman's stupid staring competition. Her eyes harden perceptibly. "Ah, the fake fiancée. I was bummed to hear you survived the explosion that took out your home. But how interesting to find you *here.*"

I follow Thom's lead and say nothing. So far. This woman is kind of horrendous and could do with a good dressing down. Not to mention possible death and dismemberment.

A muscle jumps in Thom's jaw. He seriously wanted me to be hidden away downstairs. Again. But it's a bit too late to go into hiding. Besides, they still need all the hands they can get. Even if I'm now among the walking, or sitting, blood-covered wounded, I can still hold my pistol steady enough.

My injury was the other reason Thom let me stay. No one's actually sure how badly I'm hurt. Only that any sort of movement of my spine or ribs feels like a fiery hell descending upon my head. Not that I let it show in front of these people. Thom isn't the only one who can hide his feelings.

I keep one hand in my lap, the other holding my pistol against the ground. My generous thighs helpfully hide the weapon from view. Though you'd be an idiot to imagine anyone present isn't armed. I return Scorpion's hate-filled gaze with a solid blank stare. Who cares if she probably banged my boyfriend in the past? And about now, I'm pretty damn sure she did. But I'm the one wearing the oversized diamond ring, thank you very much. Suck it, bitch.

Probably, I should care more that she's currently aiming a gun at me. Show a little fear or something. But honestly, it's just been one of those overwhelming kinds of days. A woman can't be expected to do everything. Talk about emotional labor overload.

"You do realize you were just a sham. A cute way for Wolf to hide away in the suburbs without any risk of having his cover blown." Honest to God, this woman is a cunt. Her eyes all but twinkle with malice. I've never seen malice twinkle before, but here you have it in the flesh. Wonder if she practices in front of a mirror. "That must have hurt, finding out he'd betrayed you and lied to you. Did your little heart break when you found out he didn't actually give a shit about you? That it wasn't true love after all?"

I scrunch up my nose. "Dude. Seriously. None of this is any of your business. You're coming across as petty as fuck right now. On behalf of the sisterhood, I have to tell you, it's not a good look."

Any hint of twinkle or sparkle instantly disappears. We're so not going to be friends.

The smallest hint of a smile tugs at the corners of Thom's mouth.

Archie raises a nonchalant hand as if he's become bored with the exchange. Immediately, Scorpion's mouth clamps down on whatever nasty reply she was devising. She steps back into formation and places her gun back into its resting position. Just another good little soldier.

"You wanted to talk face-to-face, Helene. Here I am."

"So kind of you," she says. "Though it's not as if you'd have gotten inside without an invitation, is it? You blow a few holes in my walls; I blow up a few of your people. We're rather at a stalemate here, aren't we?"

Archie's gaze turns every bit as enraged as Scorpion's. But he doesn't deny her words. Helene's assessment of the situation must be right. Obviously, her gamble on exactly how many more people he has to throw at us is correct. Good to know.

"But none of that matters now," she says, and then clears her throat. "Something's worrying me, Archie. I hate to admit it in front of everyone, at a time like this, but I think I've made a terrible mistake."

"You think?" Archie laughs, looking around at all the destruction that used to be her house. At all her exhausted and injured protectors. He smirks, and the smugness radiating off him is just sickening. "You always did underestimate me."

"You?" She smiles. "Oh dear, no, not you. Charlie."

He frowns. "What are you talking about?"

She looks at him hard, as if trying to gauge if his surprise is genuine. "I was wondering how he got you to come here, to your certain death. But you don't even know. He's been pulling your strings without you even suspecting."

"You're babbling," Archie snaps, but his eyes look worried.

"Don't feel bad. He fooled me too. Got me to place my entire estate into his hands two days ago, telling me we'd use it to put such a massive bounty on your head that, even if you got to me, you'd never sleep another night of your short life in peace. And I fell for it."

"Bounties don't scare me." Archie's nostrils flare. "Besides, I really thought Charles would no longer be an obstacle. Must have a word with my man on that job."

Helene shakes her head. "You don't understand. There will be no more words and no more jobs. Charlie's already won, the cunning old fox. It never occurred to me that he was the only one who knew. He told me to come here. Off the grid and defensible, he said, and I never suspected."

"Suspected what?" Archie looks furious now. The tip of his nose has turned bright red.

She smiles up at him, but this time her smile is sad. Almost sympathetic. "About the dynamite."

"What?"

Slowly, she turns her right hand over, revealing a little black device nestled within her fist. It's whatever Thom passed her, and when they see it, Archie's whole little army stiffens. The two at the back exchange a glance.

I'm guessing Helene's holding some type of dead man's switch, so if she dies or releases her hand, everything goes up in smoke.

My insides clench in fear, and the only useless, stupid thought I have is that I wish Thom were next to me. So that if it all ends in a blazing inferno, at least I can be in his arms at the end. But he's way on the other side of the room. He'd never reach me in time.

Helene continues, talking calmly, as if she weren't holding everyone's lives in her fingertips. "The whole property's been laced with it ever since the 1990 renovation. All the way from the basement out past the driveway. And Charlie knew about it from the very start. He was the one who put me in touch with the team to rig it up."

"You're bluffing," Archie says, almost spitting out the words. "You wouldn't kill all your people."

"Oh, please. They were dead the moment they agreed to come here, and you know it." She lets her left hand fall to the floor beside her, the gun tumbling from her fingers. "Face it, Archie, we've been outplayed. Charlie got us to pool all our resources and people together in the one place he knew you could successfully attack, and I could successfully destroy. It's over for all of us. You thought you were the one taking over, but it was him all the time. He knew I'd be willing to die to preserve the organization if pushed to it. Ah, well. At least I get to be the one who kills you. That's some small consolation, I suppose."

"Boss?" says Scorpion. She's looking worried now.

"Quiet," Archie snaps at her. Half his team is shuffling their feet nervously. "Just let me think for a moment. Let me think!"

"The only thing that truly makes me sad is the Vermeer. It's hanging in the master bedroom." Helene looks up at Archie hopefully, and then looks at me. "We've got a civilian here. None of us are getting out alive. But we could send her down the road with it. She could probably get far enough away in time. After all, there's only thirty-four of his paintings in the world."

"Wait, what?" I blurt, shocked by the sudden turn of events. "No! I'm not going anywhere."

To be honest, with my injuries, I'd be surprised if I could even make it out of the house, much less all the way up the driveway. But no way am I leaving Thom. Whatever is coming, we'll face it side by side. Or at least vaguely in the same room.

"Ah, well." Helene nods and looks down at her right fist, knuckles white, grip tight around the detonator. "It was just a thought."

"Wait, you stupid bitch—" Archie reaches out a hand toward her.

"Fuck this! I didn't sign up for a suicide mission." That voice comes from behind Archie, from one of his team stationed nearest the exploded wall. The guy turns and runs.

"What are you doing?" Archie turns in alarm. "Stand your ground!"

Four of Archie's remaining team members turn their heads, toward the mercenary hightailing it out of here, the poor sap obviously hoping to get clear of the blast zone before Helene blows us all to kingdom come.

And without a word Thom, Bear, Crow, and Fox all raise their guns in unison. They start firing, in that tiny moment when all of the enemies are distracted. Several of the bad guys hit the ground and don't move again.

But not Scorpion. She never turned her head. And as the shooting starts, she pulls Archie down behind the kitchen island and returns fire.

Everything is happening too quickly. Thom's gun is shredding the kitchen island. Everyone is firing their weapons, running for cover, and generally all hell has let loose.

I get even lower, lying on the ground. But not because of a new injury. It's what Thom told me to do. Only, while he's busy trying to flush out Scorpion and Archie, I'm perfectly positioned to wriggle my way around the other side of the island to do some good. If trying to kill someone can ever be called good.

Fox is engaged in hand-to-hand combat a few yards away, a huge guy slamming her head against the stovetop until she slides limp to the ground. Before this dude can shoot me or someone else, however, someone paints a bloody circle in the center of his forehead.

Thom ducks out from behind the remains of the wall between the kitchen and great room. Every time, he fires off some shots at Scorpion. Safe to say all of her attention is currently taken up by my man. Not far away, Helene has raised her pistol again and is firing back gleefully. But she's right out in the open, just sitting there, and it's only a moment before she's struck, the impact of the bullet spinning her tiny frame as she slumps to the floor.

Her eyes meet mine as blood flowers from her chest, and the dead man's switch tumbles from her hand.

Time freezes.

A couple of the bad guys throw themselves to the corners of the room, probably hoping to have a chance of surviving the building's collapse.

But Helene just winks at me.

Nothing happens.

A bluff. The whole thing was a fucking bluff. Charlie, the dynamite, handing over her estate, all of it. All to buy them that one-second advantage.

Thom, Bear, and Crow don't stop shooting. Two more of Archie's men drop. Then a couple of flash bang grenades go off and a stunned silence follows. I'm not even sure which side threw them. Dust fills the air, gray noise piercingly loud in my ears. Now is my chance.

I crawl forward on my elbows and knees. Whatever injury I sustained to my back is howling in bloody anguish. Although, the one on my arm isn't much better. Bullets continue to fly, though none in my direction. Everyone's mostly busy at the other end of the room, where the kitchen opens onto the living area—where Thom, Bear, and Crow are still giving them hell.

Pain levels going berserk, I get far enough around the island to see the douchebag in the three-piece suit. I pant out every breath, the edges of my vision growing dark. But I can still see clearly enough to get the job done. Hopefully.

Archie holds a pistol, his hands shaking. You can tell the moment he sees me. Because he lets out a startled shriek and tries to point the weapon at me. Only he's fumbling so badly he makes *me* look like an expert.

I squeeze the trigger, my first bullet slamming into his thigh. The man drops his gun, an expression of shock on his face.

Higher. I need to aim higher.

The second bullet hits his chest and he falls backward, leaving the way open for Scorpion to kill me.

Oh, fuck. She's realized that someone has snuck around her guard. The direction of her gun moves off Thom and settles straight on yours truly.

She's in the process of squeezing the trigger when Thom slides across the top of the island and tackles her. They roll around on the ground as Archie groans in pain—blood pouring out of him. Good.

Also, I think I'm about to pass out. My head is heavy, the darkness continuing to inch in around my field of vision. No. Hell no. I'm okay. Just need to hold it together a little longer. Thom needs me.

I wrench myself up to fully standing and try to aim my gun, but they're a blur of moving parts, fighting it out. Some mix of martial arts, boxing, and sheer necessity fueling their movements. It'd be impressive to watch if lives weren't at stake.

Scorpion suddenly has a knife in hand, slamming it into the meat of Thom's shoulder just as he strikes her windpipe with an open hand. He grunts and flinches, rearing back. And this gives her the chance, the second necessary, to bolt for the door, one hand on her throat.

Thom rips the knife out and hurls it at her retreating figure. Blood—Thom's blood—spirals through the air as the blade spins toward its target. There's a crunch as it glances off the doorframe as Scorpion slips through. Maybe there's a yelp from Scorpion, but she's still moving, disappearing fast into the shadows of the surrounding woods. A wise choice, given her boss is bleeding out in front of me and most of her compatriots are dead.

Her desertion isn't much of a surprise. She's already proven how loyal she isn't by joining with Archie.

For a moment, Thom and I just look at each other. With real live love. Stupid amounts of the stuff. While it's kind of annoying, Archie's moaning is easily enough ignored. Nothing can distract me from feeling all of these good things. To think I used to fall for Thom's bland and boring bullshit. He's nothing less than beautiful, and I love him. Not a single thing can take away from this. Not the debris, the few remaining shots being fired as the others ensure our enemies are indeed dead with a bullet to the head, or the general carnage surrounding us.

None of it matters. Just us.

Though apparently Thom doesn't feel the same, because he puts a bullet in Archie's brain. Then another for good measure. He does it without even looking. Just cavalierly dispatching the big bad to the great unknown. Fair enough.

Since Thom already knows I love him, I say the next thing to come into my head. "You're bleeding."

Thom's gaze narrows. "What'd you say?"

Given I'm wheezing more than actually speaking and everyone's got to be half deaf by now, this does not surprise me. "I um...you're...oh shit..."

Everything falls silent. And I fall too, my consciousness just hanging on long enough to register me planting face-first into the ground. So that's the end of that.

TEN

SO MANY BEEPING NOISES DESTROYING MY PEACEFUL SLEEP. Sheesh. Also, pretty much everything is white. Sheets, blanket, wall, ceiling.

Oh, no. My bad. When I turn my head, the monotony is actually broken up by some stupendous floral arrangements and bouquets. Peony roses, hydrangea, orchids, tulips, chrysanthemums, lilies...you name it. How overwhelming and lovely. Someone spent big-time on me. Like seriously. People can just be so amazingly wonderful sometimes. I mean, the world is really a delightfully lovely place when you stop and think about it. Just so extraordinarily great in general.

"Betty." Thom hovers over me, face pale. "Babe, I'm here."

"I know you are, silly. I can see you."

The man of my dream just blinks. "You're high as a kite right now, aren't you?"

So maybe I giggle. Who could blame me?

His smile is tired. "I'd ask them to dial back the morphine drip, but I'm afraid you've got some deep bruising to your spine and a couple of fractured ribs. But you're going to be fine. We're damn lucky the bullets that hit you in the back weren't armor piercing. They did enough damage as it was. They also cleaned up the deep graze from the bullet on your arm. That one's going to scar. I'm sorry."

Then it all hits me. The cottage and the crazy battle and

everything we went through. With my fuzzy brain, however, the pictures are distorted. Askew. I can't seem to see my way clear. "Thom. I think I killed someone. Again. Oh my God. I know we didn't have much choice, but still…"

"Shit," he mumbles, gently brushing my face. "Babe, don't cry. You only shot Archie a couple of times, remember? *He* was a terrible person. But I'm the one who killed him. Put two straight between his eyes. So it was me, not you. Okay? Do you think I'm a terrible person?"

"No. You're wonderful. The most wonderful man I've ever met."

"Maybe I should keep you drugged more often."

"I can't believe we made it out of there alive." I blow out a breath. Despite whatever happy drugs they gave me, even this small action takes a toll. "I don't think I should move just yet."

"Probably a good idea." His gaze is so warm and fuzzy. Prettiest blue eyes ever. Only then I remember something else. Thom frowns. For some reason, there's a vague long-suffering air to the man. "Why on earth are you crying now?"

"I just remembered. You got st-st-stabbed in the shoulder."

"Babe, they stitched that up hours ago. I'm fine." He's wiping my blubbering cheeks again, a little line between his brows. "Stop that. Come on, you need to keep calm. It's not good for you to get all freaked out over every little thing."

"Every little thing? We just survived a war!" I sniffle. Can't wipe my nose with the back of my hand because there's a freaking huge needle sticking out of it. Geez. Luckily, Thom recognizes my need and hands me a Kleenex. I proceed to blow my nose in a totally ladylike manner. "Thank you. How's everyone else?"

His expression stills. "Helene didn't make it."

"Oh no."

"Charles is here now. He's taken over command and is dealing with the feds and so on."

"Did they find Scorpion?"

"No. Not yet. But we will." He smooths my hair back from my face. "Betty, I've been thinking."

"Hmm?"

"I've decided after this mess is tidied up, I'm going to retire."

Color me stunned. Despite the fog in my head, his words slap a healthy though unwelcome dose of reality back into me. "Really? You're ready to give up all the excitement and running around with a gun and everything? Hang on…are you just doing this for me?"

"Of course I'm doing it for you. I'd hardly be doing it for anyone else."

"But what if you wind up all bored out of your brains and resenting me?"

"No." He shakes his head. "That's not going to happen. How could life with you possibly be boring? Besides, you were unconscious when I made the decision."

"Yet I'm still the reason you're making this decision, and it's such a *big-ass* decision."

"It's the right decision."

"Will they even let you retire? The organization?"

"After everything that happened, they're kind of in our debt right now."

"Oh." I close my eyes. Despite having only just woken, I'm tired again already. On the other hand, I like looking at him. So I open my eyes once more. "You're so pretty. But you're talking about life-altering stuff here. On the one hand, I love the idea of you not being in constant danger. On the other…ugh. I can't remember what I was about to say. Pretty sure I'm too high and wounded for such a serious discussion. I also don't want to say the wrong thing. Are you sure you shouldn't be lying down and resting too? How much blood did you lose?"

"I'm fine. Don't worry about me. And yes, that's true, it is a big-ass decision. Let's discuss it later." He kisses me lightly on the lips. "I love you. Do you believe me when I say it to you now or what?"

It hurts. But I can't help but smile. "Yes. I do."

"This is bullshit," says Jen, arms crossed, standing at the end of my bed on my second day in the hospital.

"I'm sorry."

My bestie just frowns some more. Can't really blame her. With the morphine dialed back, I'm not at my happiest either. Care of a big patch of spine that's bruised black and blue, ribs giving me hell, and all the rest, there's not much to smile about right now. Apart from being alive. And being gaga about Thom. And getting to see the people I love again. Those things still matter. It's just hard to remember that even when breathing makes me wince with pain.

"I watched those two weirdos cart you off in that ambulance," she says, voice tight with anger. "They had to push me out the door to stop me from going with you."

"I know. I'm so sorry I couldn't get word to you. Not even a message. They wouldn't have allowed it, and even if they had, it would only have put you in danger."

"So what can you say, exactly?" she asks, shoulders slumped.

"Nothing," I admit. "I'm supposed to say nothing at all. Despite this, I'm going to tell you that someone very high up in the government told me not to say anything or bad things would happen. Litigation. Jail time. I don't know what exactly. She used a very ominous tone. I'm not ashamed to say I was frightened."

And it's the truth. The woman Charles sent to debrief me kind of quietly terrified the crap out of me. With Scorpion still out there somewhere, there's always one of the guys or Thom hanging out with me. Since Thom was busy elsewhere and Fox had been on guard-the-fiancée-duty, I had to deal with the government lady on my own. In all honesty, I'd probably rather go through another gunfight than face her again. If she's taking Helene's place on the committee, I wish them all the best.

"So you can't say anything beyond telling me you're not allowed to say anything or doom will befall us all?"

"Got it in one. We never had this conversation and we will never refer back to it again. Do you understand me?" If it hadn't been for Thom searching the room for bugs and producing a thingy that blocked anyone else attempting to listen in, Jen and I wouldn't have even been able to discuss even this much. "The official story is, I was in a coma and accidentally admitted to the hospital under the wrong name, meaning no one could find me."

Jen snorts. "Like I didn't go to every damn hospital looking for your sorry ass. I would never have believed that nonsense."

"I know. That's why I'm telling you what I'm telling you. Which I'm not even supposed to be telling you."

"Which is still nothing."

"Sorry. But it's all I can give you. Please understand, I'm not joking when I say, these people…they're dangerous. We have to keep their secrets. There's no other choice."

"And Thom is one of them?"

"No." The more I think about his retirement, the more I like it. "Thom is safe. But like I said, we're never going to discuss this again. And you definitely cannot discuss it with him."

She plonks her ass on a chair, giving me tired eyes. It's going to take some serious amounts of pedicures and ice cream to make this up to her. "Are you going to tell me about that huge rock on your finger?"

"We're in love and getting married. For real this time."

Jen blinks once, twice, three times. "You were just playing when you dumped him?"

"No! Absolutely not. You know me better than that," I say, my arms now crossed too. Only it hurts my ribs and I don't want to be defensive around my best friend. This is just seriously fucking awkward. Misleading or outright lying to her just wouldn't work. Not only do I not want to do it, but what with having known each other for pretty much ever, the woman can read me like a book. No way would she believe their crap cover-up story. Getting Mom and Dad to swallow it had already required some acting on my part. "I was serious about breaking up with the man. Since then, however, we've had many and varied discussions. There was also some ass kicking delivered to him by my fine self, and now we've decided to give it another go."

"Curiouser and curiouser. What then, you love him now?"

"It kind of happened within a short period of time, but yes, a stupid amount. It's the truth."

"And he loves you?"

"He says he does, and I, for one, believe him."

"Okey-dokey," she says.

"You're letting it go that easy?"

She shrugs. "What the hell else can I say? This whole situation is beyond confusing. But on the plus side, you're alive, happy, not blown up, and mostly in one piece. As for your return to engaged status, so long as I still get to choose my own bridesmaid's dress, it's fine with me. I always liked the guy, anyway. A little on the quiet side, but you can't have everything."

"He's not actually as quiet and boring as we thought he was. We may have been just a tiny bit off on that count."

"But let me guess…" Jen raises a brow. "You can't tell me about it."

I give her a grim smile. "Got it in one."

Thom knocks gently on the door before slipping inside. "Time's up. We're about to have company."

"Who?"

His lips skew slightly. "Bear's bringing you more flowers, the suck-up."

"You know he only does it to annoy you."

My fiancé says nothing.

"What have you dragged her into?" asks Jen, voice hard again. "Don't bother telling me you can't tell me. I already heard the whole secret-government-whatever spiel. And don't worry, I'll keep my mouth shut."

"Dude," I say, ever so slightly panicking. "You said you wouldn't say anything to him."

"No, I didn't."

"Jen," I sigh.

But she's too busy giving my man the stink eye to hear me. Also, she apparently hasn't finished her speech yet, accompanied by much finger pointing. "Just know this, Thom. You better look after her or else. I don't have the required social skills to go find a new best friend. Nor do I have the time or energy. So she is not to get blown up or shot at or anything else ever again. Do we understand one another?"

Thom doesn't even blink. "Yes, ma'am."

"Just as well."

Friends…what can you do?

In the end, I don't get to pick out which of Thom's safe houses we move into. The decision is made for me due to the building's various safety features. Given that the cool, modern, concrete boxlike building is located in Venice Beach, however, I sure as hell do not complain.

"It's got a high fence, sensors, and cameras throughout the garden and interior of the house," says Thom, ushering me through from the garage into the connected open-plan kitchen/living space. "Exterior doors are made out of steel and the walls are good and thick. Should be able to withstand any number of blasts. Security system is the best available. I'll show you how to operate it later."

I shuffle along carefully since moving is still a bit of a delicate process. Ribs generally take around six weeks to heal. By then, the deep bruising on my back should be gone and the wound on my arm fully healed too. "Nice furniture. I love all of the pale wood and the exposed beams. The kitchen is like a chef's wet dream."

"Safety room is installed behind the pantry. Main weapons cache is stored there too."

"Whoever decorated the place did an amazing job," I gush. "Not that I don't want to add a few touches of my own, you know. A few cushions and throw rugs to add some splashes of color, maybe."

"Windows are all Lexan, so bulletproof."

"Oh my God, Thom, we have a fireplace and a deck! I see lots of good times ahead. Lots of socializing with Ethan. You'll enjoy that, won't you?"

A grunt.

"You said there were three bedrooms upstairs?"

"That's right. Gun safes are in each of them, along with panic buttons."

"Yeah? How about grenades?"

"Flash bangs are behind the pantry, but the others are in a

floor safe in the garage, along with some claymores and a stinger or two," he rattles off.

I give him *the look*.

"What?" He tips his chin just a little. "You want them all in the safe room?"

"Guess again."

"You don't want grenades at all?"

"What I want, my friend, is for you to chill out a little. You're retired, remember?"

"I remember. But I love you. You're the first real family I've ever had, and I take protecting you seriously. That's my job now." Arms slipping around my waist, he gets close enough to touch the tip of my nose with his own. "Without making you feel smothered or restricted, of course. Because that would be bad for various important reasons I can't recall right now, but which you've gone on about numerous times at great length."

"Hmm. You're not winning any points here."

"Yeah, but I can do that thing with my tongue. That always gets me points."

"Thom…"

"And when you do go back to work, wouldn't it be fun to have me tag along? I could be like your personal assistant."

The look sure is getting a workout today.

"Still a hard no on that, huh?"

"I love you too. I'm crazy about you. But I'd prefer we didn't *go* crazy, per se." I give him a gentle smile. "You're going to need to get a hobby outside of stalking me. This is going to be a huge lifestyle change for you, not dodging bullets all the time. As previously discussed, however, smothering me with your affection and attention would only lead to madness in various shapes and forms on both our parts."

"It might not," he says. "You can't say that for certain."

"How many tracking devices do I have on me right now? And be honest."

A wince. "One or two. Three at the very most. Okay, four. But I almost lost you and it's a dangerous world out there. Taking some precautions is just being sensible."

"I'll agree to a couple of devices. No more."

"Thank you. I appreciate that." He cocks his head. "Wait. Does that include me tracing your cell? Because that's just pretty standard monitoring procedure, right?"

I look to heaven. "Sweet baby Jesus."

"Is that a no?"

"Since I understand that it's not about trust or control issues, if it means you'll relax a little, then I'll deal with it," I say. Because I'm not completely ignorant these days when it comes to danger, but I don't want to live in bubble wrap either. It's a fine line, finding the balance. "To a degree. But don't push it, buddy. Any news about Scorpion?"

His tongue plays behind his cheek. A rare sign of nerves from my man of steel. "Crow lost her trail up in Canada. She's probably on the other side of the world by now, looking for work, regrouping, whatever."

"Probably," I say.

"We'll find her eventually. She can't hide forever."

"Are you sure you're okay with retiring? I mean, I want you safe. But I also want you happy and this life is all you've ever known."

"I'm sure."

I frown. "It just seemed such a spur-of-the-moment decision."

"Babe, listen to me." He plants a gentle kiss on my lips and smiles. "Never will my job threaten or injure you in any way, shape, or form. That cannot ever happen again. There was a moment in Helene's cottage where I thought you might have been seriously injured or dead. Nearly fucking killed me."

"I know. I do. The thought of you being in harm's way does my head in too."

"We both agree this is the right choice then."

I hesitate. I can't help it. "Guess so."

"I know so." Another soft kiss. "I choose you. No doubt in my mind about it."

"Okay," I say, trying to rid my mind of any and all anxiety. "So how about instead of planning a war, this time we plan a wedding?"

And there's something in his beautiful blue gaze. Something I can't quite read. Only it's there and gone in an instant, making me wonder if maybe I'm just being paranoid. Even more paranoid than he is, if such a thing is possible. His slow smile, however, makes me forget all about that. "Whatever you want, Elizabeth. A wedding it is."

"How's he doing?" I ask, reapplying my lipstick for the hundredth time. Not that it needs it. I'm just nervous. Ridiculously so. Or not so ridiculous, considering it's my wedding day, et cetera.

Let's do something small, I said. Let's keep it simple and low-key. Only it didn't work out that way. For starters, Thom wouldn't let me, Mom, or Dad pay for a dime of the occasion. We'd already told everyone he'd come into an inheritance and was living off investments from same. It seemed the most plausible excuse for him suddenly having money.

I'm still working, of course, and totally willing and able to contribute. Only Thom didn't agree. He wanted to spoil me. I have a sneaking suspicion he's still trying to make up for lying to me for over a year and then the whole me-getting-shot thing. Because anytime I tried to show even the mildest sort of restraint about today, he avidly encouraged or indeed pushed me on to greater excess. I'm ashamed to say it worked.

Basically the intimate, subdued occasion I envisioned became a backyard wedding fit for a Kardashian. I kid you not.

A fancy white tent stands suspended over the deck in case of bad weather, with a flotilla worth of flowers and candles suspended from the ceiling inside. A chef is on location, along with various kitchen, bartending, and wait staff, to see to all of our eating and drinking needs. Meanwhile, the string quartet is busy providing the entertainment.

A chocolate fountain also seemed like a good idea, because why not? Then there's the seven-layer cake with each layer a different flavor (there's no possible excuse for this besides me loving cake).

Honest to God, today's excess is not all my fault. This is the kind of crazy that happens when a wedding planner keeps shoving champagne and cake samples in my direction. Complete bridal mayhem. It's irresponsible and shouldn't be allowed. We've even got a goddamn rose petal cannon set to go off when we're declared husband and wife.

Pretty sure Thom just wanted some kind of explosion in the ceremony. And hey, whatever makes him happy.

"He's got his Terminator face on," reports Jen from the window.

"No expression at all?"

"Nope."

"Damn."

"It's kind of scary, actually. Like a psycho killer. I'm still not used to seeing him go blank like that." Jen smooths the black bias-cut silk frock she's wearing over her hips. Her choice, as agreed. It's a really nice dress. "Not that I'm calling your soon-to-be husband a psycho killer or anything."

"Kind of think you are."

"But not really."

"Let's agree to disagree." I shake my head. "He's just nervous."

"Of course he is. Everyone else seems to be kicking back and having a nice time," she continues. "Though the big blond hairy dude keeps thumping Thom on the back like he's encouraging him to hack up a hair ball or something. Is this typical soothing, manly behavior?"

"Not sure. But that is actually pretty typical behavior for Bear. He's probably just annoying the crap out of Thom for fun. It's how he expresses affection."

She sips from her glass of wine. "Love the name. Bear. Because he really does sort of look like one. Some parents are so mean yet so accurately descriptive."

"Yeah." I give her my best fake smile. "Aren't they?"

"He is a big dude. Decent-sized head. Maybe it was a hard birth."

"Ah, maybe."

"And who's the handsome, classy-looking dark-skinned guy standing next to them?"

"Hmm?" I move over to the window. "Oh, that's Cro… Chris. Yeah. Chris. He's an old friend of Thom's." If too many people are named after animals, Jen would definitely get suspicious. And while she knows a little bit, I'm not going to encourage her to get curious about anything else and attract the possible attention of the organization. That would be dangerous.

"The man is supermodel gorgeous."

"I know, right?"

"Oh, he brought a date."

"That's Fiona. Another friend from where Thom used to work." Mental note to tell Crow and Fox they've had a change of identity. Probably pretty normal for them.

Despite numerous lessons from Thom, my lying skills are obviously nowhere near his. Fortunately for all of us, Jen has accepted that any weirdness related to Thom and Co. should be ignored. Though today is the first time it's been "and Co." since the hospital. Guess the rest of the zoo have been kept busy working. Or they're just not the type of people to drop by for Friday night football or a Sunday BBQ. Which is sad. I think Thom misses them and the comraderie more than he thought he would. Not that he would ever admit to such a thing. Why, it would probably be considered a weakness among the hardcore operators. He has me, and I'm all he'll admit to requiring in life these days.

Thom has been…keeping busy. We now have an entire room dedicated to his whittling. What can I say, the man likes playing with knives. Everyone I know has been gifted at least one wooden squirrel or hummingbird in the last four months.

If I didn't know better, I'd say retirement is slowly driving him insane, and he's in complete denial about it. I'm not sure what to do about it just yet. Various articles said newly retired folk can take a year or two to find their stride without work to ground them.

Maybe he needs a new and different job. Something part time, perhaps. Or at least an interest outside of me, working out, sculpting wooden critters and, of course, the maintaining and cleaning of his stockpile of weapons and various safe houses. Just in case. Thom wouldn't be Thom without a couple dozen different emergency exfil plans, retired or not.

We still both go to a shooting range twice a week to practice. Even my draw has gotten faster. And when at work or anywhere outside of the house, I call or text him regularly to let him know I'm still alive so he doesn't worry.

We should be in a state of domestic bliss. But something feels off. I don't know. I worry. I love him and want him to be happy. Just not quite sure the quiet life is right for him, though. Or perhaps it's the old occasional bullshit anxiety rearing its ugly head, making me wonder if I'm enough.

Ugh. I know he loves me. Like I need that nonsense creeping up on me today of all days.

"More rosé?" asks Jen.

"Yeah. Actually, gimme the bottle."

"That's the spirit!" She laughs, handing the booze over. "Skip down the aisle, I say. Or no, rumba."

"I don't even know how to rumba. But you know, I just might." I slip it under my arm and pull out my cell, sending a quick text. "Be back in a minute or two."

"What? Where are you going?"

"Something important I have to do. Won't be long. Don't freak." I slip out the bedroom door and cross the hallway into the office or den or whatever it's called. The place where Thom stores his creations. I set the bottle of wine down among a table-top full of eagles and coyotes. His latest animal fascinations. So many beady little wooden eyes looking back at me. At least he didn't take up taxidermy or something equally gory and strange. That would have been full-on yikes.

My man slips into the room, closing the door behind him. And the look on his face, it's very gratifying. "Babe, you're be-yond beautiful. A walking dream. And that is a shit-hot dress worthy of a queen."

"Thank you." Nice to know the two hours' worth of hair and makeup were worth the effort. I swish the full skirt of my silk strapless gown. "It has pockets."

"Yeah. What's in them?"

"Wouldn't you like to know," I tease. "You look pretty damn handsome in that suit."

It's an understatement. The man is drool worthy. With the old Thom's precise, slicked-down hairdo, tepid manner, and slumped shoulders gone, he stands out as the strong, virile man he's been all along. I can't help but stare. Without a doubt, he makes my heart beat double time.

"What am I doing here, Betty?" he asks, stepping closer. "Are you all right? Is everything okay?"

"Lock the door, please."

He does as asked.

"So...my sources reported you looked somewhat tense standing down there among our guests."

"Your sources, huh? I'm fine." He sighs. "Actually, I'm more than fine, I'm great. About to marry the love of my life. There's nothing for you to worry about."

I just wait.

A groan. "Maybe I'm a little uptight about not being able to properly monitor all of the people coming and going, but it's okay. I'll live with it."

"Repeat after me. This is our wedding, not a high-threat zone."

"I know, I know." His hands slide over my bare shoulders. The pads of his fingers warm and just a little rough. "It's all good. Really."

"Tell the truth. You've got the zoo casing the place, don't you?"

He scoffs. "No."

"Yes, you do. You big fibber."

"They've been trained to monitor their surroundings. I didn't say a word, I swear."

"You didn't need to." My fingers trail lightly over the lapels of his suit jacket, his crisp white shirt. "I'm glad your friends are here for you today. And I know you think I don't take security seriously enough, but I do. I get it. I want us both to live a long, healthy life together. It's good that they're keeping an eye on things. Makes me feel safer. Now, however, you need to relax and enjoy. That's an order."

"Yes, ma'am."

My hands glide lower, over his belt buckle and onto the fly of his black slacks. Down the zip goes and in my fingers slip.

"Babe." He grins. "Do we have time for this?"

"It's important. We're making time for it. The pre-wedding blow job is a tradition. You've never heard of it?"

"Oh, now that you mention it, that does sound like an important institution that should be diligently honored," he says, cock hardening in my grip.

"Because, let's be realistic, our wedding night is going to consist of hours of you painstakingly removing bobby pins from my hair until we both collapse in exhaustion."

"There seems to be a lot of thought behind this tradition. I'm at your command."

"Are you now? Widen your stance a little, please."

He's all velvet skin and heat. And the scent of him and his cologne, it gets me so high.

Carefully, I arrange the skirt of my dress and get to my knees. One hand around the thick length of him, guiding him into my waiting lips. Much swearing from him. Some of it in foreign languages.

I tighten my lips around him, sliding them up and down his length, stopping to give him the amount of suction he loves. Meanwhile, my other hand plays inside his pants, toying with his balls. I suck and lick and take him deep, loving him with my mouth. Letting him know we're all good. The salty taste of his precum hits my tongue, and oh God, pleasuring him pleases me too. I'm already wet and ready to go. But this is about him.

However, when his dick is truly swollen and rigid, lined with veins, he stops me.

"You come with me," he breathes, hands on my arms, lifting me to my feet. "Be on top. That way we won't crush your dress too bad."

"What about your suit?"

"Fuck my suit." He slips out of his jacket, tossing it over the back of a chair. Then he lies down on the floor at my feet. A slight sheen of sweat covers his forehead. "C'mon."

My dress was not exactly designed for this, but what the hell. Straddling his body, I sink down on his hard cock. Lucky the skirt of my gown is floor length. No one need ever know about the carpet burn I'm about to get on my knees.

A small sigh slips out of me. "Damn, that feels good."

"Ride me," he commands.

"We have to be fast. All of those people downstairs…"

He laughs. "You're the one on top. What are you waiting for?"

I set my hands on his chest, my hips rising and falling, finding the right rhythm. Even grinding against him every so often. It's all so good. The way he stretches me just so. The feel of him heavy and hard inside of me. Everything about this is perfect. I love him so much it hurts. But if my complicated updo actually manages to come out of this intact, I'm going to owe the hairstylist extra. Because soon enough, I'm riding Thom for all I'm worth.

Like mine, his breath comes in harsh pants. "That's my girl."

"Yeah."

"Always feels so damn good."

Hands squeeze my thighs, beneath my dress, as he silently

urges me onward. Harder, faster, I bounce up and down on his cock. His hips rise and fall in sharp little movements, pushing his dick into me deeper. The warmth spreads and builds and finally burns in the sweetest way possible. My lungs working hard, my heart close to bursting. Until finally it hits. And it's one hell of an orgasm, racing through me, taking me over. My pussy squeezes him tight, greedy to keep him forever.

"Babe," he moans beneath me, coming hard too.

And I'm conscious just enough to stop me from face planting against his white button-down. Thank God. No one would believe he had a shirt full of makeup by accident. Jen must be suspicious as all hell already. Not that it's illegal to screw your betrothed before the ceremony. But we've definitely thrown the old don't-see-the-bride-before-the-ceremony thing right out the window. Oh well.

Thom's smile is dazzling and wide. "God, I love you."

"See," I say, taking a deep breath and trying to set myself to rights. "You're all relaxed and happy now, aren't you?"

"Sure am."

"This is what I keep telling you. I do know best. When are you going to believe it?"

"I believe it now."

"Well, about time."

"Pretty sure you just fucked good sense into me."

"Nuh." I grin. "You already had good sense. You're a smart guy. You're marrying me, aren't you?"

"Kiss me," he demands, raising his head.

I do as asked. It's both a duty and pleasure. Something I intend to do for the rest of my natural life and beyond, if I can manage. "I better go fix my makeup. Then how about I see you downstairs?"

"You're on."

ELEVEN

THOUGHTS ON MARRIAGE CEREMONIES. HERE WE GO. SO, IT'S really weird to actually be walking into your own party without having welcomed anyone. Plus, there's the everyone staring and smiling at you part. Like you've just done something really wondrous such as save the world to deserve this level of attention. When all you've really done is spent a bomb on a dress and heels. Normally, throwing money to the wind in this way on stuff you'd probably never wear again would earn you some small amount of censure. But when you're a bride, it's all fine.

None of this matters, however, in the face of Thom's love-filled gaze and radiant smile. The blow job and cowgirl sure have loosened him up. He actually seems to be enjoying himself now. Can't help but feel that we're getting off to matrimony on the right foot.

Among those assembled, Crow smiles, Fox smirks, and Bear grins. My family and friends all seem pretty much generally delighted too. It's lovely. But my gaze keeps returning to Thom, because he's my everything. He reaches out as I move to the end of the aisle, his big warm hand gently holding mine. This is it. We're really doing this.

"You okay?" whispers Thom, leaning closer.

I nod. "Yes."

"No second thoughts?"

"Hell no."

We both turn to face the lady celebrant, who stands tall and calm in her nice neat suit. She opens her mouth to speak—and that's when it happens.

The horrible yet familiar bang of a gun going off.

People scream, the crowd scattering or falling to their knees.

A waitress stands on the other side of the deck, behind the wedding guests and back near the house. In her hands is a pistol, pointed straight at me. From this distance, all I can see is that she's a brunette with a puffy face, but something about her feels all too familiar.

"Scorpion," shouts Bear, reaching beneath his coat.

Her gun swings toward him, and he hits the ground ahead of her volley of shots. There's no time to check if he's okay. There's no time for anything. And it's so loud. The moment seems so fast yet so slow. I'd forgotten what this is like. But there's a fucking good reason my dress has pockets. A reason beyond lipstick and Kleenex and all the other necessities.

I meant it when I told Thom I was serious about security. Both his and mine.

Scorpion turns back to me, hurriedly firing off another shot. And I swear the bullet is so close, I can feel it fly past. Close, but not close enough.

Now someone else is firing at Scorpion, forcing her to take cover behind the nearby bar. My ears are ringing from all the noise, people fighting to get back inside the house. To escape the violence and confusion.

So much for our beautiful wedding.

With everyone clearing out or keeping low, my line of sight is clear. I draw my gun and aim, hands steady. Another thing practice has improved. The small pistol is one I've taken to the shooting range often. My grip is good.

Meanwhile, Scorpion is so busy worrying about Crow and Fox, she doesn't see me. Doesn't think I'm a danger to her. Not yet. And the next time she appears above the top of the bar to return fire, I shoot.

Red splatters onto the sliding glass door behind her and her body tumbles back. Fox just turns to me and nods. Crow carefully approaches Scorpion's position, bending down to check the body. But she's dead. You'd have to be pretty damn lucky to take a hit to the head and live.

"Okay. Wow. That was unexpected." I relax my shoulders and lower the gun. "Thom?"

His body is sprawled on the deck at my feet.

My heart stops. I swear it. Except then he blinks.

Oh, thank God, still alive. "Thom!" I gasp.

"Call an ambulance!" someone yells.

On my knees beside him, I push back his coat. There's so much blood soaking into the fine cotton of his shirt, but it's not in the region of his heart or lungs. At least, it seems a bit lower and to the side. I tug up his shirt, trying to get a clear look at the wound.

The bullet hit him in the back on an angle and came out just below his ribs. I use my big stupid flouncy skirt to apply pressure to the entry and exit wounds, to try to slow the bleeding. All I can see and smell is his blood, spreading out through the white cotton frighteningly fast. This is horrible.

Thom's face is pale, his gaze pissed. "Babe. Hey. You okay?"

"Yes, and so are you."

"Really? 'Cause it feels a shitload like I just got shot."

"How can you make jokes?" My throat tightens, but I am not going to cry.

"I'm still alive. Why not make jokes?"

"Scorpion's dead." Fox stands nearby, gun in hand. "Seems she was working alone."

"No civvies were hit, but Betty, there's blood all over your gown," says Crow. "Are you sure you weren't clipped?"

I shake my head. "It's Thom's, not mine. Where's the ambulance?"

"On its way," reports Bear. "Sorry she got past us."

"Not your fault. I told you I didn't want to intimidate our wedding guests with full surveillance and security." Thom winces in pain. "Well, this sucks."

"Surprisingly good shooting, Betty," says Fox. At least none of the zoo seem to be overly impressed or alarmed by Thom's wound. There's a positive. "I thought she had you there for a minute. Another second and you might have been bleeding dramatically all over the floor alongside your fiancé. What a wedding that would be."

"She had you in her sights too?" Thom asks me through gritted teeth. "I thought it was just me she was after."

"It doesn't matter. She didn't hit me," I say. "It's over."

Thom does not look appeased.

"Guess she didn't like either of you very much to take on a suicide mission like this." Fox keeps perusing the crowd, gun at the ready. "She had to know we'd all be here."

"Yeah, but she also knew she was dead anyway. It was only a matter of time before she'd slip up and we'd get payback for Helene. She probably felt she had nothing to lose," says Bear. "Fox, you got this under control?"

"Sure."

"Okay. I'm going to go check the perimeter. Keep the pressure on him, Betty, and try not to worry. I know it looks bad, but he'll be fine." Bear strides away without waiting for a reply.

For a moment, no one talks. Thom just lies there bleeding, brows drawn tight. While I try to calm my breath and recover from what feels dangerously like a near heart attack.

"This is the problem with going civilian," says Fox. "Expecting a normal life can be just as hazardous to your health. Thinking all your old enemies have forgotten you."

"You're not helping," I say, voice tight.

"Fox is right. This should never have happened," says Thom. "If it hadn't been Scorpion it could've been any number of other skeletons from my closet. Me being here put a target on your back. I'm sorry, babe."

"Nothing to be sorry for. This isn't your fault."

"You just had to kill someone again. Because of me."

"Yeah, but she needed killing."

He smiles at that, or maybe he's just wincing in pain. "Can't argue with that."

I try to smile back, but it doesn't really work. My hands are shaking, but I do as told and keep up the pressure. The bleeding seems to have slowed. At least, I hope so. "Anyway, she's dead now so it's over. We can go on with our lives."

He's looking really pale now. Scarily so. Nothing from Thom. Then a whisper. "I love you."

"Where the fuck is the ambulance?" I yell.

Nearby, Crow is busy yelling things at our guests. Things like everything is all right, stay back please, and clear a path for the emergency medical personnel. Jen does likewise while giving me worried looks.

"Everything's going to be fine," I say again. But no one answers.

Hospital coffee is pretty much the worst. This is a fact. So is waiting for Thom to come out of surgery. I sit in the waiting room in my bloodstained wedding gown, watching the hours slip by on the wall clock. Jen and Crow fetched some food for us all a while back. But I'm not hungry. Mom and Dad sit on either side of me, trying to be supportive. Not that there's much you can say. Fox already took them aside, gave them the secret government business line. So far it's worked. They haven't asked a single question about who'd want to shoot up our wedding.

I rode in the ambulance with Thom, though once we got into the ER they whisked him away into an operating room. Nothing I said made any difference. I couldn't stay with him. Then we started waiting. None of the doctors or nurses will tell me a thing. At some stage, Bear and Fox disappeared. Who knows what they're doing? You can't really blame them. It's not like sitting here is accomplishing anything.

When the police arrived at the hospital to get a statement from me, Crow and a woman in a slick gray suit dealt with them. Someone similar is no doubt at the house, dealing with any inconvenient law enforcement types there. The organization is obviously used to dealing with difficult situations. Because the detectives here never even got the chance to ask me any questions. Jen took this as a matter of course. But Mom and Dad were a little weirded out. Generally, when someone opens fire at a wedding and shoots the groom, you'd assume there's going to be a thorough police investigation. That statements would be taken from everyone in attendance. Oh well. Thom can figure out what to tell them later. He's good at that stuff.

"I'm sure he'll be fine," says Mom, squeezing my hand.

I still have blood beneath my nails. Thom's blood. Even after washing my hands until the skin was wrinkled, it's still there. It's dried to that horrible dark reddish-brown color. Visible even beneath my soft pink French polish. So much for the happiest day of my life.

Don't get me wrong, I couldn't care less that we're not legally bound or that the party got interrupted. I don't even care that we never got to use the flower cannon or eat the cake. I just want to see him. To know that he's okay. Then I'll be able to breathe properly again.

"Try not to worry, honey," Dad joins in. "He's being given the best care possible. Are you sure you don't want anything to eat?"

"No. Thanks." They mean well. But five hours. Five fucking hours. Why would it take this long? Bear said he would be fine. He said so.

Finally, a doctor walks in wearing blue scrubs. "Elizabeth?"

"Yes?" I'm already on my feet and moving toward her. "Where is Thom? Can I see him?"

Only her face remains carefully blank, her gaze full of a gentle kind of sorrow. Professional through and through. She's done this many times before. "I'm so sorry."

"No."

"There were complications—"

And suddenly Crow's holding me up, his arms wrapped tight around me. He's the only thing keeping me off the ground, in fact. "Thom isn't dead. He can't be. We're getting married."

"I'm so sorry," the doctor repeats. Like it makes a difference.

Everything I love is dead.

"Open up," yells Jen from the other side of the bathroom door. "I know you're in there."

With a groan I get to my feet and flip the lock. "Is something wrong downstairs?"

"No. Your mom's got everything under control." She wanders on in with a bottle of scotch and two glasses in hand. This is why she's my best friend forever and ever. "But if you're going to hide at your own fiancé's wake then I'm not letting you do it on your own."

"I just couldn't handle it anymore. All those useless platitudes from people who didn't even know him. Not the real him."

She pours out two hefty shots, passing one to me with a sad smile. "Get this into you. You got through the service. Some days are better if you don't try to handle the whole twenty-four hours sober. Today definitely falls under that category, I think."

"Thanks." I try to smile and fail miserably." I can honestly say, the absence of him is the worst fucking thing I've ever felt."

"Oh, B."

I sit with my back against the tub, smoothing out the wrinkles in my fashionable black suit. My heels sit discarded on the other side of the room where I'd thrown them earlier. A shattered heart and sore feet were too fucking much to deal with in one day. I down a good half of the scotch, lighting my throat on fire. Not that it isn't great scotch, Thom had excellent taste in these things. It's just a lot of scotch at one time.

"Shit," I wheeze. A peaty smoky taste lingers in my mouth.

Jen joins me on the floor and we both drink more. This time, I take it easy. On an empty stomach, the alcohol's going to work fast. Ever since the hospital, not quite a week ago, I've been lost. Depressed as all hell and going through the motions, eating when Mom or Dad puts something in front of me, going to bed when they do. At night in bed alone I cry, my face buried in his pillow. But the rest of the time…I don't know. The thought of eating breakfast this morning was a big no. Couldn't do it.

Mostly these days I just stare at the walls. Nice, blank, and boring. Nothing there to remind me of Thom. Or at least, not as much as almost everything else in the house and the world at large.

"So tell me about him," says Jen. "The real him."

I lick my dry lips.

"I know there's stuff you can't say. But work around it." She takes another sip. "You know you've hardly talked about him at all. Not since it happened."

"He's gone. What's the point?"

"The point is to remember the good things. To hold onto the memories of your love, even if he had to leave you."

"He didn't leave me; he was stolen from me." Still not regretting killing Scorpion. I'd happily do it again a dozen times or more. But even this anger is muted, dulled. Sadness is an ocean and I'm drowning.

She nods.

I lean my head back against the edge of the bathtub. "He was loyal and strong and hard at times. Brutal even. But he could also be sweet and funny."

Jen's small sad smile is back.

"And he was brave. Brave and smart. I know he didn't tend to talk much, but honest to God, he was probably one of the smartest people I've ever met. Wouldn't have wanted to play chess against him. Though he wasn't perfect. He could be incredibly stupid about some things too. Usually things having to do with our relationship, which he was always messing up. But he always wound up fixing them too. The man just wouldn't quit." I sigh. "Until this."

Jen raises her glass to her lips. "He loved you very much, you know?"

"That I do know. And fifteen or so minutes more and we'd have been married. I'd officially be Mrs. Lange, the widow."

"I think you can call yourself a widow if you like. No one's going to argue with you."

I shrug one shoulder. "I don't really care. It's just one of those stray thoughts. Would have been nice to have some good memories of the ceremony as opposed to everything instantly going to hell. To have a document where he signed on the dotted line promising he was mine. That would have been nice."

"Have you given counseling any more thought?"

"Grief counseling or you-killed-someone counseling?"

Jen's eyes widen for a moment. "I'm thinking probably you could use both."

"Eventually, maybe. I'm not ready to talk about it to a stranger yet." Though there'll definitely be no mentioning of specifics when I do. News reported it as local man gunned down on his wedding day. An unmotivated attack, apparently. And now here we are on the day of his funeral.

"I tried so hard not to fall in love with him." I take another sip of liquor. "Knew it wasn't smart. But what can you do?"

Jen's gaze is somber. "I'm so sorry."

"I know. Me too." I raise my glass. "To Thom Lange. Love of my life and the best man I ever met."

"To Thom."

We both drink.

Whoever is at the door sure is determined. When constant ringing of the bell fails to get me off the sofa, they start banging on the door instead. Hammering, actually. Fortunately for me, my powers for ignoring things, people, and everything else, are mighty these days. Bear and Crow keep turning up, wanting to watch movies or just generally hang out. Something I was most definitely not in the mood for. And they were obviously only monitoring me and my security for the sake of their fallen comrade. What they didn't get, was how they were just another reminder of Thom's absence. Of my messy broken heart. The way they'd check all the doors and windows, and offer to clean my gun for me or take me to the shooting range. No thank you. Thom was gone. Surely his enemies had gotten the message and would leave me the hell alone.

The abuse to my front door continues on for several minutes. Much more of this and the neighbors might complain. Not that I care.

"It's steel, dumbass," I mutter. "You're not getting in."

At last, the noise ceases and all is quiet. Just how I like things. Except then the front door swings open and Fox is strolling on in like she owns the place.

I sit up straight. "How the hell did you get through that door?"

"Forked tension wrench."

"Huh."

"If you really wanted to try and keep me out you should have used the dead bolt."

"I'll remember that for next time."

"Well, now. Don't you look a bloody mess?" Her British accent really is perfect for this sort of put-down. "They told me you were bad, but this…have you even washed recently?"

"Go away."

"I can't, unfortunately," she says. "Bear and Crow are busy elsewhere and I was the only one available to check on your sorry self today."

"I don't need to be checked on."

"Whatever you say, my dear."

"I don't even like you."

"You're far from being a favorite of mine either, but here we are." She sniffs the air near me, nose wrinkling, before taking the seat opposite. "It's been a month, Betty. He's gone. You need to stop being pathetic, pull your shit together, and get on with life."

"Thanks for the feedback." Jen, my parents, and everyone else I know have been a bit more forgiving, giving me time to mourn. It figures that spies and killers like Fox and Bear would get over these things a bit quicker. But all I want is to be left the hell alone, thank you. Apparently, however, that is too much to ask amid my misery and grief.

"Crow thought I might start teaching you some self-defense moves," she says.

"Not interested, thanks. Not yet, at any rate."

"Do you even have a gun nearby?"

I wave a hand in the air. "There's bound to be one around here somewhere."

A pained sigh from the immaculate woman across the room. "Dedicating the rest of your life to breaking the world record for general stupidity combined with the highest used pizza box stack is a less than impressive idea."

"I know. That's why I'm working on building a pyramid of empty pickle jars too. Pickles rock. And if someone does break in and try to kill me, they'll make for a handy projectile."

"Don't you have a cleaner?"

"What part of me not answering the door failed to clue you in to the fact that I don't want people around me right now?"

An even heavier sigh. "Wolf is gone. You need to accept it and move on."

I jump off the sofa and start pacing back and forth. This is not a conversation I want to have sitting down. She's right about me reeking. A fact probably not helped by my week-old pajamas.

"I'm not ready to accept it. I just can't believe he's dead," I say. "It was all so sudden."

"Denial. That's the first stage of grief."

"But—"

"Betty, get a grip. His ashes are in the urn on the kitchen table. You saw the body. We all did."

I hate her for saying it. For reminding me. Bear didn't want to let me see him at all. He said it would be too traumatic. He was right about that. It's one thing to see a dead body when it's all made up nicely in an open casket, where the person looks so peaceful and perfect they might just be sleeping. But laid out in a morgue, Thom just looked cold and lifeless. I screamed and shook, and in the end Bear needed to carry me out, lifting me up like a husband carrying his newlywed across the threshold.

Ironic, really, given the way the day started.

"I told him it wasn't a high-threat situation." I could feel my voice rising in volume with each word. Back and forth I march, gaining even more momentum. It hurts to feel this much. Just like it hurts to be without him. "Maybe if I hadn't ignored his concerns, this wouldn't have happened."

Fox, however, simply inspects her nails, calm as can be. "Anger. Stage two. This is such a sad process to watch."

I stop cold, lips pressed tight together. "He left me a lot of money. More than I know what to do with. But I'd give every cent of it to get him back."

"Bargaining. Stage three," she says. "It's heartbreaking to see you this way. Truly. But at least we're progressing."

For fuck's sake. I'd attack her if I thought there was even the slimmest chance of getting a hit in. So instead I slump back onto the sofa, the fight gone clear out of me. "Guess he didn't love me after all if he could leave me this way."

"Depression. Stage four. Please hurry up and move on to acceptance. I don't have all day to deal with your mopey ass. Bear and Crow can tiptoe around your delicate little feelings all they want, but I have better things to do."

"Oh, go away, would you?" I groan. "I'll clean the house and take a shower, I promise. I'll even track down a gun or two. Just leave me alone."

"You promise?"

"That's what I said." I half-heartedly lob a throw cushion in her general direction.

Fox plucks it out of the air neatly. "Really, now. No need to get hostile."

"You broke into my house!"

She rises from her seat, takes a deep breath. "Yes, well, make sure I don't have to again. I'm a busy woman and girl talks aren't really my forte."

"Whatever. Get out."

"I'm gone. Remember your promise. And take a walk—get some sun." She heads toward the door. "Put on the alarm once I've left and let's never do this again."

"On that at least we agree."

Her reply is the slamming of the door.

Truth is, I don't know how to pick myself up from this. But I guess showering and getting some fresh air is as good a start as any. And if it stops Fox from breaking into my home, that's a positive. Then there's everyone else always popping in for a visit and giving me worried looks. At least I'll be able to say I did something and hopefully get them off my back for a while. I don't want to build a life without Thom. But no one's giving me much of a choice.

"Fine," I say to an audience of none. "I'll go for a walk."

It's your typical beautiful spring day in California. The sun shining in a blue sky, the birds singing their hearts out. It's been almost four months since the horrors of my wedding day, and just as I'd promised, I actually pulled my life together. I cleaned myself and the house. I got some sun. None of it had been easy, but staying busy helped. And at least Crow, Bear, and Fox have stopped watching me constantly—checking that I'm using the security system, making sure I'm being careful when I go out. All of that got old real fast.

Jen helps me carry the groceries in from the car. Lots of organic fruit and vegetables since I'm looking after myself these days. I turn off the house alarm, hit the button for the garage door to close, and head into the kitchen. That's when it happens.

Clad in all black and wearing a balaclava, the man dashes in beneath the slowly descending garage door with a gun in his hand.

Jen screeches in fright, dropping a basket of food. Apples and oranges roll across the floor. His gun is matte black and long, care of the silencer fitted to the end. He aims and fires.

It all happens so fast. Jen staggers backward into the kitchen. She tumbles to the floor, but not before I can see red blossoming across her chest.

"No!" I shout. "Jen!"

The garage door shuts and the man's on me in an instant, grabbing me by the arm. Not that I could do anything anyway. My handbag with my small pistol inside is still in the car and all of Thom's weaponry is gone. The guns, the flash grenades, both stockpiles from the safe room and the safe in the garage floor. A few months ago I'd tracked down Henry in his bunker in the forest, and said he was welcome to anything he could find in the house. The wily old survivalist promised me his immortal soul after he found the contents of two more weapons caches I hadn't even known about. It's not like I knew how to use or would have use for the bulk of the stuff. Though I did keep a few other pistols. Unfortunately, they're in gun safes upstairs, likewise beyond my grasp.

If only I had them now.

The guy's grip is strong as he ushers me into the house. He pulls me past Jen's body without a moment of pause. The front of her shirt is almost completely red.

My breathing is heavy and sobs come from my chest. "What do you want? Who are you? Why did you have to kill Jen?"

"Move it," he orders in a deep, rasping voice. At the kitchen table, he drags out a chair. "Sit down."

I do as told. "Please don't hurt me."

In no time at all, my hands are tied behind my back, linked to the wooden chair so I can hardly move. "There's some jewelry upstairs. Some money in my purse."

But the man just growls. "I don't want your damn jewelry or money."

"Then what? What?"

"Information. You're going to talk. Your late husband's friends are causing problems for me. You know who I'm talking about. I got to one of them, but she wouldn't break. Then I found out about you." In case the point needed any further elaboration, he slaps me across the face with the back of his gloved hand. "You're different. Very breakable."

I'll be honest with you, it hurts. My cheek damn well throbs.

"Start talking."

"Please, I don't know anything." I hear my voice shaking. This is all horribly reminiscent of Spider torturing me in the basement while Fox looked on.

"We'll see, won't we?"

"You're going to kill me, whatever I say."

"Not necessarily. You haven't seen my face and I'm using a voice distorter. So if you prove helpful, there's no reason we can't part amicably."

"I don't believe you."

"Think about it. You're far more use to me alive. Civilians are so hard to protect. The organization obviously cares about you, however, and that makes you an asset. My asset." He puts the glass down. "Now, we can do this the hard way or the easy way. Your choice. Are you ready for us to have a little chat?"

"All right." My voice answers, almost of its own accord. I don't want to die. "Okay."

"Then let's go back to the very beginning. When did you first meet Wolf?"

"Thom. That's his name. The name he used."

"Thom, then." He leans forward, hunching over into my space, his arms linking around my neck. "Go on."

"It was—"

Suddenly the bang of another gun comes from nearby. The man in black staggers back as he's hit once, twice, in the back. His weapon drops from his hand and he staggers back a step before hitting the floor, his breathing ragged.

Thom moves into the room with catlike grace, his lips set in an angry line.

All I can do is stare. It's him. Really him.

His hand clutches my shoulder. "Are you okay?"

And I'm still staring.

He surveys the room, first taking in the downed man, then stopping on my best friend. "Betty, why is Jen still breathing when she's taken two bullets to the heart?"

The man on the floor coughs and groans.

Thom strides toward him.

"Don't hurt him," I yell. "Don't shoot him in the head."

Thom looks back at me with a hard glare. Then he reaches down and yanks off the man's balaclava. "Henry."

"Hey, kid." Henry groans and winces. "Fuck. I'd forgotten how much I hate getting shot."

Jen's eyelids open, her head still lax against the kitchen cabinet. "Damn," she says, looking at Thom in disbelief. "She was right. You really did fake your own death. That's so messed up."

Thom hangs his head, hands on hips.

And at first I'm just smiling. So much smiling it hurts. Though so does the cheek Henry struck. Not that it matters. We had to make it look believable and apparently we did. Yay, team. Though directly underneath my happy, there's a huge chunk of pissed off and irate.

"You set this up?" He turns, giving me a dour look. "This whole thing, just to trick me?"

"Yes and it worked. You bastard."

"I…fuck." A muscle jumps in his perfect jawline. "What if I'd taken Henry out with a head shot, huh?"

"Why'd you think I was hunched over her like that, just as you came in? Giving you a nice clear shot at my back." Henry chuckles. "And I knew you wouldn't shoot with anything that could get past my bulletproof vest, not when a through-and-through might ricochet into the love of your life. If I was still alive after that, you'd probably want to question me. Find out who sent me and if anyone else was coming after Betty. Odds are, you'd at least hesitate before firing again so long as I didn't go for my piece. Just like I trained you. Face it, kid. We played you like a boss."

"That was a fast reaction time. You must have been close," I say, cocking my head at Thom, my voice cold. "Where were you exactly? No…wait…don't tell me. The silver sedan parked down the street. I've seen it in the local area a couple of times over the past few months. Never stays put for long though. Same with the white SUV and blue hatchback."

"You missed a few."

"Ah, but you didn't expect me to notice any of them. Did you?"

206

"No," says Thom, wryly. "I didn't."

"Untie me, please," I order. "This is getting uncomfortable. Henry's knots are far too realistic."

Thom pauses for a moment. I'm not sure if he was thinking of making a crazy dash for it while I'm still incapacitated. But eventually he gives a resigned sigh and starts tearing apart Henry's work. One thing I'll say for mad survivalists, they know their knots.

"Thank you. You know, I'd punch you if I thought you'd stand still for it." I flex my hands, encouraging the blood flow. "It's funny, really. Fox told me to get some sun, to get out and live my life. So I started going on walks around the neighborhood. And Bear and Crow were always lecturing me about being aware of my surroundings. Making sure I noticed changes or patterns in the local area and letting them know if I was worried about anything."

"Yet you kept it to yourself."

"Actually, I thought it was just them being overly cautious and watching me at first. The baseball caps and sunglasses and all the rest you wore threw me for a while. But then I started to wonder. Your shoulders aren't quite as broad as Bear's. Yet you seemed to have short hair, unlike Crow."

His lips form the expected unimpressed fine line. "I needed to see you, to be close to you. Even if down the street was the closest I could get. Thought I could stay away, that I'd be able to do it, but I couldn't."

Jen and Henry, meanwhile, stand nearby, hanging on every word. Guess we're quite the dramatic spectacle. And they played their roles admirably. Can't blame them for wanting to see things through to the end.

"Lucky for me that you didn't," I say, crossing my legs. "It got me thinking. Those last words you said to me back at the wedding, about blaming yourself for putting me in danger. They kept running through my mind. Then there was the way Bear held on to me when we saw your body. Something about that always felt odd. How he wouldn't let me touch you at all. A little later I find out through a bit of internet research that there are drugs that can slow the breathing and heart rate down so far they're almost undetectable."

Thom nodded. "It's risky, though. That's why we couldn't let you get too close. I had a pulse monitor on my ankle and an anesthetist in the next room. After Scorpion had tracked us down like that, tried to kill you…I couldn't risk anyone else coming after me. I had to protect you."

I ignore his excuses. Typical male. Of course he believes he did the right thing, but I know he's wrong. And right now, it's only my opinion that matters. So there.

"I didn't know you were alive for sure, however, until I had Henry go over the house looking for your weapons. I gave him strict instructions not to look like he saw any surveillance gear, especially if it looked recently installed. But to tell me everything he found."

"You found out about the cameras I installed?"

"It's you, Thom," I snap. "Of course there would be cameras. No respect whatsoever for a person's privacy."

"I just wanted to make sure you were doing okay."

"I almost didn't spot them either," Henry says. "But whoever did the install was too perfect. I just had to work out where exactly I'd want the fiber-optic cameras for best viewing and minimum chance of detection, and there they were. Down to the inch."

"Great. I'll have a word to Fox about her technique."

"Right then, time to be going." Henry eases into a sitting position, pulling off the thick black sweater to reveal the bulletproof vest beneath. "We're all square then, Betty?"

"Absolutely, Henry. You were brilliant."

"I want my weapons back," says Thom.

Henry just laughs. "You're not getting 'em back."

"You think he did all of this for free?" I ask, head cocked. Henry moans and groans, stretching out his doubtless bruised back. "I'm afraid I found your two extra weapons caches too."

"Just the two? Well, that's a relief."

"Wait, what?" Henry stopped short. "There was a third? Where?"

"See you, Henry."

Henry scowls and stomps off, offering me a brief wave before heading for the still-open front door.

"Thanks again, Henry."

"Guess that's my cue to leave too," says Jen, climbing to her feet. She grabs a tea towel off the counter to wipe off the fake blood. It's a hell of a mess. "Not to be judgey, but I think you two might need couples counseling or something. Normal people don't tend to pull this sort of shit, just F.Y.I."

"True. And I owe you a new T-shirt."

"It wasn't a favorite."

"Thank you," I say. "I mean that. You know, the drama summer camp when you were fourteen really paid off."

"Right?" She grins. "Should have gone into acting. I have a gift. You, on the other hand, sucked. *Why did you have to kill Jen?* Honestly, B. The worst."

"I didn't think I was that bad."

"The actual worst. Later." Jen wanders out of the house, still dabbing at the fake blood on her chest with a tea towel.

"Bye." The smile falls off my face as soon as she's gone.

Thom closes the door after her, flicking the lock and turning on the security system. When he wanders back my way, he's reverted to his blank-face special, giving nothing away. In silence, he starts picking up the spilled fruit from the floor.

Whatever. I caught him. I win. He's mine. After I kick his ass, of course.

"You tricked me," he says.

"You tricked me."

He shakes his head. "This was a dangerous stunt to pull, babe."

"Do you have any idea how angry I am at you right now?"

"What if something went wrong and someone actually got hurt?" He piles the fruit into a big bowl on the table. "And your cheek is red."

"He had my permission to do that."

Thom's jaw is set. "If he ever does something like that again we'll be having words."

"He's never going to need to do something like that again. You're totally missing the point," I say, somewhat exasperated. "I'm fine, Henry and Jen are fine, everyone's fine. And you're alive—what a surprise. Why don't we talk about that for a minute, huh? That and how fucking furious I am at you."

He sighs. "I did it for your own protection."

"You do *not* get to make major decisions that impact both of us on your own. That is not love and togetherness. It is just assholishness!"

He just looks at me.

"I'm serious, Thom. You broke my fucking heart."

"I know and I'm sorry. But Scorpion may not be the last person who ever comes after me."

"Then we'll deal with it together."

"You don't understand," he says. "I'm working again. Consulting only at this stage. Low threat level and lets me stay close to home. But it's still dangerous."

"Crossing the street is dangerous. Riding in a car is dangerous. I never needed you to retire. It was just another decision you made assuming you knew what I needed."

Still, he doesn't look convinced. Idiot. "How'd you get in contact with Henry? I've been keeping a pretty close eye on you. Didn't see that one coming."

"Those couple of girly weekends at Jen's. I left my cell there and borrowed her neighbor's car to go searching up north. Took me a while to remember the right trail to his place, actually. It's pretty well hidden."

"That is super sneaky."

"Thank you."

Then he just looks at me. And it's all there in his gaze. All of the love I want from this man. "This isn't a good idea, babe. For lots of reasons."

"Let me ask you one question, Thom. Just one," I say. "Do you love me?"

And there's no hesitation. "You know I do."

"There you go, then." I nod. "We're having a baby and we're staying together. I've already made my mind up. Besides, who the hell knows what I'd do next if you try to disappear again? You'd never get another good night's sleep from worrying about what shenanigans I might be up to."

"A baby?" he asks, face frozen.

"Yes."

For a long moment, he says nothing. "A baby. Wow."

"Turns out dealing with all the organization required for a wedding and having your fiancé supposedly up and die on you plays havoc with remembering to take the contraception pill."

"From when we had sex before the wedding?" He comes over and stands in front of me. "Holy shit."

"That's right. In approximately five months' time."

"You're pregnant."

"I'll probably be insanely pissed at you for at least half of that. But then I guess I'll let it go. If you're lucky."

"We're going to be parents."

"Though I'll warn you now, Thom. After this, I automatically win every fight ever. It doesn't even matter if I'm wrong. Is that understood?"

He reaches out and touches my belly, almost in wonder, though I'm barely showing.

"Are you all right? You're not going to puke or faint or something, are you?" I ask.

"No." He shakes his head. "Just need a minute."

"Okay."

At long last, he raises his gaze to meet mine. "I love you, Elizabeth."

"I know. I love you too. But if you ever pull this sort of shit again I will kill you myself."

"You will, huh?"

I shrug a shoulder. "Well…not kill you exactly, I suppose. But I'll at least shoot you. Somewhere none lethal, but quite painful just the same. Am I understood, Wolf? Are you reading me and all of my threats loud and clear?"

He smiles and it's perfect. "Roger that."

EPILOGUE

"**O**H."

"Oh, what?" I ask, stacking the last of the dirty glasses in the dishwasher. Dinner was tacos because everything is better with tacos. Not that life isn't awesome already.

Thom stands behind me with a baby in hand. A baby with a bare ass, actually.

"It fell off again?" I ask, incredulous.

Lines crease his forehead. Fatherhood and marriage have taught him how to express himself fully and often in lots of different ways. "I don't know what I'm doing wrong."

"A man with your skillset and you can't work a diaper? For real?"

"Thought I got it right this time. Not too tight, not too loose."

"Wow. Seriously. I mean, you can defuse a bomb, but your small child's pants situation is somehow beyond your capabilities. I am officially amazed."

"In my defense, nobody's managed to provide me with a circuit diagram for this one."

Six-month-old Henry takes his fist out of his mouth long enough to giggle and smile at me before peeing down the front of his father's shirt. I try not to laugh. I really do.

"Well, I guess that was inevitable," I say. "I'll go get some wipes and a towel."

"Here. You take him," my husband offers, holding our son toward me.

"No way. What if he does a number two next?" I maneuver around the dynamic and now wet and smelly duo. "He's all yours, buddy."

"Great."

Thom returning to official live status meant some changes. It's not easy to bring someone back from the dead without it becoming a big deal. Only Jen and my folks (who are still being told the whole secret-government-business-please-don't-ask-any-questions line) know about his return, for starters. I told everyone else that I was moving to get a fresh start and eventually that I'd met someone new. We relocated to a roomy modern log-cabin-style home on a couple of acres on the outskirts of Boulder, Colorado. My official favorite of all the safe houses. In the basement is a secure workstation, safe room, and weapons locker... just in case.

We also got quietly married and changed our last name to Ferguson. Thom works mostly online from home, handling the everyday management of the zoo and doing all sorts of interesting research, with a few short trips now and then. I, meanwhile, work part-time at a local florist shop. But while I can come home and tell him all about my day, his must remain top secret. And I've accepted this. In turn, he's accepted that I require a certain level of privacy and has eased up on the surveillance. I even occasionally let him win a fight when I'm feeling particularly gracious. Guess all relationships require a certain amount of compromise.

Occasionally, I fly out to see my old friends in L.A. But more often than not, Jen comes here to visit her godson. Fox, Bear, and Crow also have a habit of dropping in now and then and also claim godparent status. The original Henry prefers to Skype once a month or so from his bunker. He was delighted at our choice of name and gifted our son a rocket launcher, which my child shall never receive if I have any say about it.

I like to think our baby boy will grow up to be an accountant or a lawyer or a dermatologist. Something safe and far from explosives. But we'll see. People can only be themselves. And after everything we've been through, I know I'm my best self with Thom and he's his best self with me. Life is good.

The end.

PURCHASE KYLIE SCOTT'S OTHER BOOKS

Repeat
It Seemed Like a Good Idea at the Time
Trust

THE DIVE BAR SERIES
Dirty
Twist
Chaser

THE STAGE DIVE SERIES
Lick
Play
Lead
Deep
Strong: A Stage Dive Novella

THE FLESH SERIES
Flesh
Skin
Flesh Series Novellas

Heart's a Mess

Colonist's Wife

Find Kylie at:

www.kyliescott.com

Facebook: www.facebook.com/kyliescottwriter

Twitter: twitter.com/KylieScottbooks

Instagram: www.instagram.com/authorkyliescott

Pinterest: www.pinterest.com/kyliescottbooks

BookBub: www.bookbub.com/authors/kylie-scott

To learn about exclusive content, my upcoming releases and giveaways, join my newsletter:

kyliescott.com/subscribe

Keep reading for a free sample of

REPEAT

CHAPTER ONE

THE SHOP SITS ON A BUSY STREET IN THE COOL DOWNTOWN neighborhood of Portland, Maine. *Larsen and Sons Tattoo Parlor* is written on the window in elegant script. Inside, music plays, two guys lounge on a green velvet chaise flicking through books. It's all very clean and neat and awesome looking. And there's a sound like an electric drill in the air.

The girl behind the counter stops, mouth gaping when she sees me. She's pretty and petite with a shaved head.

"Hi," I say, attempting a smile. "Can I speak to—"

"Are you fucking kidding me," a deep voice booms.

I meet the eyes of a tall man covered in tattoos. Shortish, light brown hair, lean but muscular. He wears jeans and designer sneakers, a T-shirt advertising some band. For sure, he'd be handsome if he wasn't scowling at me. Actually, strike that. He's handsome period, irrespective of his glare. His angular jaw is covered in stubble and it frames perfect lips. Straight nose, high cheekbones. Unlike me, this man is a work of art.

"No, not happening," he says, striding over. His large hand wraps around my upper arm, grip firm though not cruel. "You don't get to come back."

"Don't touch me." My words are ignored as he marches me back toward the door. Panic bubbles up inside and I slap his chest hard. "Hey, buddy. Do. Not. Touch. Me."

At that, he blinks, a little startled. "Buddy?"

I don't know what he was expecting, but he lets go. It

takes me a full minute to get my breathing back under control. Dammit. Meanwhile, everyone is watching. The girl behind the counter and the two guys waiting on the chaise. The woman with brown skin and big beautiful hair holding a tattoo gun and the older woman she's working on. We have quite the audience assembled. The man screaming about being back in black over the sound system is the only noise.

"You need to leave," he says, voice quieter this time, though no less harsh.

"I have a few questions I need to ask you first."

"No."

"Did you do this?" I ask, pulling up the sleeve on my T-shirt to display my shoulder. It's a beautiful piece. A cluster of violets with olive-green stems and leaves. It's almost like a scientific drawing, but missing the root structure.

His gaze narrows. "Of course I did it."

"I was your client. Okay." That's now a definite. Good. Definites give my world structure and help things make sense. Unknowns just piss me off. "Did I not pay you or something?"

"'the hell are you talking about?"

"You're angry."

And it's obvious the moment he sees my brow. The hostility and confusion in his eyes changes to surprise.

I immediately smooth down my bangs, trying to hide. Stupid to get self-conscious, but I can't help it.

He gently brushes my hand aside, parting my hair to see. An intimate gesture that sets me on edge. As hands-on as tattooing must be, the way he's touching me and getting in my space is … more. I try to step back, but there's nowhere to go. Besides, he's not actually hurting me, just making me nervous. And as much as I abhor being crowded, some part of me doesn't mind him touching me.

Weird. Maybe I need sex or something. Maybe he's my type. I don't know.

Deep lines are embedded in his forehead as he studies me. This is exactly the reason I cut my hair in the first place. The scar starts an inch into my hairline, ending below my right eyebrow. It's wide and jagged, dark pink.

That's enough. I put a hand to his chest, pushing him back. Happily, he goes. A small step, at least.

"So you *know* me?" I ask, trying to clarify things. "Like, as more than a customer."

The man just stares. I don't know what his expression means. A mix of unhappy and perplexed, maybe? He really is quite handsome. A new song starts, this time it's a woman singing.

"Well?"

Finally, he speaks. "What the fuck happened to you?"

A week earlier …

"Are you ready?"

I stop kicking my feet and hop down off the hospital bed. "Yeah."

"Good. The car's waiting in the drop-off zone and we'll go straight home. Everything's organized," says my sister, a confident smile on her face. "There's nothing to worry about."

"I'm not worried," I lie.

"Did you want to see the photos of my house again?"

"No. It's fine."

My sister's name is Frances (not Fran or Frannie), and she's a police officer who lives in North Deering. She blames herself for what happened. It probably comes with the job.

At thirty, Frances is five years older than me. We have the same strawberry-blond hair and blue eyes, small breasts and child-birthing hips. Her words, not mine, and I told her it was a shitty descriptor. But given my current condition, there's something to be said for relying on others' descriptions.

Anyway, my sister and I look alike. I've seen this in various photos and in the mirror, so it's a definite.

"Hey, Clem." Nurse Mike sticks his head around the doorway. "Everything's sorted; you're good to go. Any last-minute questions or anything?"

I shake my head.

"Call Doctor Patel's office if you have any problems, okay?"

"Yes."

"Keep in touch, kid. Let me know how things go."

"Okay."

Mike disappears.

"Did you want to bring the flowers?" asks my sister.

I shake my head. This is it. Time to go. Frances just stands by the door, waiting.

My first memory is of waking up in this hospital, but really, I was born late at night on an inner-city street. A couple found me unconscious and bleeding on the sidewalk. No identification. Handbag and wallet missing. And the weapon, a blood-splattered empty bottle of scotch, lay abandoned nearby. Walter, half of the pair who found me, gets teary every time he describes that night. But Jack, his partner, did two tours in 'Nam and has seen far worse. They're the first ones who brought me flowers. Not that I got many. My friends are few.

Previous me had, apparently, gone out to dinner alone. Her last meal consisted of cheese and spinach ravioli in a pumpkin sauce with a bottle of Peroni. (Detective Chen said it's a yeasty Italian beer that goes well with pasta. It sounds nice. I might try it sometime.) From there, security cameras have her withdrawing a hundred and fifty dollars before walking off into the night. There were no cameras on the quiet side street where she'd parked the car. No one around apart from the attacker.

That's how Clementine Johns died.

Out in the hallway, there's a mix of patients, visitors, and medical staff. Same as always for midmorning. I wipe my sweaty palms on the sides of my pants. It's nice to be wearing actual clothes. Black sandals, blue jeans, and a white T-shirt. Nothing too exciting; nothing that would make me stand out. I want to blend in, watch and learn. Because if we're the sum of our experiences, then I'm nothing and no one.

Frances watches me out of the corner of her eye, but doesn't say anything. Something she does a lot. I'd say her silence makes me paranoid, but I'm already paranoid.

"Sure you're all right?" she asks while we wait for the elevator.

"Yes."

The elevator arrives and we step inside. When it starts to move, my nervous stomach swoops and drops. Through the crowded lobby we go, then out into the sunshine. Blue summer sky, a couple of green trees, and lots of gray concrete. Nearby traffic, people, and lots of movement. A light breeze ruffles my hair.

The lights on a nearby white sedan flash once and Frances opens the trunk for me to deposit my small suitcase. Anxiety turns into excitement, and I can't keep the smile off my face. I've seen them on TV, but I've never actually been in a car since that night.

Now ...

"Amnesia," he mutters for about the hundredth time. Usually, 'fuck', 'shit', or some blasphemy follows that statement. This time, however, there's nothing. Maybe he's finally getting used to the idea.

I sit on the opposite side of the booth, inspecting the cocktail menu. It's as gross and sticky as the table.

"Can I get you guys something else?" asks the waiter with a practiced smile.

"I'll have a piña colada."

"You hate coconut," Ed Larsen informs me, slumped back in his seat.

"Oh."

"Try a margarita."

"What he said," I tell the waiter, who presumably thinks we have some kinky dom-sub thing going on.

Ed orders another lite beer, watching me the entire time. I don't know if his blatant examination is better or worse than my sister's furtive looks. He'd suggested going back to his place to talk. I declined. I don't know the guy, and it didn't feel safe. So instead we came here. The bar is dark and mostly empty, given it's the middle of the afternoon, but at least it's public.

"How old are you?" I ask.

In response, he pulls his wallet out of his back pocket and passes me his driver's license.

"Thank you." Information is good. More definites. "You're seven years older than me."

"Yeah."

"How serious were we? Did we stay together for long?"

He licks his lips, turns away. "Don't you have someone else you can ask about all this? Your sister?"

I just look at him.

He frowns, but then sighs. "We saw each other for about half a year before moving in together. That lasted eight months."

"Pretty serious."

"If you say so." His face isn't happy. But I need to know. "Did I cheat on you?"

Now the frown comes with a glare.

Despite his don't-fuck-with-me vibes, it's hard not to smile. The man is blessed in the DNA department. He's so pretty. Masculine pretty. I'm not used to being attracted to people, and he's giving me a heart-beating-harder, tingles-in-the-pants kind of sensation, which is a lot new and a little overwhelming. Makes me want to giggle and flip my hair at him like some vapid idiot.

But I don't. "It's just that I'm getting some distinct vibes that somehow I'm the bad guy in all this."

"No, you didn't cheat on me," he growls. "And I didn't cheat on you either, no matter what you might have thought."

My brows jump. "Huh. So that's why we broke up?"

"This is fucked. Actually, it was fucked the first time." He turns away and finishes the last of his beer. "Jesus."

I just keep quiet, waiting.

"You have no memories, no feelings about me whatsoever?"

"No, nothing."

A muscle jumps in his jaw, his hands sitting fisted on the table.

"It's called traumatic retrograde amnesia," I say, trying to explain. "What they call my 'episodic memory' is gone—all my memories of events and people and history. Personal facts. But I can still make a cup of coffee, read a book, or drive a car. Stuff like that. Things that were done repetitively, you know? Not that I'm allowed to drive at the moment. My car's sitting outside my sister's house gathering dust. They said to give it some time before I got behind the wheel again, make sure I'm okay. Also, apparently the part of my brain in charge of inhibitions and social restrictors, et cetera, is a bit messed up, so I don't always react right, or at least not necessarily how you'd expect me to behave based on previous me."

"Previous you?"

I shrug. "It's as good a label for her as any."

"She's you. You're her."

"Maybe. But she's still a complete stranger to me."

"Christ," he mutters.

This is awkward. "I'm upsetting you. I'm sorry. But there are things I need to know, and I'm hoping you can help me out with some of them."

Our drinks arrive, the glass of the margarita lined with salt and smelling of lemon. I take a sip and smile. "I like it."

He reaches grimly for his beer, the ink on his forearm shifting with the muscle beneath. His tattoos cover a variety of topics. A bottle marked "poison" with skull and crossbones set amongst roses. An anatomical heart. A tattoo gun (very meta). A lighthouse with waves crashing below. I wonder if it's the Portland Headlight, the famous one at Cape Elizabeth. There was something on TV about it the other day. His tattoos are hypnotic in a way. As if, combined, they tell a story, if only you could understand.

Ed pushes his beer aside. "So, because you don't remember, I should just forget all the shit you pulled and help you? Because that was all the 'previous you' and not the girl sitting in front of me?"

"That's your decision to make, of course."

"Thanks, Clem." His voice is bitter, full of a kind of controlled rage. "That's real fucking big of you."

I flinch, unused to people swearing at me. Not that he hasn't been swearing in my general vicinity since the moment we met, but for some reason, this time it has an effect on me. Can't help but wonder how angry does he get, exactly? The man is taller than me, his shoulders broader than mine. And I've already had a small taste of the strength he holds in his hands.

"Shit." He sighs at my reaction. "Clem, don't … don't do that. I would never hurt you."

Unsure of what to say, I down more of my drink.

"You don't know me; I get it," he says, voice softer, gentler. "Look at me, Clementine."

When I do, his eyes are full of remorse and he's sad now. Not angry.

"I would never hurt you, I swear it. You're safe with me."

"Okay." Slowly, I nod. "It's a stupid name, don't you think?"

"Yours? I don't know. I always liked it."

I almost smile.

"You're staying with your sister?"

"Yes."

"How's that going?"

"It's all right."

The side of his mouth lifts briefly. "You and Frances were always fighting about something."

"Actually, that makes sense." I laugh. "Did she approve of you?"

"You'd have to ask her that."

"Oh, I have lots of questions for her."

This time, when he looks at me, it's more of a thoughtful kind of thing. Like he's processing. I've given him a lot of information, and I know it takes a while to sort things out in your head. So I drink my margarita and watch the woman behind the bar, the two men sitting on stools, chatting. Even though their hygiene standards are lacking, I like the place. It's relaxed.

Maybe it's my kind of place.

"I don't seem to have many friends," I say, a question popping into my head. "Was I always like that, a bit of a loner?"

He shakes his head. "You had friends. But apparently you cut them all off when you left me."

"Why?"

"I don't know," he says, shoulders dropping slightly. "Maybe you wanted a fresh start. Maybe you just didn't want to talk about the breakup and shit. Maybe you just wanted to be left alone."

Huh.

"Give me your phone; I'll put my details in." He holds out a hand. "You would have deleted me from your contacts."

"Oh, I don't have one. My bag and everything was taken in the attack."

His brows rise. "You're walking around without a cell? Clem, that's not safe."

"Pretty sure having a phone didn't make much of a difference last time."

"Finish up your drink." He tips his chin at the glass. "I'll give you a lift back to Frances's place. We'll stop by a shop on the way and get you some things."

It's an interesting idea. And he seems like a nice man, one who used to care about me. But from what little he said about the breakup, it sounds as if it was a special level of hell. Despite his assurances, he might very well have cheated on me. Crushed my heart. Torn apart my life. Shit like that.

After all, what would a cheater say?

"You should have a can of mace on you too, given they haven't caught the bastard who did this to you. One of those keyring ones." He pulls some money out of his wallet, setting it on the table. Then he stops. "What?"

"Just thinking."

"Yeah?" He cocks his head, a lock of brown hair falling over one of his eyes. "What about?"

"Lots of things," I say. "You're being very helpful all of a sudden. It makes me suspicious. I mean, why would you even want to be friends with me, given our past?"

"I have no interest in being your friend."

"Oh?"

"Trust me, that's definitely not going to happen." He settles back, watching me with a faint smile. Holy crap, his smile … it's just a bit mean yet still wholly affecting.

I squirm in my seat. "I see."

"No, you don't," he says. "Clem, you fucked me up. You fucked *us* up. And I'm not going to forgive you for that whether you remember doing it or not. But nobody deserves to be assaulted and have their mind messed with. So I'll answer your questions, make sure you've got a cell and something to protect yourself with. Then you're on your own."

"You're only helping me today?"

"No, that's why I'm giving you my number. Like I said, you think of a question you need answered, you can text me and I'll answer it for you if I can."

"I can text you with any questions." If he wants to define any future interactions, I can work with that. "But that's all."

"That's right."

"Okay. That makes sense." I nod. "Ah, thanks. Thank you."

"One or the other is fine. You don't need to say both."

I smile, nervous again for some reason. "Yeah, I just … never mind."

"Whenever you're ready," he says, sliding out of the booth. Which means he wants to go now. I don't know why people don't just say what they mean.

I finish off the margarita, then wipe the salt off my lips. When I catch Ed watching, he turns away with a sharp sort of motion. Odd. For a big man, his movements have been mostly fluid, almost graceful. Guess he really wants to get rid of me. Can't say I blame him.

* * *

"Hey, how was your day?" Frances flops down onto the other end of the couch with a bottle of water in her hand. "You got a phone?"

"Yeah. I was careful when I went out," I say, heading off the next inevitable question before it can be asked.

"Good."

My sister would probably be happiest if I'd hide at home for the rest of my life, staying safe and sound. Bubble-wrapping me isn't out of the question. But it's never going to happen. I need my freedom, the space to figure out my life for myself.

She picks up the TV remote and starts flicking through the channels. Some drama about people on a spaceship, the evening news, a woman singing about a dude named Heathcliff, and a tennis match. Finally, she settles on a wildlife documentary.

"Poor gazelle," she mumbles, taking a sip of water. "What did you want to do for dinner?"

"Pizza."

"Again?" she asks with a smile.

I'm working my way through the local pizza place's menu, figuring out my favorite. It's taken a week, but I've got it narrowed down to either the pumpkin, spinach, and feta, or the tomato, basil, and mozzarella. For some reason, the vegetarian options appeal to me more. Sometimes I get a bit fixated on things. Happily, pizza has been one of those things.

"I met Ed today," I say.

Her whole body tenses. "You did?"

"Why didn't you tell me about him?"

"Because he broke your heart." She sets down the water bottle, turning sideways to face me. "Clem, you were a mess, absolutely miserable, crying all the time. It was almost worse than right after Mom died. With everything that's happened, the last thing you need is him back in your life. The one silver lining of this whole disaster has been that you've been able to stop tearing yourself up about it."

"He says he didn't cheat on me."

She sighs. "I honestly have no idea about that. In the month leading up to the attack, you refused to talk about him or what went down between you two. So basically, I was just following your wishes."

"Hmm."

"You were crazy about the man. Can't imagine you'd have left him without a damn good reason."

Was Ed the type to cheat? Thing is, he didn't appear to be lying, and watching people is kind of my thing these days. The things they try to hide. The things they're not saying. What comes out of people's mouths versus what they do is often way off. With Ed though, I hadn't gotten that feeling. In fact, I'm not even sure he cares enough about what I think of him these days to lie. Not like the man would have too much trouble finding someone to take previous me's place, if that's what he's after.

"How did you find out about him?" she asks, voice low.

"What? Oh. I went down the street for coffee and someone in line there recognized his work. Apparently his style is quite distinctive." I nod in the direction of my tattoo. "So I went to his shop. He was not happy to see me. But we talked, and he answered some questions. Doubt I'll see him ever again."

"I actually used to like the guy," she says. "Always seemed like a straight shooter, but I guess I read him wrong. Still, I would have taken you to see him if I knew you wanted to go."

"I'm a big girl, Frances. I can get a cab."

She rests her head back against the couch, staring at the ceiling. "He wasn't involved in what happened to you. I checked him out. Photos of him at a tattoo convention in Chicago were all over social media."

"Why would you even think he was involved?"

"Just being careful."

"Another woman was attacked and robbed in the same area as me the week before. The police officer who interviewed me at the hospital said there's a good chance the attacks are linked." The words come faster and faster, until they start to run into each other. "It was random. Not directed at me personally."

"Don't get worked up. Like I said, just being careful." She shrugs. "It's part of the job description. As a cop. As your sister. No harm in that."

"Was he ever … " I swallow. "Was he violent with me? Or anyone?"

"Tattoo parlors are not the most peaceful places in the world, in my experience." She frowns. "But no, violence was not one of Ed's faults."

"From what I've seen on daytime TV, people screw around on each other all the time. It's not that uncommon and it rarely leads to trying to kill the other person."

Frances squeezes her eyes shut for a moment. "I realize your knowledge is limited, but trust me when I tell you that life is not accurately reflected by daytime TV. And I've seen enough victims of domestic violence to be wary of situations involving a recent breakup. Though, as I said, he never gave me those kind of vibes."

She has a point. Two, actually.

The pained look on her face is familiar. Same goes for her favorite wide-eyed and mouth slightly open expression. That one is used for shock or surprise. My sister is a pretty dominant-personality type. And I'm guessing previous me was quieter, less prone to speaking her thoughts regardless of consequences. Doctor Patel warned me it could be a problem.

On the screen, a crocodile drags a zebra into the water. Lots of thrashing and blood. At least it's not pointless violence, since the crocodile needs to eat. I like to think whoever assaulted me was desperate, starving, and alone. Out of their mind on drugs, maybe. It's still no excuse for the ferocity of the attack, but it helps a little. I can't spend the rest of my life in hiding, afraid of everything, and hating on civilization.

"He bought me a small can of mace," I say.

"How romantic." My sister grabs a pillow, stuffing it behind her head. "Actually, that's a pretty good idea, now that you're going out again. Same with getting you a phone. Things have just been so hectic, I hadn't gotten around to it yet."

"You've done enough already. I need to figure out how to look after myself."

She doesn't speak for a moment. "Did he pay for the cell too?"

"No, I did."

"Hmm." She sighs. "You would have had to find out about him eventually. Your name is still on the mortgage for the condo you two shared. He owes you half the down payment back."

"Really? He didn't mention anything about that to me."

"It can be hard for people to remember that you don't remember."

"True."

She says nothing for a moment. "So far as I know, he was in the process of getting the paperwork sorted to take your name off the deed, and I think you were giving him time to pay you back the money. But you'd have to ask him what the actual agreement was. It's what you sank your half of Mom's life insurance into."

"So, I'm a homeowner ... sort of. Not that I'd be welcome there." I stare at the TV, letting all of the new information settle inside my head. "I've never had anyone look at me with such animosity before. He really doesn't like me."

"And how do you feel about that?"

It always makes me smile when she tries to play therapist. Like I haven't spent a good chunk of my second life around the real thing. "I feel very little regarding him, Frances. Why would I? The guy's a stranger. And before you ask, no, nothing looked familiar."

She just nods.

"You should have told me about him."

"I would have gotten around to it eventually."

No apology is offered for her lie of omission. For not telling me about Ed. This is why I need new sources of information. My sister can't be allowed to pick and choose what I know. To try to dictate who I was, or the person I might become.

Whatever her reasons for keeping things from me, it can't be allowed. We're family, but sometimes I'm not exactly sure we're friends.

25886313R00144

Printed in Great Britain
by Amazon